VALLEY 2

LOVE ME IF YOU DARE

Love Me If You Dare

Carly Phillips

**WHEELER
CHIVERS**

This Large Print edition is published by Wheeler Publishing, Waterville, Maine, USA and by AudioGO Ltd, Bath, England.
Wheeler Publishing, a part of Gale, Cengage Learning.
Copyright © 2010 by Karen Drogin.
The moral right of the author has been asserted.

LIBRARY OF CONGRESS CATALOGING-IN-PUBLICATION DATA

Phillips, Carly.
    Love me if you dare / by Carly Phillips.
    p. cm.
    ISBN-13: 978-1-4104-3367-1 (hardcover)
    ISBN-10: 1-4104-3367-6 (hardcover)
    1. Large type books. I. Title.
PS3616.H454L55 2011
813'.6—dc22   2010042412

BRITISH LIBRARY CATALOGUING-IN-PUBLICATION DATA AVAILABLE

Published in 2011 in the U.S. by arrangement with Harlequin Books S.A.
Published in 2011 in the U.K. by arrangement with Harlequin Enterprises II B.V.

U.K. Hardcover: 978 1 445 83606 5 (Chivers Large Print)
U.K. Softcover: 978 1 445 83607 2 (Camden Large Print)

Printed in the United States of America
1 2 3 4 5 6 7 15 14 13 12 11

ACKNOWLEDGMENTS

Some books write like a dream. Others? Not so much. The ones that are a little tougher are usually the most worthwhile in the end. Getting there is a challenge, though! For helping me through this challenge, I want to thank the Plotmonkeys: Janelle Denison, Julie Leto and Leslie Kelly. You are my friends and my saviors!

A special thanks to Brenda Chin — you know why!

As always, this one is for my family — Phil, Jackie and Jen — the reason for everything I do. I love you!

And a special thanks to Lynda Sue Cooper for answering my cop-related questions and not telling me to go away! Any mistakes in details are my own. Lynda, you're a treasure. Thank you!

CHAPTER ONE

As the elite of Manhattan sipped champagne and whispered in hushed tones, Rafe Mancuso patted the Glock hidden beneath his tuxedo jacket. Relaxed but alert, he strode through the room, certain he wouldn't need the gun in this highbrow crowd. Still, the Lancaster Foundation was paying him to remain vigilant at their auction of outrageously priced jewels. Instead, he was distracted by the woman who'd recruited him to work security, Sara Rios, his one-time partner at the NYPD.

She walked through the double doors, and he couldn't focus on anything else. They'd had a unique connection, working together like a well-oiled machine. Spending hours in a car together led to an immediate friendship and an emotional intimacy Rafe had never experienced before.

Not even with his fiancée.

He and Sara had never acknowledged let

alone acted on the feelings simmering between them, but that hadn't lessened the impact. And if Rafe thought Sara had been a dangerous temptation back then, he was blown away now. The woman who'd worked alongside him in a police uniform had never looked this hot. In a sparkling silver dress that hit toned midcalf, her long blond hair draped over her shoulders and full breasts he hadn't known existed, Rafe couldn't tear his gaze away.

"Hey there, stranger! Long time no see." She greeted him with a wide smile.

"Hey, yourself."

She leaned over and pressed a kiss on his cheek, her soft lips and sweet scent intoxicating him, reminding him of why he'd switched shifts and broken up their partnership last year. Rafe's father had almost destroyed their family with an affair, and Rafe had sworn he would never follow in those footsteps. To an engaged man, Sara presented a temptation that simply had to end. Ironically, his relationship with his fiancée had imploded not long after, but as far as Rafe was concerned, breaking up the partnership was the smartest thing he'd ever done.

Sara would never commit to any man for

the long haul, and Rafe demanded nothing less.

"I'm glad you took me up on this gig. It's good to see you." She tucked a strand of hair behind her ear and met his gaze, her brown eyes sparkling with pleasure.

He smiled. "It's good to see you, too."

"You dress up nicely," she said.

His stare never left hers. "I can honestly say the same about you. And as a bonus, it should be an easy night." He inclined his head toward the other side of the room, where the jewels were on display.

The Lancaster Foundation had insisted Rafe and Sara blend in and socialize, not crowd the items for sale. As trained professionals, they'd have preferred to set the parameters, but the foundation hadn't wanted the guests to feel too intimidated to view the items up close.

"An easy night is good," Sara said. "I'm supposed to lie low until I testify at a murder trial next month. And you can't get any more low-key than this."

He laughed in agreement. "I heard about your case. Started as a routine B and E on Park Avenue, right?"

"That's what we thought. Someone broke in and surprised the wife at home, hit her on the head and stole some high-priced

9

items. But the victim refused to go to the hospital and died in her sleep a few hours later." Sara shook her head at the senseless result.

They'd both dealt with their share of stubborn victims.

"As it happened, I was the last person to speak to her before she died. She implicated her husband or at least gave him motive."

"So you're the key witness at the husband's murder trial," Rafe said, repeating what he'd heard around the station.

"Yep. And it all comes down to money." She tipped her head toward the wealthy crowd. "Alicia Morley's capital was the only thing keeping her husband's investment firm afloat. He and his partners ran the firm into the ground, and she refused to continue to subsidize his bad investments. He hired someone to break in and make it look like a robbery gone bad, hoping to inherit her estate. But if he's convicted, her money goes to adult children from a first marriage."

A waiter passed by, and Sara grabbed a sparkling water from his tray. She took a sip, leaving a pink-rimmed lipstick mark on the glass.

Rafe couldn't tear his gaze away. Couldn't stop his mind from imagining other uses for those luscious, glossed lips. "Where's the

10

husband now?" he asked, his throat parched and dry.

"Still in jail. Prosecutors convinced a judge he's a flight risk. But his business partners are connected to some dangerous people, and the D.A. wants me to keep a low profile until the case is over."

"Well, I'm happy to handle this low-profile event with you." Where he could look and not touch. "I saw your neighbor, Sam Cooper, earlier."

Coop and Sara weren't just next-door neighbors: they were good friends. And since Sara let few people get close, and Rafe trusted her instincts, he automatically respected Coop. He often crossed paths with the crime-beat reporter and professionally pegged him as a decent guy who'd never compromise the truth for a story.

Since Sara was territorial about her friends, Rafe decided not to mention that he'd caught sight of Coop sneaking out of the unused coatroom not long after a disheveled-looking woman had done the same. In the dead heat of summer, nobody used that closet unless they were getting some action. Rafe was actually jealous. He couldn't remember the last time he'd grabbed a quickie with a woman in a nearly public place, but looking at Sara in that dress had him thinking about nothing else.

Sara nodded. "I came with Coop, but I hope he'll be leaving with his girlfriend, Lexie Davis. If they settle an argument they had first." She pursed her lips and glanced around the room, her frown becoming more distinct. "I don't see them."

"It's crowded. Maybe they're somewhere making up," Rafe said in an attempt to re-assure her.

Sex, then an argument, then makeup sex? Could any guy get that lucky in the span of an hour? Rafe shook his head and laughed.

"What's so funny?" Sara asked.

Rafe came up with a cover story. "Just wondering how Coop's handling his stint on the Bachelor Blog."

The online and in-print feature now in the *Daily Post* targeted single men in New York City. The blog started by picking a bachelor and highlighting him. The spotlight led to people covering the guy's every move, from where he stopped for coffee to where he worked, and usually culminated in specu-lation about his love life. Women then came out of the woodwork in droves, hoping to snag the newest, hippest NYC bachelor. Despite the fact that he worked for the *Daily Post,* Coop was the blogger's latest sucker.

"You read that trash?" Sara sounded affronted by the prospect.

Rafe shook his head. "Hell, no. But Maggie does." As Sara knew, Maggie was their daytime dispatcher, and she loved to share station gossip and, lately, Bachelor Blog news.

"I don't know how Maggie finds the time," Sara said.

"Saves her from focusing on her own life."

Suddenly a loud shriek and the sound of shattering glass broke through the dull hum of the crowd, interrupting their conversation.

Rafe whipped his head toward the sound, hand on his pocket, ready to draw his weapon.

"The waiter has a knife!" someone next to them shouted.

"And he's got Coop's girlfriend," Sara groaned.

Instinct kicked in, and Rafe met Sara's gaze, both silently acknowledging they needed to get closer to the action.

Rafe inclined his head, and Sara immediately started clockwise around the room, heading toward the waiter with the knife. Rafe went counter and worked his way through the startled crowd.

Hopefully one of them, Rafe or Sara, could distract the waiter while the other got a jump or a clear shot.

"He's got the ring!" The warning came from the woman being held hostage.

A piece from the Lancaster Foundation. Rafe swallowed a curse.

"Shut up!" the panicked waiter yelled at her.

Rafe glanced over in time to see the man prick his hostage's skin with the tip of his blade.

"Just how do you think you're getting out of here?" Suddenly Sam Cooper stepped forward. Hands in the air, he eased toward the waiter who held his girlfriend at knife-point.

Ordinarily Rafe wouldn't want a civilian trying to talk a crazy man down, but Coop wasn't stupid. And at least he was buying Rafe and Sara time to get closer.

"Who the hell are you?" the waiter asked.

"I'm with the lady. Now, just relax." Coop attempted to take another step.

"Stay there!" the waiter shouted.

Rafe still wasn't close enough, nor could he risk scaring the man who'd already escalated from stealing a ring to taking a hostage.

The waiter shifted his grip on the woman. "Look, I'm just gonna walk out of here, and nobody's going to stop me." He made his

14

way toward a steel door marked Stairwell, pulling his hostage along with him.

Rafe sought and found Sara across the room. She was close enough to confront the man, and Rafe gave her silent encouragement, knowing she could handle talking him down. They'd been in negotiation basics together, though she'd had no interest in specializing.

Without warning, the waiter shoved the hostage into the crowd, taking everyone off guard.

In the chaos that followed, he yanked the door and bolted from the room. Sara took off after him.

Rafe surged forward, but the door slammed shut before he could reach it, costing him precious time. Heart lodged in his throat, he pushed his way through the guests, opened the door and ran up a dark stairwell.

He launched through another door and onto the rooftop, gun already drawn, only to find he had a different hostage situation on his hands.

The waiter had obviously misjudged his exit strategy. There was no way out from here, and he now held Sara at knifepoint. He'd obviously been expecting company and grabbed her as insurance.

Rafe broke into a sweat that had nothing to do with the heat and humidity swirling around him.

"Drop the gun," the waiter ordered.

Rafe gauged his chances of shooting the suspect and missing Sara. The moonlight was on his side, illuminating the roof. But considering the other man held her as a complete body shield, knife to her neck, his chances were not good.

"Come on, man. Let her go. You don't want to go down for assaulting a cop," Rafe said, beginning the process of talking the man down.

The waiter's eyes opened wide, but he didn't flinch or drop the knife. "Is she really a cop?" Sweat poured down the man's face.

"We both are," Sara said, voice calm.

Rafe admired her cool and hoped she could hold on to it.

The waiter spat a curse. The hand holding the knife shook, and the blade pricked her skin. A small trickle of blood oozed onto her neck.

Nausea swamped Rafe, but he pushed the feeling aside. "Your day just gets better and better," Rafe said, his gun level with Sara's chest. "Let her go. It'll still go easier on you if you don't stab a cop."

"I need to think," the man said, obviously

shaken. Panic warred with the irrational need to go down fighting, and his indecision was tangible.

Rafe had seen it before. The guy had to make a choice. So did Rafe. Where another trained negotiator might talk his guts out until he was out of time, Rafe had the advantage of knowing the hostage.

And *she* knew how to read his mind and his cues. Acting presented a risk, but Rafe trusted his ex-partner.

Decision made, Rafe met Sara's gaze, giving her an imperceptible nod. "Drop!" he yelled at the same time as he dove for the other man's legs.

Everything next happened in a blur. Sara's body went limp, surprising the guy while Rafe barreled into him, knocking him off balance. Sara rolled free, and Rafe tackled the other man but was unable to get a grip on the knife. He wasn't sure how long he grappled and deflected before he obtained the upper hand, landing a smooth blow to the man's jaw that ultimately subdued him.

"Don't move!" Sara stood over the waiter, gun raised.

Breathing hard, Rafe rose to his feet. "You okay?"

She nodded. "I would've been better if he hadn't gotten the jump on me," she muttered. "He knocked the gun right out of my hand." She shook her head in disgust.

Light-headed, Rafe braced his hands on his thighs. "Yeah, I hear you."

"Someone probably called the cops by now. They should be here any minute."

Rafe glanced over at her. "Way to keep a low profile."

She managed a laugh.

The waiter on the ground groaned, redrawing Rafe's attention.

"Easy," Sara warned the man. She moved closer and winced as she stepped around him, pain etching her features.

"Where are you hurt?" Rafe asked her.

She shook her head. Ever stoic, she'd never admit she was injured.

Without warning, the dizziness hit Rafe harder. He dropped to his knees, everything around him blurry as he became aware of a sharp pain in his chest.

He pushed his tuxedo jacket out of the way and glanced down. Blood oozed through his white shirt.

Damn. He hadn't even felt the knife go in.

"Rafe!" Sara called out, her voice tinged with panic.

"I'm fine," he lied just as the door to the building burst open and cops with weapons streamed onto the rooftop.

A woman he didn't recognize but remembered from the guests downstairs knelt down beside him. "Officer Mancuso, I'm Amanda Stevens from the *Daily Post.* You're a hero," she said, sounding way too excited over the prospect.

"Just doing my job," he muttered.

"I've been told you and Sara Rios used to be partners. How does it feel to rescue one of your own?" the persistent woman asked.

Rafe shoved his hand against his chest, the pain more excruciating now. From the corner of his eye, he saw uniformed officers haul the suspect to his feet.

The reporter asked the same question again.

How did it feel to rescue Sara?

Easy question. *It felt damn good to rescue a gorgeous blonde with curves to die for.*

He hoped he hadn't spoken out loud — his last thought before everything went black.

"It was touch and go for a while, but he's going to be okay."

The trauma surgeon's words echoed in Sara's head, relief making her dizzy. They'd practically shut down the city to get Rafe to Lenox Hill Hospital.

Sara barely remembered having her leg X-rayed, iced and put into a brace. The pain from wrenching her knee running up the stairs was nothing compared to that of nearly losing Rafe. He'd saved her life at the risk of his own, and she'd never forget it. She hadn't left the hospital since she'd arrived by ambulance, waiting for news.

"Rios!"

Sara turned at the sound of her captain's voice. Almost the entire precinct had gathered, waiting for news on one of their own.

"Is this what you call lying low?" A large man with a spine of steel, Captain Hodges tended to sound gruff, but Sara knew he had the heart of a teddy bear.

"Sorry, Captain. Who knew an auction would lead to a hostage crisis?"

The man rolled his eyes. "You just like to be where the action is," he muttered. "The D.A. is going to have my head on a platter for approving this off-duty assignment."

"Better stay out of her way, then," Sara joked.

To her relief, the big man smiled in return. "Good news on Mancuso."

"Yes, sir."

"How long are you out of commission?" he asked, pointing to the brace on her knee.

She swallowed hard. "I'm not sure. The

X-rays were inconclusive." If she called some evidence of early arthritis and degenerative joint disease inconclusive. "They scheduled an MRI for tomorrow."

Sara already had torn-meniscus issues from an old high-school gymnastics injury. Periodic pain, clicking and swelling of her knee were a normal part of her life. But now she'd been warned that by reinjuring the joint, she could end up with permanent problems, which would make doing her job impossible. Something she refused to contemplate.

Police work was all she knew. All she'd ever wanted to do. She came from a family of cops. Dysfunctional cops who couldn't keep their marriages or families together, so being an officer defined them.

It defined her.

"Well, you're officially on medical leave until you're cleared to return. Go home and get some rest," the captain said.

She bit the inside of her cheek, knowing better than to argue. "I will."

"Good. Take care of yourself."

She nodded.

"And this time, *lie low*."

THE DAILY POST
THE BACHELOR BLOG
Our latest bachelor quit his day job for love. Sam Cooper's heart is spoken for, ladies. But luckily, there's a new heroic bachelor in the city. Rafe Mancuso stepped in and saved one of New York City's finest, getting injured in the process. I can hear you all swooning now.

Amanda Stevens, features editor at the *Daily Post,* was there live covering the Lancaster auction. She asked the hostage negotiator how it felt to save a damsel in distress. Mr. Mancuso, not realizing he'd been stabbed, answered from the heart — "Just doing my job. With the added perk of rescuing a gorgeous blonde with curves to die for," before passing out from his injuries.

Could romance be brewing between this hero and the lady he saved? Or is the field clear for the other women of our city? Only time — and the Bachelor Blogger — will tell.

CHAPTER TWO

Rafe woke up in a sterile-looking hospital room, hooked up to an IV. He immediately became aware of a deep pain in his chest, and memories came flooding back. The auction, the hostage situation, realizing he'd been stabbed and a swarm of uniforms on the roof.

He blinked, but everything was still fuzzy.

The morphine, he thought, recalling that he'd awakened disoriented and in pain a few times before. He wasn't as out of it now and wondered how much time had passed.

"You're up!"

He turned his head toward the sound of the familiar voice to find Sara sitting in a chair against the wall. She rose and maneuvered herself onto crutches before making her way toward the bed. Her hair hung messily around her shoulders, her face was makeup free and her exhaustion clear. So was the obvious relief in her expression.

Suddenly another memory surfaced. Every time he'd opened his eyes, she'd been there.

"How do you feel?" she asked, her soft gaze never leaving his.

"Like I was stabbed." He cracked a smile.

She scowled at him. "Not funny. The knife nicked a pulmonary vein. They had to go in and close it up. At least, that's what the doctor said."

"Surgery?" he asked.

She nodded, her expression serious. "You needed blood," she told him.

He tried to swallow, but his mouth was dry.

"Here." She reached over and picked up a cup of ice, spoon-feeding him chips until he'd moistened his mouth.

"I could get used to this kind of treatment."

"Something tells me women would line up to accommodate you." Her lips lifted in the first smile she'd given him since he woke up.

She placed the cup back onto the tray.

"But they'd have to fight off your mother, and she's one protective lady."

"My mother? She's here?" he asked, shocked.

Sara nodded. "You know the drill. The captain made sure your folks were notified

24

when things looked serious. They drove down from upstate and are staying in a nearby hotel."

He closed his eyes and groaned.

"Are you in a lot of pain?" she asked, misreading the sound.

"I'll live," he said of the burning in his chest.

"Good," she said softly.

But knowing his mother would be here hovering over him was enough to make a grown man cry. He loved his big, loud family, but he'd left his upstate New York hometown so he could love them from a distance.

"What about our waiter friend? What happened to him?" Rafe asked, changing the subject.

"The bastard's in custody and not about to make bail anytime soon," she said with a satisfied nod.

"At least there's some good news."

"More than some. You made it," she said, reaching for his hand.

Her touch was warm, her grip soft and sure. Comfort filled him as she held on tight.

"You scared me to death. First there was all that blood, and then you passed out. . . ." Her voice trembled, and she sucked in a deep breath. "The paramedics said your pressure dropped dangerously low, and you were bleeding internally." She paused again for a few heavy beats. "You saved my life."

Her gratitude made him uncomfortable. "We're a team. I yelled drop, you reacted. It was no big deal."

"Tell that to the newspapers."

"They exaggerate," he muttered.

"I won't tell Coop you said that." Sara grinned.

Rafe almost laughed but stopped before he could cause himself pain. He stared up at the white ceiling. "Do I want to know what day it is?"

She let out a sigh. "Monday morning."

He'd been out of it for two days. And if he wasn't mistaken, she'd been with him the whole time. The rush of emotion in his chest replaced the pain.

"What about you? How bad is it?" he asked her, staring pointedly at the crutches.

She waved away his concern. "I just wrenched my knee running up the stairs. I'll be back at work in no time."

"Then how come you can't look me in the eye when you say that?" he asked her.

She frowned but didn't reply.

A glance at her clothing told him she wore navy NYPD-issued sweatpants. Large and bulky enough to cover a brace. "Is it your bad knee?" he asked.

She rolled her eyes. "You're like a dog with a bone, Mancuso. I said I'll be fine. Let it go."

His worry increased, but she wouldn't talk about it until she was ready. "I never even felt the knife go in," he said, changing the subject. He still couldn't believe he'd been stabbed.

"Adrenaline will do that to you." She met his gaze, innate understanding in her expression.

Comfortable silence descended around them. He'd missed that, Rafe realized. His current partner, Jake Riordan, liked to talk to pass the time. Rafe often wished for the peace and quiet that filled the car when he and Sara had been a team.

A knock sounded on the door, and a nurse walked in. "Good morning, Mr. Hero," she said in a cheery voice. "I'm glad to see you really awake! It's time for me to check your temperature and blood pressure. I also want to take a look at the bandage," she said.

"Only if you cut the hero crap," he muttered.

Sara grinned. "Behave and be polite to the nurses or I'll sic your mother on you."

"I like your sister," the nurse said, pointing to Sara. "But she still has to wait outside."

"My sister?"

Sara leaned closer. "I told them I was your sister so they'd let me stay as long as I wanted," she whispered. Her eyes twinkled with mischief. "Your mother seemed okay with it, since she didn't blow my cover," she added, reading his mind. "Now, be good and do what the nurse says." She brushed a kiss over his cheek, and her hair tickled his skin.

He felt the tingle of both clear down to his toes. "You should go home and get some sleep," he said, his voice gruff.

"Now that I know you're okay, maybe I will."

As she maneuvered toward the door on her crutches, Rafe was unable to tear his gaze from her behind. Even when they'd worked together, he'd never stared at her ass. Yet she looked as good to him now as she had at the auction in the sexy, cleavage-showing dress.

The nurse waited until the door shut behind Sara to continue. "That's a nice *sister* you've got there." The older woman winked, letting him know she was onto them.

"Yeah. I lucked out," he said with a

chuckle he immediately regretted. He shut his eyes against the pain.

"Sometimes it helps if you hold a pillow to your chest, but let's wait till we get you up and moving a bit."

He swallowed a groan, knowing he had a rough few days ahead of him.

"That young lady hasn't left your side for more than a few minutes since you were brought down from Recovery," the nurse said as she adjusted the blood-pressure cuff around his arm.

A warm feeling that surpassed gratitude flooded through Rafe. One he wanted to keep with him for the rest of the day.

Sara stepped out of Rafe's hospital room and exhaled a sigh of relief. Her body ached from the long hours in the chair by his side, but now that she'd seen him awake, had spoken to him and knew he was going to be okay, her heart finally beat normally again.

She shifted the crutches, getting comfortable for her trek down the hall to the elevator and then outside where she'd hail a cab to take her home.

As she passed the nurses' station, the women were huddled together over the newspaper, all talking at once and gesturing toward Rafe's room. When Sara paused at the desk, the women fell silent and pretended to look busy.

An uneasy feeling took hold, and Sara always trusted her instincts. "What's going on?"

"I have to go," one of the women said.

"Me, too." Another one bolted for a patient's room.

"Fine," said the third and only woman who remained. "I'll tell her." The young nurse handed Sara a copy of the *Daily Post*. "The Bachelor Blog," the woman said.

"Oh, no." Sara drew a steadying breath and glanced at the paper, which had already been folded open to the correct page.

Rafe's official department photograph stared back at her. It had taken less than forty-eight hours for his heroics to land him the spot. Rafe was a man who valued his personal space and privacy. He wouldn't appreciate the attention, and Sara knew firsthand just what kind of attention he could expect. Ironically, she'd already had experience with the fallout when her neighbor, Coop, had been picked as the blog's featured bachelor. Pathetic women had sent perfumed letters, candy and underwear. All of which merely reinforced Sara's belief that only a desperate woman would find the Bachelor Blog the answer to matchmaking in the new millennium.

With a sigh, Sara placed the newspaper back on the counter. "Do me a favor and try to keep this news from him as long as possible." She pointed toward Rafe's room. "He'll just get upset, and he needs all his strength focused on recovering."

The nurse nodded. "I'll do my best and spread the word. Although between the newspapers passed around and the people walking in and out during different shifts, there are no guarantees he won't hear it anyway."

Sara nodded. "I appreciate you trying." She turned to leave, but the nurse cleared her throat.

"Umm . . . did you read the blog article?" the other woman asked.

"No." Sara had just looked at the photograph.

The uneasy feeling returned as she picked up the paper once more and this time read through the entire blog, leaving Sara feeling blindsided and raw.

The blogger had actually speculated that she and Rafe had *romantic potential.* All because of some words he'd apparently uttered before passing out on the rooftop.

It felt damn good to rescue a gorgeous blonde with curves to die for.

Words Sara hadn't been aware of before now.

Words she'd never be able to forget.

In all the time they'd worked together, she and Rafe had shared chemistry on many levels. Some they'd acknowledged, like their in-sync partnership and ability to read each other's minds — those had made his transfer so much harder to accept. As much as she'd understood his desire to spend more time with his fiancée, partnerships like theirs were rare. She'd yet to click with her new one even after a year.

Then there was the sexual chemistry, the zing that traveled from her head to the pit of her stomach, then deliciously lower, whenever she so much as looked at Rafe Mancuso. That chemistry she'd ignored, thinking it had to be one-sided.

Now he'd given her reason to think maybe it wasn't. Maybe he shared those feelings and desires.

"Are you okay?" the nurse asked, breaking into Sara's wayward thoughts.

"I'm fine. Just surprised by the lengths people will go to in the name of news." She tossed the paper onto the desk, attempting nonchalance. "Do me another favor? Tell the other nurses not to believe everything they read, okay?"

The woman smiled. "Sure thing. Although I have to say, if that man thought I was gorgeous, I'd make sure I scooped him up before some other desperate woman stepped in for me."

Sara cringed. "I take it no one here believes I'm his sister?"

The nurse shrugged. "What can I say? Everyone figured he'd want you to stay, and his family didn't argue."

Sara rolled her eyes. "What a crazy couple of days. I really need some sleep."

"Well, you can rest assured he's in good hands."

That's what worried her. "Thanks," Sara said, preoccupied, her mind still whirling with Rafe's words.

He thought she was gorgeous?

He'd noticed her curves?

So what?

She forced herself to calm down and focus. Even if his words were honest and true, even if he was no longer engaged to be married, nothing between them could change. Rafe was a man who believed wholeheartedly in the idea of family and permanency, while Sara didn't hold any illusions about romance or happily ever after.

Life and relationships were hard enough for normal people. Her family history was proof that cops couldn't sustain long-term relationships of any kind. Generation after generation on every branch of the family tree merely cemented the mantra she lived by — job first and revolving-door relationships when she had time. Although lately there hadn't been any of either.

She gripped her crutches tighter at the reminder — her job was all she had. Which made this injury and its potential career-ending repercussions so damn scary.

THE DAILY POST
THE BACHELOR BLOG
Nothing is more sexy than a reluctant hero, and that's Rafe Mancuso. The police officer/hostage negotiator rescued one of New York's finest, earning him the next most-eligible bachelor status. And based on what he said before passing out from his injuries, his heart might already be spoken for. Still, ladies, anything can happen, so watch for him on the street and send me updates! I'll post them as they come in.

Rafe liked his privacy. Coming from a big family, he'd learned the value of being alone, away from the constant questions and attention. After college, he'd moved away from his small upstate town and the many relatives who'd been interested in his every move. Of course, he stayed close with his older brother, Nick, and his three adoring sisters. But he loved and appreciated them more from a distance. Here in Manhattan he'd found anonymity in the large crowds — until that damned blogger picked up the hostage story. Now the women of New York City seemed focused on his every move, and he hated it.

After a week's postoperative rest, Rafe began to take small walks for exercise and to slowly rebuild his stamina. But the Bachelor Blog had made him a spectacle, no longer the anonymous person he'd enjoyed being.

A trip down the hall resulted in female neighbors eyeing him like fresh meat. They coyly batted their eyes and talked in a stage whisper about how they were single and available. For anything. When he walked into the Starbucks he frequented, the guy behind the register shouted a hello, customers turned around and silence descended. The barista making his coffee slipped him her number. And the precinct called and said they'd been receiving packages and perfume-scented deliveries for him. Disgusted, Rafe told them to get rid of them.

All the while, the Bachelor Blogger continued to speculate on Rafe's relationship with the woman he'd rescued. Day in and day out, reminding Rafe she existed. As if he could forget anything about her. She'd been by his side day and night until he was finally coherent and out of the woods. She looked as good to him exhausted and disheveled as she did made up and glamorous. So, no, he didn't need the blogger to remind him of what he'd said about her before he'd passed out.

He thought about her all day.

He saw her in his dreams at night.

And wondered constantly what would happen if they gave in to the desire neither had ever mentioned aloud.

Rafe hadn't heard from Sara since he'd left the hospital, but he remembered everything — from the warmth in her eyes to the relief on her face when he'd finally come to. But the last time he'd seen her, she'd been cool and distant, a far cry from the woman who'd sat by his bedside and held his hand. He had no choice but to respect the boundaries she'd erected. Because as much as he was attracted to her, they wanted different things out of life. And he'd rather keep her friendship than lose her after an affair ended.

He was on medical leave until cleared for return — at least four to six weeks, he'd been told. To add insult to injury — literally — he'd also been reprimanded for violating his negotiator training by taking down the subject before exhausting every peaceful option first. There was no way to explain how he'd known for certain Sara would anticipate his action and duck. No way to justify his actions.

All of which left him stuck with too much time on his hands to think about that night. He was going stir-crazy sitting around the apartment, and he was miserable with the attention when he stepped out. For the first time in a long time, he missed his place by the lake and the privacy and serenity it offered. Missed the smell of Lake Ontario, where he'd grown up and spent hours with his father and siblings and cousins, learning to swim, playing ball and often doing nothing but annoying the crap out of each other. The very thing he'd moved away from was the thing he needed now.

Maybe it was getting knifed and facing his mortality. Maybe it was the stifling feeling created by the Bachelor Blog, but Rafe needed to get away. It was summertime, and he craved fresh air and sunshine. The house he owned on Lake Ontario beckoned to him.

His parents would be thrilled if he came home for a while. They'd left the city once he'd been discharged from the hospital, but his mother called a few times a day to make sure he was eating, resting and taking care of himself. She'd feel much better knowing he was close by while he recuperated, but in truth he needed it for himself.

Decision made, Rafe thought. The Bachelor Blogger would just have to make do without him.

CHAPTER THREE

Sara tested her weight on her leg, the same way she'd done every morning for the last two weeks. Once again, pain shot through her knee. She groaned and waited for it to subside. The neoprene brace she'd been given in the emergency room provided support but did nothing for the throbbing, aching discomfort she lived with constantly. She was still icing the swelling and taking anti-inflammatory medication. And still hoping her medical leave would be temporary, not the end of her career.

She glanced at the painkillers on the kitchen counter and shook her head. Being woozy wasn't her thing. She'd suffer through.

It was only nine-thirty in the morning, and she'd been up for hours. The rest of the day loomed long before her, so a knock at her door was a welcome distraction.

She hobbled over to the door, leaving the

crutches behind. The doctor had said weight-bearing as tolerated, and she needed to tolerate more and more.

She glanced through the peephole. "Coop!" she said, opening the door for her friend.

"Is this a good time?"

She nodded. "It's a perfect time. I'm sick and tired of sitting around feeling sorry for myself, so come in and take my mind off my problems."

Coop followed her inside, shutting the door behind him.

"Why aren't you at work?" she asked. He was usually out the door early and back home late at night.

"I took the day off. How are you feeling?" he asked, glancing at her knee. "And the truth this time."

Sara frowned. Though she'd been avoiding answering anyone's questions about her injury, pretending she was fine, she couldn't lie to her friend.

She wasn't okay. And it wasn't just her leg that hurt. If the knee didn't heal properly, her days at the NYPD were over.

"I'm scared it won't heal enough for me to return to active duty. It's all I can think about or focus on."

He looped an arm around her shoulder.

As an only child, Sara thought of Coop as the brother she'd never had. He was dark-haired, good-looking, charming, smart, and she'd never slept with him. Never wanted to. Together they made a lie of the claim that men and women couldn't be *just friends,* and she was grateful to have him in her life.

"I won't tell you not to worry, but I am going to suggest you do something to keep busy and not think about it all the time."

"Easier said than done when I'd rather be active than sitting around staring at the four walls."

"How about reading the paper, then?" he asked, gesturing to the *Daily Post* on the table, still wrapped in delivery plastic.

She glanced at the dreaded paper and shuddered. Ever since Rafe had been named the newest bachelor, she'd stopped reading that particular newspaper. She still had it delivered for Coop's byline, nothing more. Of course ignoring the paper didn't mean she wasn't thinking . . . and dreaming about Rafe. She hadn't been this obsessed when they were partnered together, because back then he'd been off-limits. He'd belonged to someone else. A free Rafe, one who'd admitted he noticed her as a woman, was dangerous to her peace of mind.

41

Coop cleared his throat. Obviously he had something to tell her.

"This isn't just a social visit, is it?" she asked warily.

He shook his head. "Not entirely."

"Let me have it." She gestured for him to talk.

"You know that low profile you're still supposed to keep?" He tapped on the newspaper with one hand.

Sara stiffened. "Don't tell me. The blog's writing about me again?"

"See for yourself."

He remained silent while she opened the newspaper and paged through to the correct section.

THE DAILY POST
THE BACHELOR BLOG
Our newest bachelor hasn't been spotted around town in over a week. Looks like he made a clean getaway. In the past, this would pose a challenge to yours truly, but no longer. Beginning next week, the Bachelor Blog will be in syndication, appearing in select newspapers around the country. So if Rafe Mancuso is spotted, hopefully we'll know it. In the meantime, keep your eyes on his lady friend, Sara Rios. She might hold the clues to our bachelor's

whereabouts. And if not, she's certainly a single, beautiful bachelorette.

"That's just freaking fantastic. Turn the city's attention on me now," she muttered. "This blog is just . . . wrong."

"Maybe it's right."

She whipped her head around to face him. "Excuse me? Aren't you the man who was inundated with women's underwear thanks to the blog?"

"I did meet Lexie." He raised an eyebrow, as if daring her to argue.

"You met Lexie thanks to being featured on the TV news after you stopped a robbery. The blog had nothing to do with it."

He shrugged. "Whatever. The point is, I met Lexie. And that's another reason I'm here today. I have something to tell you." The beginnings of smile pulled at his lips.

"What is it? Are things good between you and Lexie?"

"You could say that." The smile turned into a full-fledged grin. "We're going house-hunting in the suburbs."

She blinked, startled. "Wow. I knew you'd settled things after the auction, but . . . moving? White picket fence and all?" She leaned back in her seat, more than a little stunned.

He hadn't mentioned marriage, but,

divorced once, Coop still believed in the institution. Lexie, the world traveler, had obviously come around despite her initial reluctance for anything permanent. Sara couldn't think of anything more permanent than buying a home together.

"It's called compromise. We'll travel and have a home base." The light in his eyes told the whole story.

"I'm happy for you, Coop. I really am. I will miss having you as my neighbor, though."

"Hey, I work in the city. At least for now. That's another piece of news. I may give my fiction writing a real shot. You know, full-time in between world traveling. Lexie and I are still working out the details."

Sara shook her head. Things had changed almost overnight, she thought. "I hope all your dreams come true. You deserve it. So, she'd better treat you right." But Sara no longer worried about Lexie's motives for being with Coop.

They were truly in love. Apparently, it had existed for some. Ever the cynic, she still wasn't a believer.

"Back at you," Coop said. "Don't forget you'll come visit us. We'll see each other all the time."

Sara forced a smile. She knew that once

he moved out, their lives would take very different paths.

"You could have the same thing, you know," Coop said. "If you would ever open yourself up."

She rolled her eyes. "Here we go. A critique of my belief in marriage."

"Lack of belief," he corrected her.

She gripped the armrest even harder. "I guess I need to explain my family tree to you again. Police work and marriage can't coexist," she reminded him. "My grandparents fought over the hours and danger, broke up, Grandpa moved out, the kids suffered. They'd make up, he'd move back in and everyone would be miserable. One of my uncles is a divorced and unhappy SOB because his wife never let him see his kids. My aunt holds the distinction of being the first female cop in the family. She was so proud. Her husband wasn't. He took off because he couldn't handle his wife being the more powerful one. He hated the danger, too. One of my cousins died in the line of duty, leaving his wife to raise their baby. She's resentful, angry and not the best mother at this point. And we won't even mention my parents. . . ." She paused for a long, deep breath.

Coop, who'd been eyeing her, just waiting

for a chance to jump in, finally spoke. "What about the one and only success story? Why deliberately leave them out?" he asked, challenging her the way only a nauseatingly happy man in a relationship could.

Her cousin Renata — Sara had called her Reni since they were kids — she and her husband *were* happily married.

So Sara couldn't argue the point. "They have to work damn hard to make their marriage work. And in my opinion, life is hard enough. Being a cop is stressful enough. Why add more strain to the mix when the odds are stacked against you?"

"Because happiness is worth it?" Coop challenged.

"Ugh." She threw her hands up in the air. "Okay, enough sappy conversation."

Her gaze fell to the newspaper, and a more important subject took precedence in her mind. "What am I going to do about this?" She pointed to the department-issued photo of herself after the stabbing alongside one taken of her in her gown the night of the gala. "If your experience with this blog is any indication, the lunatics are going to turn out in droves," she said in disgust.

Coop let out a knowing laugh, but he didn't contradict her, either.

She pulled her hair off her neck and knotted it on top of her head. "Is it me, or is it hot in here? I thought the super said he'd fixed the AC problem."

"He says a lot of things. It's warm," he agreed. "But I think you're more nervous about being the center of the Bachelor Blogger's attention than anything else."

"Of course I'm nervous. I'm supposed to lie low. When my captain and the district attorney see this . . ." She glanced at the paper, the cause of all her trouble. "This anonymous person works for your newspaper. Any idea who it could be?"

He shook his head. "And whoever knows, nobody's talking."

"Swell."

Sara's telephone rang, interrupting her. She glanced at Coop and picked up the receiver. "Hello?"

Captain Hodges was on the other end.

Sara listened, her stomach cramping more with every word he spoke. "No, I understand. Yes, I know, and I'll let you know what I decide. Thanks for calling." She hung up and faced Coop. "Know a reporter named Mark Pettit?"

Coop nodded. "A guy with few scruples. He'd sell his own mother for a story. Why?"

"He sold *me*. The *Journal* just published a

story about the lady the Bachelor Blogger mentioned and her link to the notorious Morley murder. The entire city now knows I'm the star witness. And thanks to the Bachelor Blog, it'll be easy for Morley's partners or their associates to find me here."

She shook her head in frustration, her mind already whirling with possibilities of how easily someone could get to her.

"Do you really think they'd go after a cop?" Coop asked.

"They stand to lose everything once I testify." She held her hands out in front of her, weighing their choices. "Money versus murder. If I disappeared without a trace, who could prove John Morley, who's in jail, or his partners had anything to do with it?"

"What are you going to do?" Coop asked.

Sara paused. "I'm really not sure." She drummed her fingers on the nearest table.

"What did your captain say?" Coop gestured to the telephone.

"He thinks my injury puts me at greater risk." She rose and paced the small length of her apartment, limping her way across and back, each step reinforcing his point. "He says with this knee, I'm a sitting duck."

Sara normally didn't panic or overreact. She was a cop. She could handle herself in any situation. Except one in which she couldn't protect herself. Thanks to her bum knee, she was in a position of weakness, not strength.

Sara hated feeling weak. "This whole situation pisses me off. The last thing I want to do is let someone run me out of my own apartment."

"Pride could get you killed," Coop said, concern in his voice. "Can they assign someone to watch you? Protection?"

Sara shook her head. "We're shorthanded due to budget cuts, and the captain can't waste men or man-hours babysitting me." She groaned and rubbed her aching temples, the only alternative becoming clear.

"You need to get out of town," Coop said.

"Maybe." If the threat became real.

Although, where could she go? The cops in her family could handle the potential danger, but they were all scattered around the city, which didn't help her escape from strangers who'd recognize her and report in to the Bachelor Blogger.

"It's only until after you testify. Once Morley's convicted, you can come home."

She leaned against the side of the couch so she could prop her knee on the cushion and rest. "I know, and I'll think about it."

"Seriously consider it?" he pressed.

She nodded. "I don't have a death wish."

He inclined his head, satisfied. "Good. So. Have you heard from Rafe?" Coop named the one person she hadn't been able to push from her mind.

She narrowed her gaze, wary of why he'd bring it up now. "What does Rafe have to do with anything?"

Coop shrugged. "I'm just curious."

Sara didn't trust his motives. Happy coupled-up people always tried to push others into relationships, too. "Once Rafe was discharged from the hospital, we went our separate ways."

More like she'd kept things cool during her last few visits so he'd be sure not to call. She told herself it was better this way. He took his relationships too seriously for her to risk dabbling. No matter how much she wanted to. And she did. Badly.

Coop shook his head. "You froze him out, didn't you?" he asked in disgust.

He knew her too well.

"Don't be ridiculous," she lied. "We're friends, that's all. But these days we only speak to each other when there's a reason. Like when I asked him to work security at the auction."

Coop stared at her. Unwilling to break eye contact, the reporter in him obviously willed her to crack and admit she wanted more from Rafe than friendship.

The cop who was a master at interrogation met him with a blank look of her own.

"Don't you see how he looks at you?" Coop asked.

"Are you telling me you noticed?" she asked, secretly thrilled at the prospect that Coop might be right.

He grinned. "No. But Lexie did. And she said the sparks across the ballroom were electric. So why are you fighting what could be a good thing?"

Sara expelled a long breath. "Because Rafe is into commitment. Marriage. Family. That's what he wants out of life. And I don't." But she wished he were here now.

He was the one person she trusted to keep her safe. When on patrol, she'd never worried, knowing he had her back. Just like on the rooftop, she'd known precisely what he intended, dove for cover at the right time, then assisted him in collaring the perp. He'd know what to do, and she'd feel better just knowing he was around.

"I get it. Lexie loved travel and swore she'd never give it up for any man. Yet, we're going house-hunting. Draw your own conclusions." Coop spoke in a patronizing voice.

Sara gritted her teeth, ignoring his comment.

Finally Coop glanced at his watch and rose from his seat. "I've got to go meet Lexie."

Sara smiled. She never stayed mad at him for long. "Say hello for me. And good luck finding the right place."

"Thanks." He leaned over and kissed her on the cheek. "Even if you don't want to give things with Rafe a try, he might still be the solution to your problem. You need to stay safe, and he's already out of town. Maybe you could join him."

As much as Sara hated to admit it, Coop just might have a point, but she needed to be convinced. "He's recovering from a stabbing and major surgery." She glanced at Coop, wanting him to play devil's advocate with her.

"We both know Rafe at minimal capacity is worth a lot. Look at it this way. Between the two of you, you're the equivalent of one healthy person." Coop chuckled.

Hadn't she just thought the same thing? Together they were the perfect team. Professional team, she silently amended.

"I'll think about it," she promised. She had a hunch she wouldn't be able to concentrate on anything else.

"Do that. Because it's going to get crazy for you in the city. You won't know the lunatics from the murderers."

Sara shivered at his accurate description. "Even if I wanted to join him, according to the Bachelor Blogger, nobody knows where he is."

Coop rolled his eyes. "As if that's an issue. I'm sure a resourceful cop could figure it out. If she really wanted to."

She groaned and shook her head. "You're impossible," she said, laughing.

"*Nothing* is impossible."

Sara didn't rush to leave town. She still had things to take care of before she could disappear for a while, including visiting her physical therapist and making sure she had the rehab exercises she'd need while she was gone. She also wanted to see the fallout from the blog for herself before making any rash decisions to run.

Over the next few days, Sara learned what it meant to be the focus of the Bachelor Blog. Someone had gotten hold of her unlisted phone number and called her at odd hours, seeking phone sex, which forced her to disconnect her landline. Gifts accumulated at the station house and outside her apartment *door.*

Her walk-up apartment, without a doorman for security, provided crazy people with easy access inside her building. All it took was a resident exiting the otherwise locked door and strangers casually slipped inside, leaving her creepy notes and pornographic gifts. Not a good thing, especially now, when as Coop said, she couldn't distinguish the crazies from the murderers. She wished she had the luxury to ignore the gifts, but she needed to know if there was a valid threat from Morley or his people.

An innocuous-looking gift, wrapped in plain brown paper left outside her door along with a computer-generated label, finally convinced her it was time to go. The package looked identical to many others she'd received, but the note inside was different:

We can get to you anywhere, anytime.

She was now officially scared. Being held at knife-point by one lunatic was enough to convince her not to take stupid chances with her life.

There was only one man she trusted to keep her safe. The same man who'd never been far from her thoughts and dreams. She'd kept up on Rafe's progress through the station grapevine and knew he was feeling better each day. He'd already successfully eluded the Bachelor Blogger's reach. She needed to do the same. As a bonus, she'd be able to spend time with him and discover whether he'd meant the compliments he'd uttered before passing out.

But first she needed to find him.

She'd been using her cell phone for personal calls, but someone as well-connected as John Morley, someone willing to kill for money, would find a way to track her cell. She purchased a disposable phone with limited minutes, and in between packing, she called Rafe's cell. He didn't answer. Her call went directly to voice mail, and though she left a message, by the end of the day he hadn't returned her call.

Out of options, she either had to surprise him or not go stay with him after all.

She stalled leaving for another day.

Then the assistant district attorney in charge of the case called to tell her they'd had a tip from John Morley's cell mate, seeking favors in exchange for *helpful* information. Morley mentioned how he *hoped* something would happen to that pain-in-the-ass cop before she could testify. And as the inmate pointed out, people with Morley's connections knew how to make their wishes come true.

No more waiting to reach Rafe.

Sara rented a car with a good GPS system and headed north. It wasn't hard to figure out where Rafe had gone. He used to talk about his cabin on Lake Ontario, in his hometown. The perfect getaway in the middle of a scorching summer heat wave. And since he also would complain about how the village of Hidden Falls was so small everyone knew everyone else's business, finding him there should be as easy as a map and a few targeted questions on arrival.

She couldn't imagine him turning her away.

CHAPTER FOUR

Rafe met his brother, Nick, at Billy's Bar, an institution in Hidden Falls. With the vast amount of wineries in the area attracting the summer tourists, Billy's was the place where the locals met and hung out. Billy was older than dirt and had long since turned the running of the bar over to his son, Joe, who, like his father, knew everyone's choice in drink with no need to ask.

While Rafe nursed his first beer, Nick was already on his third.

"Angel giving you trouble again?" Rafe asked his brother.

Nick narrowed his eyes and rumbled an unintelligible answer.

"I'll take that as a yes."

To the horror of the older generation in the family, Nick and his wife had separated. Angelina, or Angel as everyone called her, had moved into her father's empty home. Empty because her father, Pirro DeVittorio, had recently married Rafe and Nick's Aunt Vivian, a widow of five years, and lived in her house.

Aunt Vi was their father's sister, an aunt who Rafe had always felt close to over the years. Together, Aunt Vi and Rafe's father ran the Spicy Secret, the family business, while Pirro was head of shipping and delivery. Add in Nick as vice president, and the family's business and personal connections were definitely messier now.

Rafe glanced at his older brother. Nick's current foul mood went beyond the separation, which was six months old.

Unlike Rafe, who'd gotten out of town and broadened his horizons as well as his beliefs, Nick was still a traditional man who'd expected his wife to stay at home or work in the family spice business only until she had children. But after Angel had a miscarriage, she'd decided she needed something more out of life.

She wanted to open her own business. Nick didn't agree. Angel went ahead with her plan anyway, and when the arguing became too much, she moved into her father's house and turned the upstairs rooms into guest rooms. She'd joined the chamber of commerce and now ran a successful bed-and-breakfast. On the surface, it seemed like Nick just couldn't deal with a businesswoman as his wife, and until he did, Angel wouldn't budge on reconciliation.

Rafe sensed there was more going on.

"Women know how to make you crazy," Nick said, finishing the last of his beer.

"I hear you," Rafe muttered. A woman who wasn't even his had him tied up in knots.

Sara still occupied his thoughts, day and night. He'd hoped by coming here and getting away from the damned blog and its innuendos, maybe then he'd stop wanting a woman he couldn't have. He'd accomplished part of his goal. He was relaxing and recuperating, feeling stronger every day. But even without the blog, Sara was constantly on his mind.

Nick raised his hand to order another drink.

"Hey. You've had enough," Rafe said, waving away the waitress. "Let's talk first. Then, if you still want to keep drowning yourself in alcohol, I won't stop you."

His brother rolled his eyes. "I hate it when you use that psych degree on me."

Rafe shook his head. "You don't need a shrink. You need common sense knocked into your thick skull. It's the twenty-first century. How's the caveman attitude working out for you?" He deliberately provoked his brother, hoping for a reaction. For something that would explain why Nick was acting like a Neanderthal and not a smart guy who could compromise with the wife whom he loved.

Nick glanced up, eyes red and bleary. "Hey, smart-ass, did you forget my wife had a miscarriage? It's not cavemanlike to want her to deal with the loss instead of burying her emotions in work."

Finally. Now Rafe understood. "You never talked about it except to tell me it happened."

Rafe lived five hours away, and his brother was the least-communicative human being he knew. Which explained why there were missing pieces to this story.

Nick glanced down. "It's not the easiest thing to talk about. The doctor said she probably would never carry to term. That's when she started talking about turning her father's house into a bed-and-breakfast. Then she set about doing it. If she grieved for the loss of the baby, the loss of our dream of having a big family, I never saw it."

Rafe placed a hand on his brother's shoulder. "Everyone grieves differently."

"I know that. But that business stands

60

between us. She's buried herself in it, and now we're at a stalemate." He ran his hands over his hair.

Rafe had seen Angel since he'd been home. She looked healthy and happy except for the pain in her eyes caused by her disintegrating marriage. "She's handling the responsibility of the business well. The B and B is thriving. Especially with the festival starting in a few days," Rafe said.

The Hidden Falls Wine Festival, an annual summer event, had started out as a summertime town festival sponsored by a local vineyard and other homegrown businesses, including his family's. Eventually, larger, national companies got in on the action — a weeklong event featuring up-and-coming local bands, a carnival and booths run by locals. Angel's B and B was small, but it offered people a down-home place to stay, and this was her first time with a full house courtesy of the festival.

"So you agree with me. She's overworked, stressed and unable to focus on what's really important."

Rafe set his jaw. "Uh, no. She seems to be coping just fine. You, on the other hand, are a miserable, unhappy son of a bitch."

Nick narrowed his gaze. His curled his hands into fists, clenching them tight on the table. "I can't believe you're taking sides."

"I'm telling it like it is, which nobody else in the family is willing to do. They're all too busy hovering over Angel, reminding her you're waiting for her to fail and come home." Rafe drew a deep breath. "What's really eating at you? Because until you figure it out, nothing's ever going to get better."

Nick didn't answer. He merely raised his hand for another beer.

Rafe was finished nursing his and ready to go home. Nobody could help Nick except Nick.

Rising from his seat, Rafe pulled money from his pocket and dumped it onto the table. "See you at dinner at Mom's tomorrow night?"

"I'll be there."

"Angel going?" Maybe there'd be a chance for the two of them to talk.

"Nope. She says it's time we start acting like we're separated. She's not coming to family gatherings unless it's for her immediate family — like her father or Aunt Vi. My family doesn't count." He stared into his empty glass.

"Come on. Let me take you home," Rafe offered.

Nick shook his head. "I'll be fine. It's not

like I'm driving. I'll walk home after this last beer."

Rafe shrugged. "See you tomorrow night."

Sara knew driving five hours in a car would be tough even if she stopped every sixty minutes to stretch her legs. She just hadn't known how tough. Her leg was cramped, her knee aching by the time she arrived in Hidden Falls, near dinnertime. As she pulled off the exit, she saw a billboard advertising the Hidden Falls Wine Festival coming up this week. She hoped that wouldn't impact her finding a place to stay until she located and spoke to Rafe.

As if divine providence was at work, the next sign advertised Angel's Bed-and-Breakfast.

"Pretty name," Sara mused. And if the accommodations were as heavenly, she'd soon be resting her knee.

She followed subsequent signs until she pulled into the gravel drive leading to a Victorian house painted in a robin's egg–blue with white trim.

So far so good.

Leaving her suitcase in the trunk, she limped up the path to the front porch. Although she'd begun walking better, the drive had stiffened her muscles.

She rang the bell, and in no time the door opened and an attractive, raven-haired woman greeted her with a welcoming smile. "Can I help you?"

Sara nodded. "I saw your sign off the highway and was hoping you had an available room."

"You can stay for two nights," the woman said. "But after that, I'm booked. The Wine Festival is starting, and we've been fully booked for months."

"Two nights works fine."

She'd come here hoping she could stay with Rafe anyway. On the off chance someone discovered where she'd gone, he'd be right there as backup. But she'd be safe here at Angel's for a short time. She felt certain nobody had followed her out of the city. She had been extremely careful, taking a long detour around Manhattan, stopping for errands, doubling back, making sure nobody was on her tail.

She'd rest her knee, and by the time Angel needed the room, she'd know whether Rafe minded having a visitor or if she had to make alternate arrangements.

"Okay, then, come on in. I'm Angel Mancuso, and I'm the owner. Chief cook, maid and companion, when you want one. And if you'd rather be alone, I can accommodate that, too. Do you need help getting your bags from the car?"

Sara barely heard her spiel. She was stuck on the woman's last name. "Did you say you're Angel *Mancuso?*"

"Yes. Why?" Curiosity etched her features.

It couldn't be a coincidence. "I'm here to visit a friend. Rafe Mancuso?"

The other woman's eyes widened in recognition. "Rafe is my brother-in-law!" Angel said. "I'd say it's a small world, but around here everyone knows everyone and is potentially related somehow." Angel laughed. "So, do you know Rafe from the city?"

Sara nodded. "We used to be partners."

Angel studied her, her eyes narrowing. "Actually, you look familiar."

"I can't imagine why. I've never been here before."

The other woman paused in thought. "I know!" Angel snapped her fingers. "You're the one Rafe was with the night he was injured! My mother-in-law showed me the articles from the hostage crisis. You're prettier in person."

"Thank you. Those department-issued pictures aren't very glamorous," she said, laughing.

"The whole family appreciates how you took such good care of Rafe, staying by his side and all."

A heated flush rose to her face. "We used to be partners. He would have done the same for me." She turned away, taking in her surroundings. Paintings adorned the walls; an area rug covered the hardwood floor in the entryway.

"So, do you and your husband live here?" Sara swept her arm, gesturing at the lovely house.

The light in Angel's eyes flickered and dimmed. "No. I'm afraid we're separated," she said, obvious pain in the admission.

"I'm sorry." Something about Angel inspired an easy rapport, and Sara reached out, touching the other woman's shoulder in comfort. ·

"Thank you. Why don't you come on in and get settled?" Angel asked.

Sara nodded. "First I need to get my bag from the car."

A few minutes later, bag in hand, she followed Angel upstairs to a floral-wallpapered bedroom. Fresh flowers filled a small vase on the dresser, and an antique lamp sat on the nightstand.

"This is beautiful," Sara said, running her hand over the lemon-colored comforter on a four-poster bed.

"Relax and enjoy."

"I intend to! I desperately need a nap," Sara said. "And can I bother you for an ice pack or a bag of ice?" She pointed to her knee, over which she now wore a lighter brace than the original one given to her in the emergency room.

"Of course!" The other woman turned to go.

"Angel?"

"Yes?" She braced her hand on the door frame and turned back around.

Sara swallowed hard. "Can you possibly tell me where to find Rafe? I tried to reach him to let him know I was coming, but I couldn't get through to his cell. I'd like to stop by after dinner."

Angel smiled. "Of course. I'll write down the address where you can find him, along with directions."

"Great. I'd appreciate it."

"So, dinner is at six. I hope you like fried chicken and mashed potatoes."

Sara's mouth watered at the thought. "Perfect."

"Okay, then. I'll be right back with the ice." She stepped out, leaving Sara alone.

She collapsed onto the comfortable bed. A light lemony scent permeated the room, and she relaxed, allowing her body to absorb the softness surrounding her, feeling calmer and safer than she had in New York City.

Rafe's parents still lived in the house he'd grown up in. Except for some updates and renovations, everything remained the same. Until the family descended. Then the noise level and chaos exceeded anything he remembered or could tolerate. Rafe was thirty-one and ready to settle down, while his sisters were married and lived within half a mile of their parents and each other, as did Nick. With the exception of Nick, they all had children. To most people, the sheer numbers would be confusing. To Rafe, it was normal.

His oldest sister, Joanne, had six years on him and always acted like his mother. She had a thirteen-year-old daughter and two rambunctious ten-year-old twin sons who currently wrestled in the den. Nick came next, then Rafe. Carol was three years younger than Rafe and had gotten an early start on her family. She had three adorable kids that Rafe called the Steps due to their ever-increasing height, girls ages two, four and six. Andrea was the most spoiled and self-centered, but she was learning how to give, thanks to her new baby boy.

And they all loved their fun-loving single

uncle Rafe. He managed to maintain that status by living in the city, visiting when he could and not allowing himself to be over-whelmed by family all the time.

When the noise level in the living room reached epidemic proportions, Rafe escaped onto the front-porch swing for some peace. The summer air was hot and humid, but at least the noise dimmed. He had only a few quiet minutes when his thirteen-year-old niece, Toni, joined him.

An adorable kid with light brown hair, her mother's serious eyes and a mini-adult personality, she immediately started talking.

"Hey, Uncle Rafe." She began kicking her feet back and forth beneath her.

"Hey, kid. Noise too much for you in there, too?" He pointed inside toward his parents' living room.

She nodded. "But I also wanted to talk to you alone."

"Shoot," he told her, gesturing with his hands.

"Okay." She drew a deep breath. "You're a guy, right?"

"Last time I looked," he joked.

She didn't laugh.

Rafe glanced at her. Her hair hung straight over her shoulders, and an intense expres-sion, much like his sister Joanne's, had settled on her face.

Okay, this was important.

"What's up?" he asked her.

"What do I have to do to get a boy to notice me?" She didn't meet his gaze, merely focused on her swaying feet.

Rafe was in over his head here. He didn't have kids. Didn't know how to give relationship advice to a teenage girl. But she obviously wanted a guy's perspective and couldn't talk to her father about boys unless she wanted him to lock her up until she was eighteen.

That left Rafe, her single uncle, to do the job. "Want to know what I think?"

She nodded, and this time she watched him carefully.

The pressure of getting it right settled on his shoulders. "I think any guy who doesn't already notice you has rocks in his head and isn't worth your time."

She blushed. "You have to say that. You're my uncle."

"True. But I'm saying it because it's a fact. You're special." He resisted the urge to reach out and ruffle her hair like she was a little kid. "So, maybe this boy has noticed you but he's too shy to talk to you?"

She shrugged. "Maybe. He's new around here, and he goes to the same camp as me.

The girls play the guys in softball, and he's really good!"

The obvious solution dawned on him. "Ask him to help you hit."

"But I don't need help." She rolled her eyes like he was a dunce. "I'm already the best hitter on the team!"

Rafe bit the inside of his cheek to keep from grinning. "Ask him for help anyway. Guys like to feel needed. Maybe then you can get to know each other."

She paused for a minute, seriously thinking about his suggestion. "Okay, good idea!" she exclaimed at last. "Hey, who's that coming up the walk?" She pointed toward the street.

He exhaled in relief. Subject obviously closed. A new attraction had captured her attention.

And what an attraction it was. Sara slowly made her way up the cobblestone path leading to the porch. He'd been so distracted by his talk with Toni, he hadn't heard the car pull up. But he noticed it parked on the street now.

He couldn't have been more surprised to see her. If Toni hadn't noticed her first, Rafe would have thought he was dreaming. He was relieved to see the crutches were gone and her limp was obvious but not terrible.

She was a vision. She wore white jeans and a ruffled tank top. Her long hair flowed loose, softly around her shoulders. Once again, he was struck by the stark contrast between the uniformed partner he'd known at work and the woman she was outside the job — and his body's immediate reaction to her.

She waved at him with a hesitant smile, obviously unsure of her reception, which was ridiculous. He might be shocked, but he wasn't disappointed. In fact, adrenaline pumped through him, filling him with anticipation and sheer delight.

"Who's that?" Toni asked.

"A friend of mine from New York," he said, just as Sara reached them. "Sara Rios, this is my niece Toni. Toni, this is my friend Sara."

He heard the question in his voice. *Why was she here?*

"Hi!" Toni said.

"Nice to meet you." Sara treated the girl to a warm smile.

"Hey, why don't you go inside and tell Grandma to set an extra plate at the table for company?" Rafe suggested to his niece.

He wanted to get Sara alone.

Toni nodded, turned and headed inside.

Before Rafe could speak, Toni's voice traveled back to him, loud and clear over the usual din. "Nana, Uncle Rafe has a girlfriend coming to dinner!"

Amused despite himself, Rafe shook his head. "She's thirteen," he said, figuring that explained it all.

Sara grinned. "She's cute."

"She has her moments. And there are seven more kids inside," he said by way of warning.

If Sara was going to survive his family, she needed to know what she was in for.

"I'm really sorry to show up uninvited. Angel said I'd find you here." She nibbled on her bottom lip. "I ate, so there's no reason to worry about putting out an extra setting. In fact, I should go. We'll talk later." Obviously embarrassed and rethinking her visit, she turned to walk away.

Rafe reached out to stop her. She hadn't driven over five hours to get here just to leave now. "Wait. My mother would love to see you again." In fact, Mariana Mancuso had found many excuses to ask about the pretty girl who'd slept in the chair while he was in the hospital.

Rafe had found just as many excuses to avoid answering. But that didn't mean he'd forgotten what Sara had done for him, or what those actions indicated about her feelings for him. Then there was the lingering curiosity about what would happen if they took things further and tested this *thing* that had been simmering between them since their days as partners.

Now she was here.

"Are you sure?" Sara asked hesitantly. "It sounds like there's an army of people inside."

"That about covers it," he agreed with an exaggerated shudder. "You'd be a welcome reminder of my life in New York. So stay."

"Okay. I just wish Angel had mentioned I'd be intruding or interrupting a family gathering."

He placed his hand on her bare shoulder, the warm skin singeing his fingertips. "You're not doing either. Angel knows another person is always welcome. Mom likes to say she cooks in the bathtub. In other words, there's enough for an army. But first, tell me. What brings you to this corner of the world?"

She raised her beautiful gaze to meet his. "Actually, you do."

Before he could reply, the front door swung open wide. "Toni said you have company. I came out to meet our guest," his mother, Mariana Mancuso, said as she joined them, her timing impeccable as ever.

"Hello, Mrs. Mancuso," Sara said. "It's nice to see you again."

"Sara! This is a pleasant surprise!" His mother stepped down onto the porch and pulled Sara into an embrace.

Sara's eyes opened wide as she hugged his overly affectionate mother, but she quickly relaxed and readily returned the gesture.

"I'm so sorry to show up uninvited."

"Nonsense! You're always welcome here! And that hug just showed me you're too skinny, so come in, meet the rest of the family and eat!"

Rafe glanced at the cleavage peeking from the top of Sara's shirt, now askew thanks to his mother's big bear hug, and thought her curves were just about perfect.

"We weren't finished talking," he told his mother. "I'll bring Sara inside in a minute." First he wanted to know why she'd come to see him.

What she wanted.

Whether or not she wanted *him.* The thought, once lodged in his brain, wouldn't go away. She was wrong for him on every level except the one that mattered most. He desired this woman like crazy. He wanted to know what would happen if they indulged the banked desire and took what they both wanted.

But he didn't get the chance.

His mother ignored his request to go inside alone. Keeping an arm around Sara's shoulder, she steered her into the house, where the entire clan had gathered by the front door, eager to meet Uncle Rafe's *girl-friend.*

Thanks to Toni, the designation was sure to stick.

Whether it was true or not.

CHAPTER FIVE

Rafe had a big family. A really big family. As in a lot of people sitting around the dining-room table all talking at the same time. Thanks to the fractured dynamics in Sara's family, she'd never been part of one big happy clan. The scene in front of her was a foreign one, but she couldn't say she minded. Food passed from person to person until Sara lost track of what she'd put on her plate. Although she'd already had dinner, she felt too guilty saying no to Mrs. Mancuso's generosity.

And truth be told, everything smelled delicious.

"You can pick at what you want and just push the rest of the food around," Rafe leaned in close and whispered.

At his husky tone and heated breath against her ear, warm flutters took up residence in the pit of her stomach, and she couldn't focus on anything but Rafe. His nearness. The raw, masculine scent of his cologne.

But rapid-fire questions shot at Sara from all corners of the long dining-room table, drawing her attention.

"Are you originally from New York?"

"Did Rafe really save your life?"

"What's it like to be a female cop?"

The questions came fast and furious, giving her little if any time to answer before another one was lobbed her way.

"Do you like living in Manhattan?"

"Are you really Rafe's girlfriend?"

The last question stopped her cold. Unfortunately, it had the same effect on the rest of the table, because everyone grew silent and turned her way, waiting for a reply.

"Sara and I are friends," Rafe said, jumping in to save her from embarrassment. "*Good* friends." He reached down and squeezed her leg.

He meant to relax her, but his big hand, fingers splayed over her thigh, had the opposite effect. Tension spiraled through every corner of her body.

Sexual tension.

Yearning.

Desire.

Since they'd been ushered inside the house, they hadn't had any time alone for her to explain why she'd come. Or that she'd need to stay with him while she was here.

One look at him on the porch with his niece, looking gruff and sexy, yet kind and gentle all at once, had her thinking crazy thoughts about exploring the obvious chemistry between them. Seeing where this need took them. And it was obvious now. There was no more wondering if he reciprocated. No more other woman between them.

She tried to swallow, but her mouth was dry. She lifted a crystal glass, taking a long sip of cool water.

She felt a poke and glanced down into inquisitive brown eyes.

"Do you like Uncle Rafe?" Toni, the young girl she'd met on the porch, asked her.

Sara bit the inside of her cheek. "I like him a lot," she said honestly.

"Me, too. Uncle Rafe is smart. He even gave me advice about a boy."

"He did, hmm?"

Toni nodded. "He said guys like to feel needed and that I should pretend I need help swinging the bat in softball to get him to notice me."

"What are you two ladies talking about?" Rafe braced his arm behind Sara's chair and leaned closer.

His body heat nearly swallowed her whole. "Toni was telling me you gave her advice about boys."

He grinned. "I was a little out of my element. It's been a while since I've played games with the opposite sex."

She wondered if his statement was true literally or figuratively. Since his broken engagement, had he sought comfort with other women? Or had he been alone?

"But I did my best to help out my favorite thirteen-year-old niece." Rafe laughed.

So did Toni.

Sara found herself tongue-tied.

"Well, I have camp on Monday. I'll let you know how it goes. Can I be excused? I'm finished eating," Toni said, switching subjects like a pro.

"Go!" Her mother waved from across the table.

"You heard that?" Rafe glanced at his sister in surprise.

The woman nodded. "Mothers hear every question their kids ask, whether they're paying attention or not. Sara, do you have a big family?"

"Umm, no. It's always been just me and my father."

"Oh, I'm sorry. I didn't realize your mother passed away."

80

Sara forced a smile, not surprised by the assumption. "She didn't. She walked out on us when I was fourteen."

Beside her, Rafe stiffened. "Joanne, cool it with the personal questions."

Sara appreciated him getting protective of her feelings, but she didn't need it.

"I'm sorry. I'm just trying to get to know her!" Joanne shot Sara an apologetic glance.

"It's fine. I'm fine. Don't worry about it," Sara said, surprised that she meant it.

Though she didn't normally discuss her personal life in public, this anything-goes attitude was a refreshing change, and she found herself wanting to answer the question. "My mother didn't like being a cop's wife. The danger and the panic when the phone rang while he was at work." Sara shrugged. "It just wasn't her thing."

In truth, her mother probably hadn't been able to cope with being a mother, either, as she'd taken off for *greener pastures.* She'd gone west to L.A. and had never looked back. Or called, for that matter. But Sara had her father, and they'd been a tight unit. Still were.

Joanne shook her head sadly. "Her loss."

Sara shrugged. "You're probably right."

"If you're finished, do you want to get going?" Rafe asked. He'd obviously had his fill of family.

"Whenever you're ready."

It took over half an hour to say goodbye to everyone and answer questions about how long Sara was staying and where. When Angel's Bed-and-Breakfast came up, Rafe's brother, Nick, stormed out of the house, the screen door banging closed behind him.

"Ignore him," Rafe whispered, his hand on her back. "He's going through a lot."

Sara nodded, feeling sorry for the estranged couple. Here were two people, not cops, who couldn't hold their marriage together. More proof not to expect happy endings and forever after.

Finally, she and Rafe escaped and drove in his open Jeep Wrangler to his house. Though less than a mile away, she was amazed at the remote location. He drove nearly out of town, turning on so many streets she couldn't keep track until they came to a sign marked Private Road, No Trespassing. He made a sharp turn on an unpaved road she wouldn't have noticed on her own. From there, they drove through what felt like a forest, the road unlit and surrounded by trees and foliage.

Rafe remained quiet and focused, while she enjoyed the wind blowing through her hair and the music blasting around her. The silence between them was comfortable as always.

He finally came to a stop in front of a dimly lit house and shut off the motor.

"Well." She spoke into the sudden silence. "This is about as remote as you can get."

He nodded. "Just the way I like it." He leaned an arm on the steering wheel and turned toward her. "Is your leg bothering you, or are you up to a walk on the beach?"

"I'm up for it. Light walking is good for me."

"Okay, then."

Together they walked the shore of the lake behind his modest home. She found it difficult not to watch his graceful stride as they strode the sandy shore.

Harder still to tear her gaze from his handsome face. "This place is beautiful. I don't know how you could ever leave it," she said.

He smiled. "The lake? The house? Those are hard to leave. The family? Not so much."

The chaos and noise level earlier might have been extreme, but there was no missing how much they all cared. "They're warm and loving. They care about you. And they're fun!"

Kids talking over adults. Adults yelling over each other. They were a vision of a life she'd never even glimpsed growing up.

"Fun?" He stopped in his tracks, turned and placed his hand over her forehead.

"What are you doing?" she asked.

"Checking for fever."

His grin did crazy things to her insides, and his touch . . . oh, his touch was hot, stirring up emotions and desires she'd dreamed about so often it was hard to believe they were real.

"So, tell me. Why are you here?" His husky voice spiked her body temperature even higher.

"I had to get out of the city," she said, then told him about how the Bachelor Blogger had targeted her after he'd left, the ensuing article tying her to the murder case and the subsequent threats.

"I'm sorry I left you twisting in the wind. I never thought that blogger would go after you."

"I know. The thing is, there's no one else I trust to have my back. I knew I'd be safe here with you." She glanced up at him, hoping he didn't read in her face the pure longing she felt in her heart.

He reached out and tucked a wayward strand of hair behind her ear. "I won't let anyone hurt you," he said in a rough and determined voice.

"I know." Because she knew him. "We do make a good team. I'm sorry I just showed up on your doorstep, but in my defense, I did try to call you."

He winced. "Service is sporadic around here, and since it's easy enough to find people, I don't worry too much about keeping my cell on hand."

"I left a message."

This time he let out a low groan. "I'm pretty lazy about listening to those. I must not have seen your number come up, or I would've called you back."

"That's because I called from a disposable cell phone."

"Smart." He nodded, approving. "Now that you mention it, I do remember getting a few calls from a number I didn't recognize."

"Well, I came anyway. I hope you don't mind the surprise."

"If you're in danger back home, I'm glad you came here."

"Like Coop said, two of us injured is the equivalent of one healthy human being."

"Way to stroke my ego." He grinned.

"I'm not too worried. Your ego is pretty solid. How's the rest of you?" she asked.

"Amazingly, I'm feeling pretty good. How about you?"

She glanced down. She'd left the brace back at the B and B. "I'm sure you noticed the limp."

"How about the pain? The flexibility? Will you —"

"I don't know." She cut him off, not wanting to discuss the future of her career. "Time will tell."

He inclined his head. "Fair enough."

Another thing she appreciated about Rafe. He instinctively knew when to back off. "Listen, there's one small problem."

"What's that?"

"Angel only has a room available for two nights. I can call around to local hotels, but I didn't realize there was a festival coming up that was such a big attraction. I may not find anything."

He waved away her concern. "You don't have to. You can stay with me."

She exhaled in relief. "I hoped you'd say that."

There was just one more thing standing between them. The words were unsaid, yet as loud as the wind. She swallowed hard, knowing she had to bring things out into the open. "What about us? What about what you said that night on the roof?"

"I said a lot of things. Just so we're clear, what exactly are you referring to?" he asked.

But from his deepening gaze, he obviously remembered.

She gathered the remainder of her courage. She couldn't stop thinking about what he'd said. What those words implied.

And she needed to know. "You said I was gorgeous. That I had curves to die for. When the blogger quoted you, I didn't know if you meant it or if it was the blood loss talking. Then we were linked as a couple, and I couldn't stop thinking . . ."

"About?" he asked, his voice gruff.

Sexy.

His gaze bore into hers.

The air around her hummed in anticipation. "About the chemistry we always had on the job. And all the things left unsaid."

His hands framed her face. "Things like this?" He lowered his head and touched his lips to hers.

She let out a soft sigh, and he deepened the kiss, letting his mouth do the talking. And he spoke eloquently, his tongue tangling with hers, kindling heat she'd dreamed about. Sparks flew between them, delicious, sweet and undeniably hungry.

Oh, yes. She hadn't imagined the chemistry. And it definitely hadn't been one-sided.

She wound her arms around his neck and kissed him back. Summer temperatures mixed with body heat. Intensity radiated from him, and she inched closer, seeking more. He complied, alternating long, lazy strokes of his tongue with deeper, faster thrusts, a prelude of what could be.

On and on it went. She didn't know how long they stood there, his hands threading through her hair, her fingers curling into the soft fabric of his T-shirt, his mouth making love to hers.

Suddenly the rumbling of a motorboat startled her.

She jumped back just as the motor shut down and a male voice yelled out. "Guess I should take my chessboard and go home!"

"You guessed right!" Rafe yelled back, gesturing at the man in the boat to leave.

He swallowed a curse. Didn't it just figure his uncle Pirro would interrupt at the best — and worst — possible moment?

He'd finally gotten a taste of what could be if he and Sara just let down their guard, and it was more explosive than he'd ever imagined. And if they hadn't been interrupted, he would have taken it to the obvious conclusion right here on the beach. He'd have finally known what being inside Sara, what becoming a part of her, felt like. But they had been interrupted, and now the reality of the situation settled on his shoulders. Of all the ironies in life, this had to be the worst. The woman of his dreams needed his protection, would be living under his roof and clearly wanted him, too. But taking what they both wanted would be a mistake, for more reasons than he had time to think about now.

The motor started up again, and the small boat turned and headed back the way it came.

"Who was that?" Sara asked, gazing toward the rippling water.

"My uncle Pirro. He's married to my father's sister. Actually, he's Nick's father-in-law. He has insomnia and often comes by for a game of chess or a talk." Rafe ran a hand through his windblown hair. "The way things are around here, I'm sure you'll meet him soon."

She smiled. "And I look forward to it." She paused and eased closer, a seductive gleam in her eyes. "So . . . where were we?"

She wanted to pick up where they left off. So did he. But someone had to think rationally and look out for both of them. As hard as it was, Rafe stepped back, folding his arms over his chest, deliberately placing distance between them.

"What's wrong?" Confusion followed by hurt flickered over her face.

The hurt hit him in his gut.

Rafe shook his head, sorrier than she could imagine. The last thing he wanted was to cause her pain, but she'd brought up their feelings, and he had no choice but to be honest.

"I don't understand. We're both unattached, right?" she asked before he could explain. And her voice cracked, making him feel even worse.

"Right." He inclined his head in a curt nod.

"And unless I'm really misreading signals, you were as into that kiss as I was."

She attacked a problem head-on. Another thing he liked about Sara — her no-nonsense attitude. "You're right. I was."

She perched her hands on her hips. "So, what's the problem?"

"We are. A quick fling can't end in anything but pain and heartache for us both."

His brother was currently living in hell over a woman who'd started out wanting the same things out of life as he did. Why willingly put himself in that position with Sara, his polar opposite, knowing ahead of time how it would end?

She drew a long, deep breath, her chest rising and falling beneath her shirt, and Rafe braced himself for an argument.

"You're right." She raised her hands in a gesture of defeat. "I've thought the same things myself." She turned her back to him and stared out over the lake, wrapping her arms around herself.

For comfort?

Or to ward off the chill?

He came up behind her, pulling her against him for warmth. And for one last touch before he took her back to Angel's for the night.

As the smell of the water mixed with her fragrant scent, Rafe wished like hell he could throw caution away and dive into her. After all, Rafe was all for affairs, and he was way overdue. He'd like nothing more than to bury his thoughts and himself deep inside Sara's sexy body. And if she was any other woman, he would.

But Sara wasn't just another willing female. She meant something to him. She had from the start. That kiss had proven without a doubt why he had to resist her — because his gut told him this limited time with her would never be enough.

And a short period of time was all she'd ever allow.

CHAPTER SIX

Rafe didn't sleep. How could he when he'd been given a taste of what could never be? He climbed out of bed early, determined to focus on the ordinary. The mundane. If he was going to have company, he needed to stock up the fridge. He showered and headed to town. First stop: Hidden Falls's doughnut shop, for coffee. Fortunately for the doughnut shop, unfortunately for Rafe, the small store was located next door to the barber shop where his aunt's husband, Pirro, and his cronies hung out every Saturday, rain or shine.

Today offered pure sunshine, as had most of the summer. Pirro wore a Yankees cap to protect his bald head from the sun and a pressed white-collared shirt courtesy of Aunt Vi. He was surrounded by his friends.

"Rafe!" They greeted him before he could speak.

"Hi, all." He tipped his head in acknowledgment. "In a rush." He hoped they'd take the hint.

"Sorry to interrupt you last night," Pirro said with a not-so-subtle wink.

"Not a problem." Rafe wasn't about to get into a conversation about his private life with the town gossips. These men were worse than the women who gathered in the beauty salon. He took another step toward the doughnut shop, but his escape wasn't to be.

"Vi tells me she's a visitor from the city?" Pirro prodded, digging for more information than his wife had given him.

"Good to know the family grapevine is alive and well." Rafe's mother had probably spoken to Aunt Vi bright and early this morning.

"You don't want to talk about it, do you?" Pirro asked.

"Nope."

Ernie, Pirro's best friend, had stepped toward Rafe. "You having trouble with your pecker? Because there are pills you can take for that. Pirro here can hook you up!" He spoke too loudly, and people on the street turned to stare.

"Ernest, you shut your mouth!" Pirro shouted.

Rafe agreed. Too much information about

his uncle's sex life, Rafe thought and shuddered.

"Not having any trouble, Ernie, but thanks for the advice. I'm in a rush, so I'll see you all later." He waved at his uncle and his friends and finally headed into the doughnut shop.

When he exited a few minutes later, coffee in hand, the men were huddled over Pirro, who was scribbling in a notepad.

"Bye, Pirro!" Rafe called out.

The older man snapped his pad shut while his cronies surrounded him, blocking Rafe's view.

"Strange," he muttered, hoping when he was their age he had better things to do than hang out outside the barber shop.

Sara spent her first day in the small town of Hidden Falls wandering the shops and getting to know the area. Main Street was decorated for the festival. Outdoor tables with umbrellas and chairs were placed on the sidewalk, and across the street on the grassy lawn, booths were being erected for everything from wine to handmade crafts to food. A makeshift stage had been set up at the far corner, with chairs lined up, obviously for a concert of some kind, and she found herself looking forward to the event.

She didn't run into Rafe, and she was disappointed. Though he'd made his feelings clear the night before, and, as hard as it had been, she'd agreed, she still wanted him. Now that they'd kissed, she knew what she was missing and found herself looking out over the street, hoping to catch sight of him. When she didn't, she consoled herself with the notion that there would be plenty of together time when she moved into his place tomorrow.

Before heading back to Angel's, she stopped at an Internet café to check her e-mail messages. She wouldn't answer them, because she didn't want anyone tracking the IP address, but she needed to know if someone was looking for her. She scrolled through the usual mass of jokes from her cousins, mail from the various stores where she shopped, and the daily account balance she received from her bank.

But there was one e-mail with a red flag that caught her eye. A warning from her bank that someone had been searching activity on the debit card linked to her account. Sara paid extra for the additional security just for times like this — the rare incident when she was working a case or lying low and wanted to be notified if someone was tracking her. Not that Morley's people would find anything. She'd taken out a lump sum of cash and wasn't leaving a paper trail.

Still, she was unnerved. Using one of the disposable phones she'd purchased the day she'd left the city, she called the bank, only to hear they'd been unable to discover who had initiated the search, just that it had occurred. She thanked them and hung up, frustrated, then called Rafe and left a message that she needed to see him. If he was going to be her backup, she had to keep him informed.

She walked into Angel's late in the afternoon to find her hostess in the family room talking to a young girl who appeared to be in her early twenties. Not wanting to interrupt, Sara waved and continued, planning to go to her room.

"Sara, wait! I'd like to introduce you to someone."

Sara walked over and joined them.

"Sara, meet Joy. Joy, this is Sara. She's a guest here now. Joy's looking to book her wedding here this fall!" Angel said, her excitement at the prospect of hosting the event tangible.

"That's fantastic. Congratulations," Sara said, more to Angel than to Joy.

But the other woman didn't seem to

notice. "Thanks. I couldn't stay here, because I decided to come at the last minute and the rooms are booked because of the Wine Festival, but I wanted to come take a tour. I'm looking for a small, intimate bed-and-breakfast where my fiancé and I can get married in a private ceremony," she said dreamily.

The woman obviously had stars in her eyes when it came to romance, Sara thought. She bit the inside of her cheek to keep from expressing her opinions on the subject. She'd learned long ago not everyone was as pessimistic as she was. Then again, not everyone saw divorce and discontent everywhere they looked within their own family tree.

"Anyway, since Joy will be around for the festival, I thought I'd introduce you in case you see her in town," Angel explained.

Sara smiled. "I'll be sure to look for you."

"Same here." Joy's gaze remained on hers too long for comfort.

"Sara, when I'm finished with Joy, I'm going to be baking a second set of apple pies for my booth at the festival. Want to help?" Angel asked.

Glad to turn her attention away from Joy, Sara glanced at Angel and nodded. "Sure. I'd love to."

"Okay, why don't you meet me back downstairs in about half an hour?"

"I will." Sara turned and headed for the stairs and the comfort of her room. Her knee ached, and she could use the time to lie down for a little while.

Sara must have dozed off. She jumped up, certain she'd been sleeping for longer than the half hour Angel had given her. A glance at her watch told her she'd been out for an hour.

By the time Sara walked into the kitchen, Angel was surrounded by ingredients, bowls and a mixer. The scent of apple pie permeated the air, and a warm, tingling feeling filled Sara, making her wonder if this was what she'd missed growing up without a mother.

The thought took hold, and she shivered, unable to escape the haunting feeling that she had missed out on something deep and fundamental. Something she'd never allowed herself to miss — or want — before.

"Those pies look tiny," Sara said, noticing the mini-piecrust holders spread out on the table.

All day she'd been forcing the unsettling news about someone trying to track her accounts to the back of her mind by immersing herself in the present, and now was no different. She'd find comfort in easy things like making small talk and baking.

Angel glanced up, her hands covered in flour as she kneaded dough. "I'm making individual pies for the festival. I'm working on the crust right now. Grab a roller. The dough will be ready in a second."

Sara glanced at the cluttered table as she settled into a chair beside her. "I haven't baked in years."

Not since she'd turned herself into a little cook for her father. Birthday cake had been her specialty. But once out on her own, she'd worked long hours, and, on her days off, she kept busy by shopping and browsing as she walked through the city. She'd never thought to use her old baking skills as an outlet to relax or keep busy.

Half an hour later, she'd rediscovered the magic. And the company was interesting. Rafe's sister-in-law had an independent streak as long as Sara's, and a good sense of humor.

"So, how was dinner last night?" Angel asked.

Sara raised her gaze. "Yours was delicious, but you're not referring to that, are you?"

Angel shook her head, a guilty smile on her face. "Sorry I didn't warn you, but I figured you might not want to show up uninvited. But I know my in-laws. They love company."

Sara nodded. "They welcomed me with open arms, but I'd have appreciated a heads-up anyway."

"Next time," Angel said with an easy shrug. Obviously, she didn't feel too badly about sending her over.

"I'd already met Mr. and Mrs. Mancuso when they came to visit Rafe in the hospital," Sara said. "I like them."

Angel gestured to the flour, indicating that Sara should coat the prep area so the mixture wouldn't stick.

Sara followed her lead with each step.

"My in-laws are good people. I just wish they'd stop pushing for Nick and me to get back together. It's not as easy as they think."

In between instructions on how to make piecrust, Angel confided in Sara about her miscarriage and the reason behind the breakup of her marriage. According to Angel, she wanted to move on and put her energy into building the B and B. Nick wanted to constantly talk about what had happened, what it meant to them both. But Angel felt that talking about the most painful thing in her life wouldn't change the fact that she'd never be a mother. Her choices were to try again and risk miscarrying over and over or adopt. Not wanting to deal with any more disappointment, she'd chosen to give birth to her business instead.

She needed the stimulation the B and B provided. And for Angel, best of all, it didn't leave her with time to think about their loss and her inability to have children.

Nick wanted the life they had had.

Angel couldn't go back.

All things Sara innately understood.

"But Rafe seems to get why I need this." Angel waved her arm around the small kitchen, but Sara knew she was really referring to the entire house and venture. "I wish Nick did, too."

Sara raised an eyebrow. "Rafe isn't on his brother's side?"

The other woman shook her head. "He says he's on *our* side." Angel paused from pressing the crust into the tin. "You sound surprised."

"It's just that I always thought of Rafe as a very traditional guy. He wants what his parents have. Marriage, family. The white picket fence." Which was what stood between them now.

Angel pressed her lips together, obviously needing time to think. A few seconds later, she exhaled a long breath. "Okay, I'm going to share something private. But I don't want you to think I'm a gossip. I'm telling you this because no woman drives five hours just to say hello to a man. You must have strong feelings for Rafe, or you wouldn't be here."

Sara bit the inside of her cheek. "Actually, I need him. I need his . . . expertise." She stopped short of saying protection. There was no reason to worry Rafe's sister-in-law by admitting there was danger looking for her.

"I'd believe you, except for one thing. His mother told me you didn't leave his side the entire time he was in the hospital. That's caring. Whether you want to admit it or not."

Sara shook her head and laughed.

"What's so funny?"

"You remind me of me." Sara had been as blunt with Lexie when she'd confronted the other woman about her feelings for Coop. Sara admired Angel's honesty and decided to open up a little more. "Okay, I care about Rafe," she admitted. It felt funny saying it out loud.

Angel smiled wide. "My gut is so good," she said, laughing. "So, I'll tell you where the Mancuso boys got their feelings on marriage and family. Maybe it will help you understand Rafe better."

Sara rested the rolling pin on the table and leaned in. "Now you've got me curious."

"When they were younger, Rafe's father had an affair." Angel wiped her hands on a damp kitchen towel. "And not a one-night stand, either — though that's how it started out."

Sara let out a low whistle. "You're kidding." She was stunned by Angel's admission, unable to imagine how a younger Rafe would have handled that.

She scratched an itch, running her hand over her nose, her focus never leaving Angel.

"It was a long time ago. He started sleeping with a woman who worked in the office. Joanne was older and on her own, but the boys and Carol were still young, so Mariana was home then. She hadn't started working in the business and wasn't there every day. My understanding is that Frank eventually fell in love with this other woman."

"Uh-oh."

Angel bobbed her head in agreement. "But Frank's a good guy, and the guilt ate him alive. He broke up with the woman so he could save his family. He confessed to Mariana, and they agreed to try and work things out. But the other woman felt betrayed and made their affair public. Even the kids knew. It was very ugly."

"But they obviously stayed together and made the marriage work," Sara said, remembering the close-knit couple from the night before.

Angel nodded. "They're stronger than ever. But the affair left scars. Sometimes I think Nick can't let go of the idea that he needs me around where he can see me, check up on me. In his mind, letting me work outside the home, especially taking in strangers, just opens us up to possible trouble."

Sara paused, thinking about what Angel had said. "Maybe it's not about cheating. Maybe he's just afraid of losing you, period. This kind of job takes a huge commitment. Sort of like mine does. It takes a rare person who can understand that. I should know. Every one of my family members who is or was married to a cop had marriage problems."

"But his attitude drove us apart, not this place!" Angel pounded on the dough in frustration.

"You said he wants to talk. Can you give him that?" Sara asked gently.

"And relive the whole thing again?" She shook her head. "No, thank you. Listen, I've been over this in my head a million times. I don't want to talk about it, if you don't mind."

The pain in the other woman's eyes was obvious. The wounds were still fresh.

"Not at all. I understand." Sara decided to change the subject to one closer to her own heart. "I bet Rafe's need for a stable marriage is based on what he experienced as a child. How old were the boys when this happened?"

"Nick was eighteen, attending college. Rafe was fifteen. Carol was twelve, still pretty young, but the boys knew exactly what was going on."

"Which tells me Rafe understood every-thing that happened all too well."

"Exactly," Angel said. "He knows what it takes to make a relationship work."

But not even he could work miracles, Sara thought.

Angel rose from her seat and looked around at the mini-piecrusts on the table waiting to be baked then filled. "Great job," Angel said.

"Thanks!" Sara said, feeling proud of herself and her attempt at playing Betty Crocker.

"Maybe tomorrow morning you can help me with the filling? I like to make them fresh before the festival starts."

Sara nodded. "I'd like that."

A knock sounded at the side door.

"That'd better not be my father or Nick coming by to play handyman," she muttered. "Excuse me a minute." She turned and headed for the door, moving the curtain to see who was on the other side.

"Rafe, come on in!" she said, opening the door, giving Sara no warning or chance to prepare.

Rafe stepped inside, looking too sexy in a navy T-shirt and worn jeans. Her stomach curled in that funny flip she'd come to associate with being around him.

"Hi!" Sara waved at him.

"Hey." He raised his hand back.

Angel leaned over, greeting him with a sisterly hug. "What brings you by?"

"I need to have a word with Sara," Rafe said, his gaze never leaving her face.

"I'll just go inside and clean myself up. Give you two some privacy," Angel said.

"Thanks," Sara murmured.

Rafe waited until Angel disappeared, her footsteps creaking the stairs. He pulled out a kitchen chair, turned it around and seated himself, straddling the back. "You have flour on your face." He grinned and wiped her forehead with his hand.

Her skin burned at the mere touch.

Though his eyes flared deeper, he didn't acknowledge the yearning that was so obvious between them. "I came as soon as I got your message. What's wrong?" he asked instead.

"My bank sent me an alert. Someone attempted to access my account and track my purchases."

He frowned. "That's not good. Any idea who?"

She shook her head. "Nope. But I've only used cash since I left. There's no way for them to find me that way."

"But if they are determined, it's only a matter of time."

Sara exhaled a long, resigned breath while Rafe's gut was tied up in knots. She'd gone from appearing like sunshine in white shorts and a yellow flirty tank top to looking like she'd lost her best friend.

He reached out, placing his hand on her shoulder. Her bare skin scorched his palm. "As far as we know, they haven't found you yet. But I think you should stay with me now. Just to be safe."

She nodded. "I thought the same thing. Your place is remote and hard to find. Angel's is right in the center of things. It's just that . . ." She wrinkled her nose.

"What?"

"I was looking forward to helping Angel with her pies tomorrow." She glanced at the uncooked crusts on the table.

He burst out laughing. "Sara Rios, are you telling me you like being domesticated?"

An adorable flush stained her cheeks, and an amused grin tugged at her lips. "Let's just say it has its moments."

"Well, don't worry. You can still help. You'll just be stuck with me watching over you. This way if someone does track you here, they won't get you alone."

She nodded in agreement. "If you don't mind babysitting?"

"Of course not. I'd be at the festival anyway." Now he just had an excuse to be by her side, admiring her long legs, sexy ass, gorgeous face. . . .

"Great! Thanks." Her face lit up in relief. "I need to clean up, but then I'll pack my bag and we can get going."

"In the meantime, I'll call the captain and see if he's heard anything from the D.A."

"I'd appreciate it. I've been afraid to check in. I know they sweep for bugs, but still." She sighed. "Thanks, Rafe. I know you didn't sign up for this."

Maybe not, but he'd never walk away.

With Sara upstairs washing up and packing, Rafe tried the captain from Angel's phone and left a message for the other man to call him back on his cell.

He was about to grab a can of soda from the fridge when he heard a noise outside the window over the sink. A loud banging sound that repeated itself again.

Cautious, Rafe headed out the side door — and nearly tripped on his brother, who was struggling to attach a garden hose to the spigot on the side of the house.

"What the hell are you doing?" Rafe asked. Luckily, he hadn't pulled his gun on his sibling.

"Replacing the leaky hose with a new one. What are you doing here?"

"Picking up Sara. Does Angel know you're here?"

Nick shook his head. "And don't tell her. Pirro mentioned the hose leaked and Sara was having trouble watering the yard."

"If she finds you here, she'll kill you."

"That's why you aren't going to tell her."

Rafe raised an eyebrow. "Do you really think she won't notice a new hose?"

Angel didn't want help. But the fact that his brother was helping instead of complaining was a good sign. Still, the fireworks when Angel discovered he'd meddled in her life would be heard around town.

"By the time she realizes, it'll be fixed and

I'll be gone. At least she won't have to struggle with the old one."

"That's awfully generous of you." Rafe paused, debating on offering advice. But this was his brother, and he wanted to see him happy. "Maybe Angel would appreciate the fact that you're taking an interest in her . . . project. Instead of you sneaking around like you think she can't handle it herself, maybe you could tell her you're coming to accept this venture of hers. I bet it would go a long way toward helping you reconcile."

"Maybe Angel can speak for herself!"

Rafe groaned and, without meeting his brother's gaze, turned to face his sister-in-law.

"Hey there." Rafe greeted Angel with a smile.

His sister-in-law scowled, her gaze reaching beyond Rafe to her husband.

Rafe wouldn't want to be in Nick's shoes right now. "I'm going to leave you two alone to talk," Rafe said, backing away and heading for the house before he could get any more involved in family drama.

Once inside, he found Sara waiting for him in the kitchen, her large rolling suitcase packed and waiting beside her — a blatant reminder he was about to bring her *home.*

CHAPTER SEVEN

Rafe might not be ready for the intimacy sure to follow from moving in with Sara, but he appreciated a woman who could pull herself together quickly.

"That was fast." He gestured to the suitcase.

She shrugged. "I knew I'd have to leave in a couple of days, so I didn't unpack completely."

"What do you say we —" The ringing doorbell interrupted him. "This place really is like Grand Central Station," he muttered.

For the first time, he could understand his brother's issues with his wife running the place alone, always distracted by one thing or another. Then again, if it came down to a distracted wife he loved or no wife . . .

No question, Rafe thought.

The doorbell rang again.

"Where's Angel?" Sara asked when she

didn't come to answer.

"Outside with Nick. I'll get it for her." He headed to the door, Sara behind him.

Two strangers stood on the other side. The festival crowd had already begun milling around town. Strangers Rafe didn't recognize browsed the local shops and eateries. Good news for the struggling economy. Bad news for his ability to spot potential danger.

Rafe crossed his arms over his chest and assessed the men on the other side of the screen door. One dark-haired, the other blond-haired, both blue-eyed and clean-cut. The preppy type who'd stand out in a town that lacked pretension. The blond guy even wore argyle.

"Can I help you?" Sara asked, stepping around Rafe and taking over.

"We have reservations," the lighter-haired guy said.

"Why don't you come in?" She pushed open the storm door, and the men stepped inside.

"Ms. Mancuso?" The dark-haired guy obviously assumed Sara was Angel, the owner. "You're as lovely as the name of your establishment." He oozed slick city charm.

Rafe set his jaw. "She's not Ms. Mancuso," he said in an annoyed tone. Because he didn't want this guy hitting on Sara or his sister-in-law.

Sara cast him a curious glance before refocusing on the men.

"Ms. Mancuso is seeing to something in the backyard, but why don't you come in and have a seat." Sara gestured to the small sitting area with a couch and a desk that Angel used to check in guests.

"*Mrs.* Mancuso is out back," Rafe stated bluntly.

"Are you a guest here, too?" blond guy asked hopefully. Ignoring Rafe, he checked out Sara's obvious assets, staring without shame at the exposed cleavage in the vee of her thin cotton top.

"No, she's not," Rafe said through gritted teeth.

Thank God he'd already convinced Sara it was time to move out. These two *gentlemen* irritated the hell out of him, and he reassessed his earlier thought about his brother accepting a distracted wife. Especially if she was distracted catering to other men. Paying guests or not, Rafe now knew why his brother was uncomfortable with his wife's new occupation.

Suddenly Sara nudged Rafe with her elbow. "I asked if you were going to get Angel or whether I should?"

Rafe wasn't about to pull Angel away from

Nick. Hopefully they could use the time outside alone to communicate in a positive manner.

"She's busy right now." Rafe turned to the two guests. "Why don't you do as the lady said and wait in the foyer until she comes back inside."

They shot each other a wary glance and stepped into the small waiting area. Good. Rafe wanted them on guard around *his women.*

The sudden thought unsettled him. Being protective of Angel made sense. He was looking out for his brother's wife and their fragile marriage. Being possessive of Sara was another story. She wasn't part of his family. Nor was he involved with her personally. Hell, he'd deliberately taken a step back from that ledge. Besides, she didn't need his protection. Rafe and everyone in the NYPD knew Sara could take care of herself. In fact, she wouldn't be here now but for her injury. He knew as well as anyone that even at less than one hundred percent, Sara was a force to be reckoned with. It was one of the things he admired about her. One of the things he didn't want any other men admiring, too.

"What's wrong with you?" Sara whispered her question so the men couldn't hear.

Before he could answer, the back door slammed shut with way too much force, rattling the pictures on the walls. Obviously there'd been no real communication between Nick and Angel after all.

"Angel, you have guests!" Sara called out before whipping around back to Rafe. "Well? What's wrong?" Hands on her hips, she tapped one foot impatiently.

Jealousy, that's what was wrong with him. He was jealous of perfect strangers who'd looked at her with interest.

Something he wasn't about to admit.

"Let's just get going," he suggested. Before he did or said something to embarrass himself further.

Sara left her car parked at Angel's. She'd pick it up another time, and went home with Rafe. He was silent on the drive back to his house. He'd been grumpy and moody since Angel's guests had arrived. Rude and obnoxious had been more like it. Maybe he was just being protective of his brother's marriage? But would that keep him in a bad mood now?

As they approached his long driveway, he reached into his pocket and pulled out his cell phone, glancing at the number before answering the call.

"Hi, Aunt Vi." He listened, shook his head. "Wait. Slow down. And speak louder. I can barely hear you over the crackling." He cast a glance at Sara. "Told you service was bad here."

She nodded and settled in to wait.

Rafe stopped the Jeep at the end of the driveway as he obviously struggled to hear his aunt yet keep her calm at the same time.

"I'll be right over, okay? See you in two minutes. Bye." He disconnected the call, then turned to Sara. "Sorry, but Aunt Vi is having some kind of crisis. I couldn't understand her through her hysteria, so I need to drop by for a few minutes."

"That's fine." Sara didn't mind.

He backed out of the driveway, and, not one minute later, they pulled onto a street directly off Main. He parked the car in front of a small Cape-styled house and cut the engine.

"I can wait in the car," Sara offered. She didn't want to intrude if his aunt was upset.

To her surprise, Rafe shook his head. "Come on in. I should warn you that Aunt Vi is prone to hysterics. Maybe seeing company will calm her down faster."

Sara shrugged. She hopped out of the Jeep and followed him up the path to the house. He rang once and let himself inside.

Another interesting part of small-town living: the unlocked doors and the easy entry and access everyone had into each other's homes and lives. So different from the city. The neighborliness and comfort had to lead to more intimate friendships. The kind Sara lacked in the big city. Once she entered her apartment, she could lock the door and not see anyone for hours, days or weeks, depending on her mood.

"Aunt Vi?" Rafe called out.

"I'm in the living room!"

Rafe led Sara to a small foyer that opened into a cozy family room. An older woman with salt-and-pepper-colored hair sat on a couch covered by a hand-knit afghan blanket, a box of tissues by her side.

"Oh, Rafe, you're such a good boy to come over." She sniffled and forced a smile at Rafe before her stare settled on Sara. "Oh! I didn't realize you'd be bringing company!"

The woman jumped up from her seat and began to fuss with her already perfectly coiffed hair. Hair that could only be done in a salon and finished off by a ton of Aqua Net hair spray.

"Aunt Vi, I want you to meet Sara Rios, my friend from New York. Sara, this is my aunt Vi."

Sara shook her hand. "Nice to meet you."

"What's wrong?" Rafe asked, walking up to her and placing a strong, comforting hand on her shoulder.

Aunt Vi gripped a tissue tighter in her hand. She'd obviously been crying.

"I'll just wait in the car." Feeling like an intruder, Sara turned to leave.

"No, no. You're the woman who stayed by Rafe's side when he was critically injured, right? My brother told me you were in town. That makes you like family, so please stay."

Sara raised an eyebrow at how quickly Rafe's aunt had welcomed her. Her own father would still be shooting questions at Rafe in order to discover whether he liked him or not.

"Thank you," Sara said. She chose a chair and settled in, remaining unobtrusively quiet while Rafe spoke to his aunt.

"Sit." Rafe guided the middle-aged woman back to the couch. "What's going on? And why didn't you call Janice or Judy?"

"Those are my daughters," Aunt Vi helpfully explained to Sara. Then she turned back to Rafe. "I called you because you're a cop. You know how to find things out about people."

Rafe narrowed his gaze. "What things? What people?"

"It's Pirro." The other woman sniffled. "He . . . he . . . he's having an affair!" she wailed, pulling tissues from the box and blowing her nose loudly.

Rafe was right when he'd said Aunt Vi was prone to hysterics. Her dramatics were enough to make Sara cautious about believing her claim.

But Rafe stiffened at the words. Leaning in close, he placed his hand over hers. "What happened?" he asked gently.

Suddenly Sara remembered Angel's description of Rafe's father's affair. Obviously Aunt Vi's claim hit a nerve. As much as Rafe complained about his family, he clearly loved them, too.

"Pirro disappears out at night." Aunt Vi sniffled.

"Where does he go?" Rafe asked.

She shrugged. "Each time it's a different story. Tonight he said poker, but I called the other wives, and their husbands are home!"

Rafe patted her hand in reassurance. "I'm sure there's a good explanation. Maybe he went for a walk. Maybe he wants to have a cigar, and he knows you get upset when he smokes."

She shook her head. "He's gone too long for it to be one of those things. It's another woman. I just know it!"

119

"Maybe he's out on the boat. Just last night he drove it past my house, hoping I'd be around for a game of chess." As he spoke, Rafe raised his gaze and locked eyes with Sara.

They both remembered what they were doing at that same moment last night.

What she wanted to repeat again.

Her heart pounded harder in her chest.

From his deep, steady gaze, Sara had the distinct sense he wanted the same thing. Despite his protestation to the contrary.

"He's not out playing chess." Aunt Vi recaptured his attention.

The woman's breathing became rapid again, and Sara feared she was gearing up for another wail.

"Listen, I know things are strained with Angel and Nick separated, but that has nothing to do with you and Uncle Pirro."

Aunt Vi shook her head. "I drove him to leave me, and now he's sleeping with another woman!"

She wailed, convincing Sara that some things were inevitable.

"Impossible. Pirro would never cheat on you with another woman."

Aunt Vi sat up in her seat. "I know that! He wouldn't cheat, cheat. Not in the way you mean."

"What other way is there?" Rafe asked.

Sara wondered the same thing.

"Didn't you hear? I said he's *sleeping* with another woman!"

Rafe narrowed his gaze. "I'm sorry, but I'm still confused."

His aunt glanced down, not meeting his gaze. "This isn't easy for me to say out loud, but if you're going to help me you need to know." She drew a deep breath. "I'm a nymphomaniac," she said in a stage whisper.

Rafe choked and began coughing uncontrollably.

Was he laughing? Or beside himself, Sara wondered. She bit the inside of her cheek and somehow remained silent.

"Do you need water?" Aunt Vi asked, patting him on the back.

"I'm fine," he managed.

"Then pull yourself together and help me. I said I'm a nympho!" She pressed a tissue to the inside of her eyes, blotting tears. "I've been reading all about it on the computer, and I think I might be a sex addict like David Duchovny. I should be put away in one of those rehab places. Oh, poor Pirro!"

Rafe pinched the bridge of his nose. Why couldn't she have called one of her own kids for this? Because he was a cop, he reminded himself, reinforcing the notion that no good deed went unpunished.

He kept his gaze on his lap, afraid that if he looked at Sara, he'd burst out laughing. His aunt didn't find this amusing. For some crazy reason, she believed the things she was saying. "I think you're watching too much Dr. Phil," Rafe told her.

She twisted a tissue between her hands, shredding it to pieces. "Your uncle Ralph, my first husband, bless his soul, he was insatiable. It was a little tough at first, but that's what I'm used to! Pirro and I have so much in common, and I know he tries to keep up with me, but he doesn't have the stamina my Ralph had. So I think he goes looking for downtime elsewhere."

You having trouble with your pecker? Because there are pills you can take for that. Pirro here can hook you up! Ernie's words from this morning repeated themselves in his mind. If Pirro didn't have the stamina to keep up with his wife, it made sense that he'd turn to Viagra or something like it. Again, more information than Rafe wanted or needed to know about his relatives. And if Pirro needed a pill just to keep up with one woman, why in the world would he go looking for another?

God help him, Rafe still wasn't following

his aunt's logic. "Keep explaining," he said to her.

"I saw that Agnes Parker coveting him in church last Sunday. Church of all places!"

Rafe resigned himself to her rambling until he could make sense of what she needed from him.

"You see, my Ralph was friends with her first husband and I know she's frigid, so he wouldn't have to worry about her wanting sex from him, too! He's going to her instead of being home in bed with me!" She started to wail again.

Sara cleared her throat, and Rafe met her gaze. Amusement and pity flickered across her face. "Maybe Rafe could follow him next time he leaves, see where he's going?" Sara offered, speaking for the first time.

Rafe swallowed hard. Following Pirro. His head was so filled with unmentionable images, he'd never have thought of it himself.

"Would you mind?" Aunt Vi asked.

He shot Sara a grateful glance. She'd given him a solution and a way out of here. "Next time he leaves, call me. Day or night. I'll follow him and see what's going on."

"You're the best!" Aunt Vi hugged him tight, reminding him of why he loved her.

She had daughters, and so he and his brother were the sons she'd never had.

She'd gone with his mother and father to his football and baseball games and to his graduations. She'd spent hours baking with his mother, and she'd often been there when he came home from school, sneaking him cookies before dinner even when his mother had said no.

The warm memories caught him off guard, and he hugged her tighter. "Don't worry," he reassured her, meaning it.

Though he didn't want to think about her sex life, he'd do his best to help ease her mind. Despite Rafe's experience with his father's affair, he still couldn't believe Pirro would cheat on Aunt Vi — with or without sex, the man was loyal. He thought the sun rose and set on his wife.

Still, Rafe didn't doubt Pirro was up to something. The writing in the notepad, the way his cronies circled around him when Rafe walked out of the doughnut shop . . .

Aunt Vi was prone to dramatics, but Rafe had no doubt the man was working an angle. He just had to figure out what it was.

Rafe parked in his driveway. Sara met him behind the Jeep, ready to pull her suitcase out of the back herself. Instead, he grabbed the handle, too.

"I've got it," Rafe said.

124

"I appreciate the gesture, but I can handle it." They each had a grip on the luggage handle, but he'd just had surgery. She wasn't about to let him do heavy lifting just for her.

She cleared her throat and shot him her fiercest *I mean business* look. "Do I need to call your mother and tell her you aren't following doctor's orders? Maybe she'll come over and supervise you."

He immediately released his hold. "Fine. Drag it in yourself."

"I will." With a grin, she yanked the suitcase, ignoring the tug in her knee. It had been a long day, and of course her injury was bothering her.

He strode ahead of her, unset the alarm and released the dead bolt. Along with the woodsy, hidden driveway, the security system made her feel much safer.

"Welcome home," he said, holding the door for her.

"Thanks." She walked past him, lifted her suitcase over the doorstep and inside. She glanced around, taking in the warm, cozy place he called home. "I love it. It's very you."

Deeply masculine and earthy, in a welcoming sort of way.

"Thanks." He smiled, pride evident in his

expression. "My family has owned this property for generations. My great-grandfather originally bought the land. He subdivided the acreage and left it for his sons, who left it for their sons and so on."

"And so on. I get it. But didn't your father want to live here?"

"Even if he did, my mom never wanted to be hidden away. She liked being in town, in the center of things. So Dad used an old cabin for fishing until Joanne got married. He subdivided the property, and we all got our portions early. Joanne is a few miles closer to town. I took the most secluded part." Rafe shrugged. "So, here we are."

She wrapped her arms around herself. "It's so nice that you have such deep family love and tradition. You can just feel it surrounding you." It was something she definitely missed.

The sense of having roots in any particular place.

"The only thing handed down in my family is being a cop." For some reason, the thought didn't bring as much comfort as she got from envisioning Rafe's family living on this land.

Rafe didn't reply.

It was almost as if he didn't want to bring his big family into the small house with them. "So, how many bedrooms are there?" she asked, respecting the boundaries he'd erected.

"Two."

"Perfect!" She glanced toward the small hallway leading to the other rooms, which appeared directly next to each other.

"The second one is an office with a daybed."

She nodded. "Great. I can sleep there."

He shook his head. "I'll take the daybed. You can have mine. It's more comfortable."

"Nope. You're the one recuperating from surgery. I'm the one intruding. I'll take the daybed."

"Don't argue with me again." He placed his hand on the handle of her suitcase and wheeled it toward the hall.

"But —"

"But nothing. Keep it up and I'll call my mother and tell her I'm sleeping in my bed while I put you, my guest, on the daybed." He threw her threat back at her. "She'll be over here in no time, lecturing me on how to treat a lady. And you wouldn't want to subject us to that, would you?"

Sara swallowed her argument. It wouldn't hurt her to be gracious. "Okay, I'll take your bed. Thanks." Although she didn't know how she'd get any sleep, imagining him there.

She wondered if he slept nude.

Sara sighed. She doubted she'd get any sleep with him directly next door, either.

Chapter Eight

Rafe couldn't sleep. How could he when the woman he desired more than his next breath was in the adjoining room? Her mere presence was making him crazy. He tossed and turned, imagining he could hear her breathing next door. Wondering what she wore to bed.

His bed.

Suddenly he bolted upright and glanced at the clock. One o'clock. He must have dozed off after all. Sounds from the other room told him there was someone in the kitchen. He assumed it was Sara, but he climbed out of bed, pulled on an old pair of sweats and headed into the other room to make sure.

Sure enough, Sara stood in front of the sink. But he was unprepared for the sight of her in a short two-piece number, all silk and lace, that was probably supposed to be cute but instead looked sexy as hell.

Her hair, tousled from sleep, hung over her shoulders. Her full breasts peeked from the low-cut V-neck and her nipples poked through the nearly sheer silk.

How much could a red-blooded male take?

Knowing he was staring, he cleared his throat.

She jumped, startled, and met his gaze. "I didn't hear you come in!"

"Sorry. I wanted to make sure it was you and not someone trying to get to you."

She nodded in understanding. "Sorry if I woke you. I just wanted to get a drink of water." She raised the glass in her hand.

He inclined his head. "You didn't wake me. I couldn't sleep."

"Me, neither."

Quiet descended; there was no noise except for the hum of the fridge and the ticktock of a clock on the wall.

"We could sit and talk for a while," she suggested. As if she weren't half-naked. And he weren't completely aroused, the blood rushing in his ears, through his head and settling in one very obvious body part.

There was no way she could miss it any more than he could ignore it. "Or we could pick up where we left off on the beach."

Her eyes widened in surprise. "I thought

130

you said it was a bad idea?"

He inclined his head. "It probably is."

They looked at life from opposite points of view. He wanted to believe anything was possible. She was a cynic, always looking for the worst. He knew better than to think he could convince her to change her mind about relationships.

But he could change his about short-term affairs.

She reached out and placed her hand against his forehead much as he'd done to her the other day. "Are you sure you're not sick?"

"I'm sure." He was burning up, but not from fever. He stepped closer. "Are you still interested?"

She didn't back away. "I could be persuaded . . . if I knew what brought on the change of heart."

He dove in completely. Meeting her gaze, he lifted a lock of her long hair, winding it around one finger. "I didn't like it when those guys tried to hit on you back at Angel's."

Her eyes darkened to a richer hue. Desire shimmered in the chocolate depths, and a pleased smile tipped her lips. "So that explains your snippy behavior."

"You sound pleased."

She shrugged. "Maybe I am. Nobody wants to be rejected, even if the reason is a sound one." She paused, biting down on her lower lip.

"I'm not turning you down this time," he assured her.

She nodded her head in understanding. "But . . ."

"What?" He couldn't take it if she rejected him, and steeled himself for whatever she said next.

"Are you sure you're up to it?" She reached out and gently drew her hand over the still-fresh scar on his chest, her fingertip delicate and hesitant as she touched his skin.

Memories of waking up and seeing her in his hospital room came flooding back. Of Sara asleep in a chair, watching over him — caring for him. Yes, they'd already bonded emotionally, and knowing she cared deeply merely assured him that this next step was right.

Necessary.

As necessary to him as breathing, Rafe thought. Because there was no way he could walk away from her.

"So, what do we do now?" she asked.

"This." Rafe tugged lightly on her hair and pulled her toward him.

She came willingly.

Her lips met his, and all the oxygen sucked from the room. This was what he'd been waiting for. Starving for. He swirled his tongue inside her mouth and found himself surrounded by her scent and her taste, aroused by the sweet feel of her lips urgent and insistent on his.

She snuggled in close, plastering her body against his until his bare chest crushed her breasts. Skin against skin, every soft curve pressed tightly into him. There was no room between them. Not even air.

She trailed kisses with her lips from his mouth to his jaw, her hot breath against his cheek, her wicked tongue whispering over his skin.

He shuddered from the arousing sensations he never wanted to end.

"Take me to bed," she whispered into his ear.

She asked for what she wanted, and he liked that about her.

Rafe grabbed her hand and led her into the bedroom. He paused by the nightstand and opened the drawer, pulling out a box of condoms.

"I like a man who's prepared." She sat on the bed and eased back against the pillows, the pose provocative and arousing: everything he hadn't let himself want, there for the taking.

His heart beat hard inside his chest. He placed the foil packet on the corner of the mattress and sat beside her, deliberately leaving the dim light on so he could enjoy the view. Her hair fanned over the pillows, her eyes hooded and pupils dilated. He watched in awe as her nipples tightened, peaking beneath the flimsy material, silently beckoning to him.

He slipped his hand beneath the thin strap of her top, his finger deliberately grazing her skin. "I never knew you liked silk and lace," he murmured. But he was damned glad she did.

Sara lifted one shoulder in a light shrug. "That's because we didn't spend much time together outside of work," she said, her voice sexy and raw.

"That's because I knew I wouldn't be able to keep my hands off you."

"And now you don't have to."

She met his gaze, her need crystal clear, so he slid the straps down over her arms until the entire camisole gave way, pooling around her waist, exposing her full breasts to his view.

He hadn't known she was so full or ripe, and he wondered what other surprises awaited him. His mouth watered, the need to taste her growing stronger. "Beautiful."

She made no move to cover herself, merely braced her hands behind her, thrusting those luscious mounds forward, teasing him, tempting him, as she waited for him to make the next move.

He cupped her breasts, letting their weight settle in his hands, her nipples puckering and pressing into his palms. Just the feel wasn't enough; he turned his attention to those tight peaks, rolling and plucking her nipples between his thumb and forefinger, watching with satisfaction as she threw her head back and writhed beneath his touch.

He'd found her sensitive spot, he thought, pleased, and continued the sensual assault.

Her breathing grew more and more un-even, and suddenly Rafe was on a mission to see how far he could take her this way. Dipping his head, he sealed his lips over one breast, pulling the distended bud into his mouth. His other hand never left her other breast, and he continued giving them equal attention.

Her breathing increased, while his body tightened more with each pant until her body convulsed and she let out a long, drawn-out moan of pleasure.

He lifted his head in time to see her slide her hand from beneath the waistband of her silk shorts.

Startled, he met her heavy-lidded gaze. "Should I be insulted?" he asked lightly.

Because he wasn't. He was even more turned on.

She shook her head, a naughty look in her eyes. "Only if you're insecure."

He burst out laughing. "I admire a woman who isn't afraid of anything."

She grinned. "I believe it's your turn now."

"I'd like mine the old-fashioned way."

"I think that can be arranged." A slow, seductive smile curved her lips. "I don't want you to exert yourself. You're still recovering, after all." She sat up and eased his shoulders down until he lay flat on his back.

Liking this show of control, he placed his hands behind his head and grinned. "Then take care of me, babe."

"I thought you'd never ask." Sara pulled the string on his sweats, releasing the waistband, then lowered the soft cotton only to discover he wasn't wearing boxers. Or briefs. Or anything but a raging hard-on meant just for her.

She glanced at his swollen member and swallowed hard. "Commando."

He merely shrugged.

"That means you sleep . . ."

"Naked."

Just as she'd thought.

"Is that a problem for you?" he asked.

"It certainly isn't."

"Good." He kicked the sweats off, leaving him gloriously naked. "Your turn." He watched her intently.

She wasn't normally self-conscious, but his admiring gaze unnerved her, in part because she'd wanted this for so long. At the reminder, she turned her thoughts off and decided to enjoy. After all, this might be the only time she had with Rafe, and she wanted to savor and remember it all.

Her top was already wrapped around her waist, and it didn't take long to shimmy both pieces down her legs and slide them off.

"Now we're on equal footing." His eyes darkened with need, his expression one of pure admiration.

She swung her good leg over his hips and settled her body over him. Warm skin against warm skin, he felt so good as she eased herself down and settled her lips on his.

He captured her head with the back of his hand, holding her in place while he thrust his tongue inside her mouth. Like everything else they did, they were in complete synch, his rhythm and hers meshing perfectly. Each kiss, every roll of their hips, the rasping of her sensitive breasts against his hair-roughened chest, was in unison.

His erection teased her, rubbing against her flesh, making her ache and want with a desperation she'd never experienced before. And the sensations were spectacular, shooting through her body, which now begged for completion.

She broke their connection only to grab for the condom packet on the edge of the bed and tear it open. She sat back, watching out for her knee, and rolled the condom over his shaft.

Her hands shook as she touched his rigid length, covered with soft skin. Her fingers lingered, feeling and learning him until his hips bucked upward, startling her.

"I suggest you get to it or it'll be over before it begins," Rafe said, his voice rough. He gripped the sheets beside him, knuckles white.

She'd obviously tortured them both long enough.

She bent her legs to lift herself over him. Pain shot through her knee, and she buckled over. "So much for me taking care of you." She spoke over the searing pain, knowing it would eventually subside.

"Maybe we're supposed to take care of

each other." He brushed her hair out of her eyes and met her gaze.

"What did you have in mind?"

He climbed out of bed. He was gorgeous, his body tanned and fit. He pulled a chair from the desk in the corner, turned it around and sat down.

Then he crooked a finger her way. "Come here," he said, his tone sexy and full of need.

She stood and walked over. "I like how you think."

As she swung her bad leg over his thighs, he grasped her hips and helped her maneuver directly over his erection, which jutted out at her, poised for entry.

He placed one hand over her mound, using his finger to spread her moisture, tease her flesh. She bit down on her lip, allowing the gentle but insistent sensations to take over, enjoying his tender touch until her good leg buckled from the weight.

"Ready?" he asked gruffly.

She nodded.

Raising her hips, he lifted her and settled his erection at the juncture of her thighs. He thrust upward at the same moment she released herself and settled onto him completely.

The shock of the connection made her pause. He was thick inside her, buried deep.

She met his gaze and saw the same sense of rightness and awe settle over his handsome face. It scared her so much she shut her eyes and rocked her hips in an attempt to focus on the sensations in her body, but for the first time she couldn't separate emotion from need. Desire from yearning.

He tugged at her hair, and she opened her eyes. He wanted her to watch. She saw it in his face and was powerless to deny him.

And then they began to move together, in unison, the rock of her hips, the thrust of his, working together to take her higher and higher. He was buried so deep, she felt all of him inside her, every thick, rigid, velvet inch as they ground together where their bodies joined.

Harder, faster, he took her higher.

He breathed deep, his exhales sounding like erotic groans in her ear.

His hips rocked against hers over and over, and she gasped at each sensual assault, the waves coming at her from all sides, inside and out. His cheeks were flushed, his eyes dilated, and every raw groan took her closer to the explosive orgasm that was just out of reach.

She wrapped her arms around his neck to thrust harder against him, letting him plunge higher and deeper. He released her hair, slipping his hand between them again and touching her where she needed it most. His fingertip slid over her, and the pressure sent her spiraling out of control as she exploded, coming in wave after never-ending wave that took him along for the ride. His last final groan reverberated in her ear and sent shock waves through her body.

Even after the contractions subsided, Sara held on to him for dear life, her arms still around his neck. But when reality came pouring back, she unlocked her hands and released him, easing herself off, careful not to put too much pressure on her bad knee.

She heard rustling behind her, and then, taking her by surprise, he wrapped an arm around her waist and pulled her back into bed.

No words were spoken as, naked, he curled himself around her, held on tight and fell asleep.

She didn't relax as quickly or as easily, the ramifications of finally making love to Rafe hitting her hard.

She'd dreamed of this, but the reality was far more potent and exciting than she'd ever imagined. Even with them both not quite at one hundred percent, he'd satisfied her like no man ever had. Because he'd breached the emotional walls she'd always kept high.

Walls she'd just have to make higher now that she knew what they were capable of together.

Because no matter how incredible, Sara knew one thing for sure when it came to relationships: all good things had to come to an end.

Rafe woke up to an empty bed and the sound of the shower running in his bathroom. He immediately processed two things. The good news — Sara was still here. The bad news — she wasn't in his bed.

He stretched, feeling the pull of muscles telling him he was alive and feeling good. Better than good. Great.

The water stopped running, and his gaze wandered to the closed bathroom door.

He eased himself up against the headboard, propped his arms behind his head and waited.

A few minutes later, the door swung open and steam trailed out, followed by Sara wrapped in one of the beige towels his mother had bought him when he'd moved in, convinced he needed her help.

"Good morning," he said.

She jumped, obviously startled. "I didn't realize you were up."

"I am now." In more ways than one, after

viewing her glistening skin, damp hair and creamy exposed skin.

"I hope I didn't wake you."

He shook his head. "Sunlight did that." He gestured to the blinds he'd forgotten to draw closed the night before. "Where are you going?"

"To get my clothes. I need to go over to Angel's to help her set up her pie booth at the fair."

"I'll drive you. I figured we could pick up your car and park it back here, where no one will notice it. Then we'll go back to Angel's." He'd hoped to coax her back to bed, but she'd already warned him she wanted to be at Angel's early this morning. "Just let me jump into the shower, and I'll meet you in the kitchen."

She nodded and started for the door.

Not too awkward considering it was their first morning after.

They hadn't discussed last night, but in his mind that was a good thing. He didn't want her running scared, and if she knew just how much he'd enjoyed her, how much he wanted to be with her again, she'd do just that. So silence on the subject suited him fine.

Silence in general, did not. "Sara."

She turned back to him. "Yes?"

"Why don't you move your things in here?"

She narrowed her gaze, assessing him.

"Did you really think I'd let you sleep alone in your bed the rest of the time you were here?"

An amused smile pulled at her lips. "Umm . . ."

"Of course, if you want to be alone . . ."

She shook her head. "I'll be right back with my things." She turned and ran out the door, leaving him laughing.

And pleased.

Not bad for a morning's work. He had her where he wanted her.

The rest would fall into place.

They ate a quick breakfast of cereal and milk before heading over to the bed-and-breakfast, bringing Sara's car back to Rafe's, and returning to Angel's, resigned to helping his sister-in-law and Sara load pies into her minivan — only to discover the two guests who'd checked in yesterday had already finished the job. The pies were securely in the van along with her price signs and flyers.

Frick and Frack and their argyle vests were nowhere to be seen. Rafe called his brother to make sure he'd be at the festival to watch over Angel. Just in case.

Sara slid out of the Jeep, an added spring in her limp that Rafe attributed to last night. He was damn well floating.

"Sorry we're late," Sara said, heading to meet Angel by the van.

Rafe couldn't tear his gaze off her short, flouncy skirt, which showed off her long legs, her skimpy tank top and beaded flip-flops. She'd skipped the knee brace, and when she wasn't looking, he'd tucked it into the backseat of the car. After a long day of working at the booth, she'd be happy to have the support.

"No worries." Angel waved away the apology. "Biff and Todd did all the heavy work so we didn't have to." She shot a grateful gaze toward the two men who'd walked out onto the front porch, dressed as preppily as they'd been the day before. They were damned odd, and his radar was on alert.

"They seem really nice," Sara said.

Rafe frowned. "What kind of names are Biff and Todd, anyway?"

"Shh!" Sara nudged him with her elbow. "They helped Angel out, so leave them alone!"

Rafe shook his head, uncomfortable with their defense of those two men. He couldn't say why they bothered him, but they did.

And instinct rarely served him wrong.

Angel glanced at her watch. "I need to get moving. Why don't you meet me at my booth, and you can help me sell?" she asked Sara.

She nodded eagerly.

He wasn't sure what had her so excited to work a pie booth, but he wasn't about to take that smile off her face. He'd just spend the day at the family spice booth, hanging out with his relatives and keeping an eye on her from a close distance.

Biff and Todd weren't the only strangers that concerned him. The influx of visitors would camouflage anyone who came specifically for Sara. But if someone was after her, they'd have to get through him first.

CHAPTER NINE

Main Street in Hidden Falls was as busy as Little Italy during the annual San Gennaro Festival in New York City. Okay, maybe that was an exaggeration, Sara thought. But for a small town near the Canadian border, the streets were pretty crowded. Throughout the morning, she'd met many locals, including Rafe's uncle Pirro, a happy, kind gentleman who obviously adored his family. She couldn't see him looking for comfort or anything else from a woman other than his wife. But as Sara knew too well, appearances were often deceiving. Who knew what Pirro did in his spare time?

Today, however, everyone was mingling together, enjoying the sunshine and the festival, including Rafe and his brother, who were watching every move she and Angel made. But they weren't the only ones. Biff and Todd were never far away, either, constantly offering to restock the pies or buy them food or drink from another stand. Their attention made Sara uncomfortable. If she didn't already know the men had made their reservations way in advance, she'd be concerned that maybe they had been sent by John Morley, but their reservation preceded her coming here. They might be too clingy and preppy for her taste, but they weren't hit men.

Joy, the woman Sara had met at Angel's yesterday, walked by and purchased an apple pie. Sara caught sight of her a few more times during the day. She mostly kept to herself, and Sara even toyed with the idea of introducing her to Biff and Todd, but then she remembered Joy was engaged. Better to leave well enough alone.

"Ladies," a familiar male voice said.

Speak of the devil, Sara thought. Biff stood in front of the booth, Todd at his side.

"Hello," she said in a deliberately cool tone.

She wanted to keep her distance from these two, mostly because she knew they annoyed Rafe, and she didn't want to instigate trouble. He was looking out for her physical well-being. She could do no less for his emotional one.

"Are you enjoying the festival?" Angel,

ever the warm proprietress, asked the two men.

"I am. It's a nice town you have here," Biff said.

"What brings you upstate, anyway?" When Sara was curious, her inquisitive nature took over.

The men met each other's gaze before Todd turned back to face her. "We work for a wine distributor in New York, and we're looking to make new contacts."

"Makes sense," Angel agreed. "We have quite a few vineyards in the area and a lot of people interested in doing business during festival time."

"Have you been successful so far?" Sara asked.

"We've met some nice people, but we've yet to hook up with the main person we want to do business with," Todd said.

"That'll come soon enough." Biff spoke with cool confidence. "But that's not the reason we came back to your booth."

"What is?" Angel asked.

"Just want to offer to get you ladies some lemonade. The day's getting hotter, and we thought you might be thirsty."

Sara had been saying no thank you for most of the morning, but Rafe was glaring from across the way. "I'd love some," she said, hoping they'd go for the drinks and forget to come back.

"Me, too," Angel said. "Thanks."

The men smiled, obviously pleased they were needed, and headed off to the lemonade stand.

The line of people who'd formed behind them edged forward, eager to buy Angel's pies. Especially the mini ones that people could eat while they enjoyed the fair, something Sara understood well. She'd snuck more than one as a snack and wouldn't be surprised if she'd cut into Angel's profits. She was definitely glad she'd worn a skirt with a stretch waist.

Apparently, sex last night made her hungry today.

Amazing sex.

Hot sex.

Sex with one very special person.

Across the crowded street, she met Rafe's gaze.

To outsiders, he manned the family spice booth along with his brother, speaking to people who came to taste their famous Italian spices on dishes Mariana had made. But Sara recognized the look on his face, the fierce determination that told her he was in cop mode, on the lookout for anyone unusual in the crowd of neighbors and strangers. His protective nature eased her own nerves and enabled her to enjoy the festival. But it was the caring, sensual looks he reserved for her alone that kept her tingling and in a constant state of anticipation.

Sara couldn't stop thinking about being with him last night. They'd had breathtaking, off-the-charts sex. He'd been everything she'd dreamed about and more. *More* referring to the bond they shared. An emotional link that went deeper than the connection between their bodies.

They'd once been partners, and she'd thought they couldn't get any more in sync.

She'd been wrong.

Sex with Rafe had been a perfect dance. As perfect as the way she'd known he'd yell *drop* on the rooftop even before the words escaped his perfect mouth.

"What are you smiling about?" Angel asked, breaking into her thoughts. "You're practically glowing!"

"I was just thinking about how delicious your pies are. And wondering if I could sneak another without you noticing." She rubbed her stomach, which was already craving another pie.

Angel shook her head. "No, you're not glowing from food, although these days that's the only way *I* can get those rosy cheeks. It's Rafe. He's putting that glow in your cheeks."

"What makes you say that?"

Angel shot her a knowing look. "The way you're staring at him. The way he hasn't stopped staring at you."

"Oh. Well." Caught, Sara raised her hands to her heated face.

"Yes. Well." Angel grinned. "I remember those days, when Nick used to put a smile like that on my face." She sighed wistfully.

"You miss him."

"Of course I miss him." She slowly lowered herself into a chair behind the counter. "You don't lose your other half and not miss them."

"Have you told him?" Sara asked. Because from where Sara sat, Nick was looking at Angel the same way. He obviously longed to be back with his wife.

Angel tipped her head to one side. "Have you told Rafe he blows your mind?" she shot back, a grin on her face.

"Direct and to the point. Now, see, this is why we get along so well." Sara laughed. "So, have you told him?"

Angel shook her head. "No. There's no point. Not until he accepts the new me, career and all. Missing just isn't enough."

"I understand." After all, wasn't that the

same reason she and Rafe had initially agreed not to get involved?

Because they couldn't accept certain things about each other and what they believed? It was also why Sara wasn't about to have a morning-after conversation with him.

"So . . . your turn. Have you told Rafe how you feel?"

"We have an understanding," Sara said vaguely.

A silent agreement — sex until it was time to go home.

She could live with that.

"I remember those days of easy sex," Angel said dreamily.

"If that's all you're looking for, Biff and Todd seem eager to fill the role."

"Eew, no!" Angel said, laughing. "I may be separated, but I'm not desperate! Besides, I'm not really single. And even if I was interested in dating other men, those preppies aren't my type."

Sara nodded. "I prefer my men a little more manly, too."

Once again, her gaze drifted to Rafe.

Her gaze locked with his, and he inclined his head in a tilt she found incredibly sexy. She could stare into those eyes forever, Sara thought.

"Lemonade as requested!" Biff said, breaking her connection with Rafe, whose expression soured as he caught sight of their returning admirers.

His brother took an angry step out of the booth, but Rafe grabbed the other man's shoulder, stopping him in his tracks.

Crisis between husband and wife averted, Sara thought.

At least for now.

Rafe had had to physically restrain more than his share of men during his career, but holding back his brother was a first. He understood the impulse that drove Nick to want to plant his fist in the preppy men's faces, but it wouldn't be cool.

"Relax," he said to Nick. "You don't want to make a scene in front of the entire town and piss Angel off."

His brother's shoulders relaxed, but Rafe wouldn't release his grip. Not until he was sure Nick wouldn't go for the men again.

"Are you okay?" Rafe asked.

Nick, still breathing hard, nodded.

"And you won't go off half-cocked?"

Nick shook his head.

Rafe loosened his grip but remained ready to restrain his brother again.

"She doesn't have to be so damned nice

to them," Nick muttered. He braced his hand on the counter in the makeshift booth.

"She does when they're paying her room and board," Rafe said pointedly.

"Don't remind me."

"Someone has to. The bed-and-breakfast is part of the problem. Your problem."

Nick let out a groan. "What does she see in them, anyway?" he asked, his gaze traveling to Biff and Todd.

Clearly it was time to knock sense into his brother's thick head. "Let's see — they're young and good-looking," Rafe said, trying not to gag on his own words. "And they're hanging around Angel and making her feel good. Why wouldn't she like the attention?"

Why wouldn't Sara?

The thought jumped out at him, and Rafe's insides curled with jealousy. The difference between himself and his brother, however, was that Rafe wouldn't let two strangers poach his woman.

His woman.

Uh-oh.

Sex does not make a relationship, he reminded himself. *Especially not in Sara's mind.*

But it did in his.

"They have no right to even look at her.

She's married," Nick said, his anger palpable.

"She's separated," Rafe qualified. "And if you don't fix things soon, she might just end up divorced and free to do whatever she wants with whomever she chooses."

"And that would kill me," Pirro said, joining the men.

"Where did you come from?" Rafe asked.

"I went back home to pick up more calzones for my Vivian." He tipped his head toward the far end of the booth, where Vivian and Rafe's mother were selling their Italian dishes along with individual jars of spices. "Vivian's calzones are *molto bene!*" He kissed his fingers and raised them in the air. "No, not just very good — the best!"

Pirro was obviously dedicated to his wife, and still smitten, too.

Rafe thought back to his aunt's claims and couldn't imagine her husband finding comfort elsewhere. But he couldn't talk to Pirro about it now. There were too many people around, and Nick still looked ready to blow a fuse.

"Now, what's this nonsense about divorce?" Pirro asked, placing an arm around Nick's shoulder. "My Angel is an independent woman, but there's no reason why you two can't work things out."

"Right now he's upset two of her guests are paying her a little too much attention," Rafe explained.

"And she's enjoying it too much," Nick said.

Pirro nodded in understanding. "Ahh. Now I understand. Nick, you have to know how a woman's mind works. When she's not getting attention at home, she becomes starved for affection. Of course she'll be flattered when other men look her way. Even if it's really her husband's attention that she's looking for."

Man, couldn't Nick see what everyone was trying to tell him? "Step up before it's too late," Rafe said to his brother.

And there was no time like the present. "Nick, let's go on over to Angel's booth. I don't know about you but I could go for some apple pie."

Nick hated it when his brother was right. Things needed to change. Nick knew it. He just didn't know how to make it happen. He headed over to Angel's booth, determined not to argue with his wife and to take a step in the right direction for a change. He sure as hell wasn't getting anywhere butting heads with her every time they were in the same vicinity.

The flow of traffic at Angel's booth had faded, and the two women were sitting on stools, drinking lemonade and laughing. They presented a distinct contrast, Angel with her long, beautiful, jet-black hair and Sara with the blond halo flowing over her shoulders. The two women had obviously become friends in the short time Sara had been in town. Nick didn't know a thing about her. He'd been so wrapped up in his own problems, he hadn't taken the time to get to know his brother's ex-partner or even find out why she was here. Though if the way Rafe looked at Sara was any indication, the reasons for her visit were extremely personal.

"How about some apple pie for two starving men?" Rafe asked, getting the women's attention.

Sara met his gaze and greeted him with a wide smile.

Angel's expression as she caught sight of Nick was much more wary. "Apple crumb or apple pie?" Angel asked politely.

Dammit, she knew which he preferred. She didn't have to question him like he was an ordinary customer.

But he'd promised himself no picking an argument. "Pie," Rafe and Nick answered at the same time.

Sara jumped up from her seat. "Two apple pies, coming up." She walked over to the back, where the pies were stored.

Rafe immediately joined her, leaving Nick alone with Angel.

Nick shifted from foot to foot, unsure of where to begin. "Good day at the booth?" he finally asked.

She nodded. "Sold a lot of pies and booked B and B reservations into the fall."

She just had to bring up the business. Testing him, he thought.

When he didn't answer immediately, she locked her gaze on his and never flinched, waiting for a reply.

He was determined not to fail. He had to work through his problems with her owning the bed-and-breakfast and with them being unable to have a baby. Getting *her* to open up and talk to him would be an even bigger challenge.

"That's great!" he said at last.

Her blue eyes grew wide and filled with hope. "Is it really?"

No. "Yes." He hoped she didn't notice he'd gritted his teeth. "Are you going to the dance tonight?" He changed the subject to one easier to deal with.

Angel's shoulders and stance relaxed. "Actually, I am."

His mood lightened. "So I'll see you there," he said, feeling upbeat for the first time in a long time. "And tomorrow night's wine tasting?" he asked.

"That, too."

In for a penny, he thought. "Save me a dance tonight?"

"Sure," she said, but she sounded uncertain.

"Hey, we've just gone all of two minutes without fighting. I figured why not push our luck?"

She laughed, a free and easy sound he missed. "I'd like that."

"Me, too." A quiet moment passed with nothing but the sound of their breathing. No arguing, no bickering. It was time to get out before he put his foot in his mouth. "So, I'll see you tonight?"

She blinked in obvious surprise. "What about your pie?"

He angled his head toward the back of the booth, where Rafe and Sara stood with their heads together, whispering and obviously lost in their own world, pie forgotten.

"Ahh." Angel grinned.

"Yeah." He grinned, too. "So, uh, I'll catch up with you later?"

She nodded. "Sure."

He shoved his hands into his pockets and

160

took a step back. "And we'll dance?"

She nodded. "We'll dance." This time she sounded more certain.

"Good." He turned and headed for the booth, hoping they could sustain the truce longer than just this night.

Pirro loved life, but his happiness was tied to his family's, and they were all an unhappy mess. His daughter was separated, his son-in-law, who he loved like his own, couldn't see past his own pain and hurt to find his way back to the wife he loved, and Pirro's own wife was out of sorts but wouldn't tell him what was wrong. His side business was the only thing stress-free these days.

Pirro, on the other hand, valued what was important, and he decided to surprise his Vivian with flowers. Maybe that would cheer her up. He purchased the nicest bouquet he could find from Manny the florist, who'd set up a booth at the end of the street outside his shop.

Pirro paid, pocketed his change and turned to head back to the spice booth, but he was stopped by two young men he'd seen around town earlier. He didn't know their names, but they were the only ones wearing argyle sweaters in the heat of summer, so they stood out even among the other strangers in town.

"Pirro DeVittorio?" the blonder of the two men asked.

"The one and only! What can I do for you? Is it my company's homegrown basil that interests you?" He'd been fielding requests all day after people tasted Vivian's calzone and asked what the secret ingredient was.

The blonde fellow eyed the darker-haired man and laughed. "Yeah, the basil."

"My son-in-law, Nick, can give you information about product. I'm just in charge of distribution," Pirro explained. "And while you're discussing the basil, please take a look at our other products. I'm sure you'll find our spices are better than any on the market today."

"Pops, we don't need the spiel. We're already sold."

Pirro grinned. "Well, that makes things simpler, but the same rules apply. My son-in-law is taking orders at the booth. Then we'll be in touch as to shipment dates and times."

The darker-haired man took a step closer. "No, we'll tell you how it's going to be. We want in on your supplier and distribution."

Pirro raised an eyebrow. "You're confused. My company, the Spicy Secret, is the supplier. Our spices are homegrown," he said proudly. He'd worked his way up in the company, starting as a delivery boy when he was in high school. He'd been a part of their growth and success.

"Pops, you don't have to play word games with us. We know you're in the drug trade. So are we."

"Drug trade?" Pirro narrowed his gaze. They couldn't be referring to his side business. Nobody but close friends knew about that.

"Our bosses in New York just want access to your Canadian supplier. Tell him you're ready to move into the harder stuff, and we'll take care of the rest."

They knew.

Pirro's mouth grew dry. His side trade had happened accidentally after he'd married Vivian. He'd been good friends with her husband, and, after his passing, he began keeping Vivian company. Their friendship progressed to romance, they fell in love and Pirro quickly discovered his old friend's tales about his insatiable wife were true. Pirro had a hard time keeping up with Vi, but he didn't want to disappoint her in bed. He confided in his doctor, who gave him a sample of Viagra and Pirro discovered the little pill was magic. But he couldn't fill a prescription and risk his Vivian finding out his stamina wasn't naturally his.

A friend told him about a friend who had a friend across the border in Canada who could get Viagra cheap. Pirro contacted the man, and soon he was meeting him monthly to pick up more pills. His barbershop group noticed his good mood, he admitted what caused the change and soon he became the Viagra king of Hidden Falls, supplying his friends with Viagra and single-handedly helping the sex life and maintaining the privacy of the town's older male population. It was a harmless side business. But what these men wanted sounded *dangerous.*

"Who told you about the Viagra?" he asked.

"That doesn't matter. The point is, we know and we want in on your supplier and use of your trucks to ship to New York."

"Who do you boys think you are, coming to my hometown and making demands?" Pirro straightened his shoulders, and though he was shorter than both men, he was bulky enough to be intimidating.

"We're the guys you don't say no to," the blond guy said, unfazed.

"Well, I just did."

"Sorry. Wrong answer," the darker-haired

one said.

"But we'll tell you what. Since we're here for a few days, take some time and think about it. I'm sure you'll do the right thing." He turned to his friend. "Let's go get something to eat."

Pirro shivered and watched them leave, telling himself they'd go back to the city after the festival and everything would be fine. He hadn't totally convinced himself, but he couldn't possibly get involved in illegal drugs.

He walked through town, stopping at various booths, waving to friends, most of whom he'd known for years. Many of whom were now his customers. Pirro prided himself on taking care of the men in this town, men like him, who had erectile-dysfunction problems that a little pill called Viagra took care of.

Although Viagra was a prescription medication in the United States, most of his friends, like Pirro, didn't want their wives to know about their little problem or lack of stamina. By purchasing across the border in Canada, there was no insurance involved, no paperwork, and best of all, no nosey Gertrude at the pharmacy to ring up their order and snitch to their wives. Pirro thought of supplying Viagra to his friends as a good deed. He didn't mark up the pills or make a profit. He just made sure the men and women in town had their happy endings.

But what those two men wanted involved hard drugs, and, to make matters worse, they obviously wanted him to send those drugs to New York on company trucks for distribution in the city.

He shook his head and broke into a sweat. There had to be five kinds of felonies involved in what they were asking. No way would he agree, Pirro thought.

No way at all.

CHAPTER TEN

Sara stepped into the shower, and as the spray hit her body, the exhaustion of the day slipped away and she found herself looking forward to the dance tonight. To her never-ending surprise, she loved the small town, the people, and the way Rafe's family had welcomed her as if she were an old friend. Most of all, she liked the way Rafe looked at her when he thought she wasn't aware. His dark eyes feasted on her body, and she reveled in the attention.

She tipped her head up and let the shower spray run over her face, washing away the grime of the day. She barely registered when the bathroom door opened, but she definitely knew when Rafe pushed the shower curtain aside and stepped into the tub along with her.

"Well, hi there," she said, wiping the water out of her eyes.

He grinned. "Hi, yourself." Taking the wet

washcloth from her hand, he knelt at her feet. With deliberate precision, he started with her toes, running the soapy cloth over her ankles, then her calves, taking his time. He let the soap accumulate and paused as the water washed it away. Slowly but surely he inched higher, teasing her as he rose ever closer to the juncture of her thighs.

She trembled at the sensual assault and closed her eyes as he continued. The washcloth, a mixture of soft and roughened material, glided up her thighs as high as possible, until his knuckles grazed her damp outer lips. She quivered and placed one hand against the tile wall for support.

Suddenly his thumb stroked her moist opening, and she nearly died from the sweetness of the feeling. As she leaned against the wall, he dropped the cloth and sealed his mouth over the place she needed him most. He worked magic with his hot tongue and gentle teeth.

She moaned and sank backward. The cold tile pressed against her skin while his tongue flickered back and forth, over and over, taking her higher and closer to a pulse-pounding orgasm that seemed just out of reach. She curled her fingers into her palms and thrust her pelvis toward him, seeking harder, deeper contact.

He understood and thrust one finger inside her.

"Yesss." The word slipped out on a sharp hiss.

"I've got you," he promised, his deep voice turning her on even more.

His long finger eased out, then in, out then in, until Sara got lost in the sensation. She could no longer tell which felt better, his thick finger inside her or the pressure he applied outside. And then he rubbed his thumb over her clit and stars exploded behind her eyes, every nerve ending coming together, sending her into erotic, perfect oblivion.

When her awareness came back, Rafe was standing, one hand braced on the wall beside her, a satisfied grin on his handsome face.

Water, somehow still hot, pelted over them.

"You look as pleased as I feel," she said.

"Not quite," he said over a strained laugh. He leaned close and kissed her hard, his mouth sealing over hers.

She tasted herself on his lips, and that fast she wanted him again, this time inside her.

He pulled her against him, his hard member pressing deliciously into her stomach, pulsing with desire. "I need to be inside you." As always, Rafe seemed to read her mind.

She threaded her hands through his wet hair. "Then what are you waiting for?"

"Your knee, my chest," he reminded her.

She winced at the reminder of her injury, something she'd managed to place at the furthest recesses of her mind while she was here.

He slammed the water shut and opened the curtain.

Pulling a towel off a hook, he wrapped it around her, and somehow they made their way to the bed.

The towel fell to the floor. They dropped onto the bed. Rafe lay over her, his body covering hers, deliciously hot, sinfully sexy.

And then he paused to look into her eyes. The world fell away, and it was just the two of them. He brushed her hair off her face and kissed her lips, so softly and reverently, with a wealth of emotion she wasn't ready to face. Would probably never be ready to deal with.

But she wanted him to know how much she desired him. She reached out and stroked his cheek. "Make love to me."

A willing gleam flickered in his gaze. "I thought you'd never ask."

He eased back, then slid in, his flesh hard

yet velvety soft, tender yet demanding. Her entire body clenched tighter, and she felt him pulsing heavily inside her. She closed her eyes, memorizing his weight, the thickness of his member, the sheer perfection of their joining.

Rafe slid out of her body, then pushed back in, slowly out, harder in, faster and faster with each thrust, their bodies rocking together in unison. The friction grew, the tension increased and she climbed closer and closer to completion. Yet somehow her climax took her off guard as sparkling stars and immense pleasure washed over her in wave after wave of perfection until he'd wrung every last sensation from her body and Sara went limp beneath him.

Rafe rolled off her, gasping for air. "Wow," he said through ragged breaths.

"I'll say." She turned her head to meet his gaze. Her cheeks were pink and flushed.

He grinned. "I'll take that as a compliment."

She laughed. "Please do."

He swallowed hard. She was so damn hot and sexy. They clicked in bed like they did everywhere else.

But there was something they'd both forgotten in the heat of the moment. "We didn't use protection."

"I'm on the pill. And we're both tested at work. It's all good," she murmured.

He wasn't worried, which ought to worry him more. His cell phone rang, interrupting his thoughts, and he rolled over to check the number. "It's the captain."

He sat upright in bed. "Hey, boss."

The other man yelled so even Sara could hear. "I thought I told her to lie low. How the hell could the damned Bachelor Blog find her all the way in Hidden Hell?"

"Hidden Falls," Rafe reminded him.

Sara started to chuckle before the reality and seriousness of the situation struck her.

"The whole world knows I'm here?" she asked, horrified.

"The blog said she came to stay there at a place called Angel's," the captain said.

Son of a — "She's not there anymore. She's staying with me. It's a lot safer."

"Well, tell her to be careful!" the captain bellowed.

"I'll take care of her, boss," Rafe promised, his gaze never leaving Sara's.

Well, maybe it left her gaze so he could take in the sight of her naked body, gorgeous breasts, large nipples . . .

"And if I find out anything about Morley, I'll let you know," the captain said, breaking into Rafe's fantasy. "But I'd suggest being extra careful. Just in case his men track her there." The man muttered a curse and disconnected the call.

Rafe put the phone on the dresser. He turned to reach for Sara to find her already there, climbing onto his lap.

"Someone told the Bachelor Blogger I'm here?" she asked.

He wrapped his arms around her, pulling her tight. "Looks like it. But to be fair, nobody here knew you were in hiding."

She pursed her lips. "I haven't noticed any dangerous-looking strangers around town."

He shook his head. "You wouldn't know a stranger from a local," he reminded her, laughing, but he sobered quickly. "We should stay home tonight."

"No, we should not! I'm not going to stop living my life."

"I know. I had to suggest it anyway."

She exhaled a long breath. "If someone's after me, they'll find me here or in town, but I won't sit home in fear. Besides, there's safety in numbers."

"And I'll be sticking to you like glue. Nobody will get near you tonight."

And Rafe was a man of his word.

The annual dance went along with the annual festival set on the great lawn on Main

Street, across the street from the row of shops. Over the years, the bands who'd played as entertainment had run the gamut from unknown locals to an *American Idol* finalist who'd returned to his hometown to perform. This year boasted a pop band with a good reputation, and the lawn was jam-packed. Unlike Sara, Rafe knew exactly who belonged in town and who didn't. But he had no idea which, if any stranger, wanted to hurt her.

He glanced around, assessing the scene. The older generation had brought lawn chairs to sit in while they listened, teens were grouped together near the makeshift stage and the rest of the town had gathered to mingle or dance.

Rafe and Sara stood together, listening to the pop music. He slipped his hand inside hers, ignoring the tug of emotion that said she belonged there, and pulled her closer beside him.

"Let's dance," she said, turning toward him and wrapping her arms around his neck.

"That's one way for me to stick close." He slid his hands around her waist, and they began to move to the music.

With a soft sigh, she snuggled closer, resting her head on his shoulder. The emotional kick in his gut grew stronger.

"This is nice," she murmured.

"I'll say." He breathed in deep and took in the light, sexy scent of her perfume.

Her lithe body slid sensuously against him. Though she was toned and in shape, she was still soft and womanly in all the right places, and he curled his fingers into the indent of her waist. He was totally aroused as they swayed to the sound of the band.

"Are you always in town for the festival?" she asked, oblivious to his physical reaction.

"When I can make it. I usually come up here for a week or two every summer, so if I can time it right, I do." Summertime was when he tried to be here most often to enjoy his house on the lake.

"And who would your dance partner be if I weren't here?" Sara not-so-subtly asked.

He laughed. "I usually just hang out with my family or old friends."

"You never brought Kim up here for the festival?" she asked of his ex-fiancée.

Was that a touch of jealousy he heard in her voice, or was it mere wishful thinking? He wasn't surprised the subject had finally come up. They'd never really talked about it before. Then again, they'd never had sex before, either. He supposed more personal

175

things were part of the deal. Even if he'd already put that part of his life behind him.

He turned his focus to Sara's question. "I never brought Kim up here at all."

"Mind if I ask why?"

"Not at all." He just didn't know how to sort through it all in order to explain.

Sara clasped her hands behind his head and moved her hips sinuously against his.

He found it difficult to concentrate on another woman with Sara in his arms, but she'd asked, so he forced himself to remember. He'd fallen fast and hard for Kim. She was sexy and had focused all her attention on him. He hadn't wanted to share her with his family and their nosey questions — the complete opposite of how he felt about Sara, he realized with no small amount of shock. He liked having her here in his personal environment and space.

But he had no time to linger on that thought. Sara was waiting for a reply. "In the beginning of the relationship, I was too busy at SWAT to come visit here," he said at last. "And I didn't want to share her with everyone and the craziness that came along with visiting. Or at least that's what I thought at the time."

But he realized now that while he'd believed he was consumed with Kim, it had been a sexual thing, not an emotional one. He got the difference now, thanks to Sara.

"What happened after?" Sara asked.

They both knew she was no longer referring to why he'd never brought Kim here, but to the end of the relationship.

He exhaled hard. "I'm not sure. I know I enjoyed her company and being in a committed relationship. And in the beginning, so had she." They shared the same taste in movies, in television shows, and though they both worked hard, they both wanted a family.

Eventually.

It was just that eventually became further and further away, at least for Kim. Something he didn't want to mention to Sara and risk bringing up their differences. As for Kim, they'd never set a wedding date, and though he'd pushed at first, she'd resisted. Because she was younger and wanted to focus on her career. He understood, and he'd had no problem easily letting her off the hook. Too easily. Because when the excitement had worn off, he just hadn't cared enough, and obviously neither had she.

"We both led active but parallel lives that rarely crossed paths," he summed up for Sara.

If he'd been too busy with work to romance Kim, she'd been too focused on her career at an ad agency in New York to spend much time with him. And neither had seemed to care.

Sara remained respectfully silent, letting him gather his thoughts, but he couldn't tear his gaze from her big brown eyes and lips he wanted desperately to kiss.

And he would, as soon as he ended this conversation. "I think Kim and I stayed together as long as we did because neither one of us asked much of the other. In the end we were comfortable, but we weren't in love."

Sara threaded her fingers through the back of his hair, and he felt the tug directly where it mattered most — reminding him that if he'd really loved Kim, his interest in his partner would have died down. He wouldn't have been so tempted by Sara that he'd had to put distance and another shift between them.

He drew a deep breath. "I think Kim knew as well as I did, convenience wasn't love. The end came too civilly and easily."

Sara nodded slowly. "I'm sorry."

He met her gaze, looking deep into her eyes. "I'm not."

Silent understanding passed between

them, sexually charged and undeniably hot, and she shifted her gaze over his shoulder, obviously unnerved by the emotional connection she couldn't deny.

What pleased him frightened her.

While he was being drawn deeper every minute, she was building walls.

Which meant he was at a crucial point. As a negotiator, he knew when to push hard and when to back off no matter what *he* wanted. And Rafe now knew sex with Sara would never be enough.

If he wanted to break through her defenses, he'd have to step up his game slowly but surely. Not overwhelm her when she was wary and hesitant. And yet he had to face facts. Even if he did everything right, he might not win. So he had to ask himself if, knowing that, he was willing to let down his guard and risk his heart.

"Look!" Sara exclaimed, interrupting his thoughts.

He followed her line of vision to where his brother danced with his wife. Neither spoke; they just danced close and enjoyed each other's company. "They're not fighting."

Rafe grinned. "Now, that's a miracle."

"Angel still loves him," Sara said with a happy sigh.

Rafe inclined his head. "And Nick loves

179

her. I just wish they could get past their differences."

Sara tipped her head to one side, her long hair brushing her shoulders, reminding him what it felt like to curl his hands around the long strands while he was buried deep inside her body.

"Nick needs to accept who Angel is now," Sara said, oblivious to Rafe's thoughts. "He expects her to be the same girl he married, but she's not. She lost a baby, and that changed her."

Rafe blinked, surprised at the wealth of information Sara had accumulated. "You got all that out of Angel in the last day and a half?"

Sara shrugged. "What can I say? Angel and I clicked, and she confided in me."

"I see," Rafe said, a sense of rightness settling over him.

Sara got along well with his family. Another thing he liked about her.

Rafe glanced at the other couple. "I think Nick needs Angel to open up to him more."

Sara nodded. "I don't see that happening anytime soon," she said, sighing again — and this time it was not a happy one.

"In that case, I hope my brother can change. Nick's stubborn."

"If Angel means enough to him, he'll

come around," Sara said with certainty. "And vise versa."

Another shock for Rafe. Sara obviously held out hope for his brother and Angel's future. "Careful, or I might think you're an optimist," Rafe teased.

Sara curled her fingers into his shirt and continued dancing, but said nothing in reply.

He let her avoid answering, content with the notion that deep inside Sara there just might be a woman who believed in the commitment she claimed not to want.

"Uncle Rafe!"

At the sound of Toni's voice, Rafe separated from Sara. "Hey, kiddo! What's up?"

"Your advice? Not so good."

"What happened?" Sara asked.

"Uncle Rafe said to pretend I didn't know how to hit a ball so Pete Goodfriend would notice me."

Pete Goodfriend? Rafe mouthed the name behind Toni's back.

Sara shook her head hard.

Rafe cleared his throat.

"Did you do it?"

Toni nodded. "He showed me how to swing. I did. And then I came up to bat."

"And?"

"I swung with all my might, and I hit it

out of the park!"

"So what happened?"

She bowed her head. "Pete was the pitcher."

Both Rafe and Sara winced.

"She never mentioned that," he said by way of apology.

Sara laughed. "Toni, listen, I know what it's like to like someone who doesn't notice you."

The young girl looked up at Sara with hopeful, adoring eyes. "So what do I do?"

"Hmm." What had Sara done when Rafe hadn't noticed her?

Nothing, because he'd been taken. But what would she have done if he'd been available? "Toni, honey, I think you should be yourself. If you like sports, talk sports to Pete. If you like music, talk about that. Be real. Pay attention to him. If it's meant to be, he'll like you back."

Toni scrunched her nose in an adorable way. Rafe stepped closer and wrapped an arm around her shoulders. "Remember what I told you. You're a great kid, and I bet he already notices you."

"Your uncle Rafe is right. Maybe he's shy, or he thinks his friends will laugh at him if he likes a girl. But you have to be stronger.

Pay attention to him first and see if it pays off."

"Cool! You're really smart about things, Sara."

She grinned, thrilled with the compliment from the pint-size teenager.

"I'm going to try now. See ya!" Toni ran back into the crowd.

Sara blew out a long breath. "Wow. She's a handful."

"You handled her like a pro." Rafe's steady gaze was filled with admiration.

She'd seen that look before, in training or when she'd taken down a perp. But she'd never seen him admire her for more personal reasons. The warmth in his gaze gave her goose bumps.

As did watching *him* interact with his niece. The man was a natural with kids, whether the advice he gave was good . . . or, as in this case, bad. He'd be the perfect man to have children with.

If she was looking for such a thing. Which she wasn't. Because they'd never make it together, and then she'd be as hurt as her father was after her mother abandoned them.

She drew in a shaky breath. "Thanks, but it's easy because Toni's such a great kid."

"Sara . . ." Rafe stretched his hand toward

her. He clearly had something to say.

Something she wouldn't want to hear, because it would mean she'd have to give him up sooner rather than when her time here was over.

"Fire!" someone in the crowd yelled.

The one word caught their attention. She turned toward Main Street and the row of buildings and the booths in front of them. Smoke billowed in the air above.

"Oh, my God!"

Rafe swore, grabbed her hand and they ran to see what was going on.

CHAPTER ELEVEN

Angel's pie stand burned down, and the fire department immediately labeled the incident arson. Pirro stood by Angel as the firefighters questioned her, but she hadn't seen anything unusual during the day, nor had she been near the pie stand at the time of the fire. Pirro said a silent prayer of thanks nobody had been hurt.

The firemen instructed everyone to clear the area, and Rafe invited Nick, Angel, Pirro and Vivian to come back to his house for a while until everyone had calmed down. Pirro sent Vi along with Angel, promising to meet them there in a little while. He couldn't stop thinking about the two men who'd approached him to sell hard drugs. Could it be coincidence that bad things were starting to happen now that he'd said no?

He didn't have to go looking for the men to find out. No sooner had his family driven off than they found him.

"It's a shame that your daughter's pie stand burned down," the blond man said, coming up to Pirro. "She was so proud of how well she was selling and how much everyone loved her apple pies."

"It's a good thing she wasn't in the booth when the fire started," the other one chimed in. "I heard the firemen say that with the amount of accelerant that was used, the booth went up like that." He snapped his finger in Pirro's ear.

"If a fire like that happened at her house, she'd have no chance of getting out," the blond man — Pirro refused to think of him as a gentleman — said.

Pirro shivered at the implied threat. "What do you want me to do?" he asked, willing to do anything to keep his family safe.

"Talk to your supplier and pave the way for us to meet with him."

"Okay," Pirro said, feeling sick as he agreed. But he'd be even sicker if he didn't. "But I don't contact him. I just meet him at a set place and time every couple of weeks. I need time."

A lie that bought him a little time to think, he thought, and his hands were shaking as he shoved them into his front pants pocket.

"It's beautiful this time of year, so we're

in no rush to get back to the city. As long as you're telling the truth, and you put things in motion, your beautiful daughter will be safe. Are we in agreement?"

"Yes. But remember one thing. If anything happens to my daughter, you two will be the first ones the cops look at, since you're two strangers staying under her roof," Pirro said to the blond man whom Pirro was convinced was the one in charge.

"Don't worry about us. We can take care of ourselves. But I think you understand what you need to do now."

The other man slapped Pirro on the back. "Relax, old man. It's all good. We're going back to Angel's. I don't know about you, but after all the excitement tonight, I can't wait to get a good night's sleep."

The two men bid him goodbye and walked away.

Pirro was sick to his stomach, and he still had to go to Rafe's. The man was a cop and could spot a lie a mile away. Pirro wanted nothing more than to tell him everything, but he needed to think things through first. Now that he'd agreed to go along with the men's plan, his family was safe, at least for now. He'd bought himself some time to figure out how to fix the mess he'd gotten himself into.

Rafe's family was in a panic, and he knew he had to take control. He sent his parents and sisters home, assuring them there was nothing more they could do to help. Then he gathered the more immediate people involved with Angel's pie stand in his den. As the cop in the family, they looked to him for answers, but he had none.

He glanced around his small den, where the entire clan had congregated, and clapped his hands to shut them all up.

They turned their heads toward him.

"First, I need everyone to stay calm. The fire department and the county police already took Angel's statement because she owned the booth. They'll continue the investigation, but I have some questions of my own." Rafe glanced around the room, and his gaze met Sara's.

"Let's start with what we know," she suggested.

He nodded. "The fire department said it was definitely arson. An accelerant was used."

As he spoke, Sara marked down notes on a pad she'd grabbed from the kitchen.

"Gasoline," Nick added. "The chief said

the area reeked of it."

Sara nodded and made another note. "That takes care of what we know about the crime itself."

"So now we move on to possible intended targets," Nick said.

Angel stepped forward. "Well, that's obvious. It was my booth, so it must have been me they were after."

Nick stepped up and wrapped a reassuring arm around her shoulder. She leaned into him for comfort. At least something good was coming out of this nightmare, Rafe thought.

Rafe glanced at his aunt Vi and Pirro, who'd arrived late. His aunt appeared worried and distraught, while Pirro was sweating and pacing beside her.

"Who would want to destroy my booth?" Angel asked. "All I was doing was selling apple pie."

Rafe didn't know enough to calm her down just yet, but he had a few more delicate questions that might help him narrow down the scope. "You were also booking reservations. Could someone want to sabotage your business?" Other than his brother, that is, Rafe thought wryly.

Angel shook her head. "Everyone claims to want me to succeed. At least, that's what they say to my face." She let out a shaky laugh.

"Except for me." Nick shocked them all by admitting the truth out loud.

"Nick!" Angel said, horrified.

Nick held up his hands in defensive mode. "Hey, I'm just stating the obvious before someone else does." Nick met Rafe's knowing gaze. "I was the one who said I was against the B-and-B venture."

To Nick's credit, he sounded ashamed.

"But you wouldn't burn down the booth!" Angel stepped up, defending her husband. "And you were with me during the entire dance."

"I agree with Angel. Nick's not a suspect," Rafe said. "Who else in the family might have someone with a grudge against them?"

Angel stepped forward once more. "Not that I want to be the target, but if the fire was aimed at the family or the business, wouldn't the person have hit the spice booth, not the pie stand?"

"Depends on how obvious they wanted to be. Sometimes someone who has an agenda will start small, with a warning, as opposed to hitting the main target," Sara explained.

Pirro began to cough hard.

"Dad, I'll go get you a glass of water." Angel ran to the kitchen and returned with a drink for her father.

Rafe nodded. "Sara's right," he said when Angel returned. He glanced around the room. "Pirro, are you okay?"

The older man nodded. "I'm fine." He coughed some more, but the sound was less harsh than before.

Still, he'd been unusually quiet tonight, probably because he was worried about Angel's safety.

"Any problems in shipping I should know about? People with a grudge?" he asked Pirro.

He rubbed his bald head. "No, no, not at all. Everything's fine. Why wouldn't it be fine?" he asked, upset and rambling.

"Couldn't it just be a random act? Teenagers causing trouble?" Angel asked.

"Anything is possible," Sara said.

But Rafe just didn't believe in coincidences, and his gut screamed this wasn't random.

"I'm sick with worry about someone wanting to hurt my Angel. It's just not right," Pirro said.

Aunt Vivian nodded her head in agreement. "Angel, darling, I don't want you alone in that house with all those strangers. You'll sleep at our place tonight." She issued the statement as if it were a done deal.

Angel glanced at Nick and subtly shook her head.

"It's okay. I'll stay at the B and B tonight," Nick said. "Angel won't be alone."

Pirro exhaled hard, obviously relieved. "You're like a son to me, Nick. You're a good boy. Thank you."

"It's been a long day. I'm exhausted and upset, and I'd really like to go home," Aunt Vi said.

Rafe nodded. "Pirro, take her home. There's nothing more you can do here, and Nick will look out for Angel."

"That's a good idea, Dad. You look tired, too. Go home and rest," Angel said. "I'll be fine."

"Okay." The older couple began to say their goodbyes.

As usual, it took another half hour for them to finally get themselves together. Rafe had hoped the seriousness of the fire would take Aunt Vi's mind off the possibility of her husband cheating or whatever else she thought he was doing. But as Rafe walked them to the door, Aunt Vi gave him one last hug and a whispered reminder that the next time Pirro went out alone, she'd be calling Rafe to follow him.

He returned to the family room, where Sara had poured everyone a cold glass of

192

iced tea. The three of them talked, looking comfortable together. Apparently she had a way with his family that won them over. She'd made herself at home in his house, serving his brother and Angel as if she were the hostess. And Rafe liked what he saw.

But he didn't have time to enjoy the moment. "Now that Pirro and Vi are gone, I need to talk to the two of you," Rafe said to his brother and Angel.

"What's up?" Nick asked.

Rafe met Sara's knowing gaze. "Before I say anything, is there any chance you know of any complaints lodged with the company? Or someone with a grudge against you who'd use Angel to make a point?"

His brother shook his head. "I checked in with Dad on the way over here and he's blank, too. Nobody can imagine anyone who'd want to target us."

That's what Rafe figured. "There's a very real possibility that Angel wasn't the target, but Sara was." And she'd worked the booth along with Angel.

"What? Why?" Angel asked.

Sara cleared her throat. "To put it simply, I'm supposed to testify against someone in New York, and he wants me too scared to come home and take the witness stand."

"Or he wants to shut her up permanently."

Rafe walked over to her chair and put a hand on her shoulder. "She came here to hide out."

"Oh." Angel's eyes opened wide.

"I still don't get it," Nick said. "If she's here to hide, I'm assuming she didn't tell anyone she was coming, so why would you think the fire was aimed at her?"

"Because the Bachelor Blog in New York posted that I'd escaped the city to rendezvous with Rafe in his hometown," Sara said as she absently rubbed her bad knee.

"Unbelievable," Nick muttered. "Rafe told me about that damned blog when he was in the hospital. But if no one in New York knew where you'd gone, then it had to be someone here who reported in."

"My thoughts exactly." Beyond that, Rafe was blank. He couldn't fathom who would have reported on her whereabouts.

"Who would snitch about where Sara had gone?" Nick asked the same question aloud.

"Me." Angel raised her hand in the air.

All eyes turned her way.

"I'm sorry! I had no idea you weren't here just to be with Rafe. I'd never have done it if I'd known you were in danger!"

Shocked, Sara met Angel's gaze. "Why? I thought we were friends."

"We are! And it wasn't personal. When

194

you first showed up and asked for a room, I recognized you from the articles in the newspaper about the hostage crisis. But I also recognized you from the Bachelor Blog. I take out ads in the New York City newspapers to generate business, so I have them delivered, too."

"That still doesn't explain why you'd turn her in," Nick said angrily.

Obviously any good feelings they'd been working toward had gone south, Rafe thought. "Why did you do it?" Rafe asked Angel with more diplomacy than his brother had shown.

"For the same reason. To get the bed-and-breakfast's name in the paper and generate business." She glanced at Sara, then Nick, her gaze full of regret. "But I would never have put the business before Sara's safety. I didn't know!"

Sara exhaled a long breath. "It's not your fault," Sara said, letting Angel off the hook. "Actually, it was a pretty business-savvy move, if you ask me."

"You're too generous." Angel rose and ran for the bathroom in the hall, slamming the door shut behind her.

Nick ran a hand through his hair. "It wasn't savvy. It was selfish and stupid, just like this business," Nick muttered.

"And you're a hothead and an idiot," Rafe said, not about to let Nick ruin the progress he'd made by picking a fight with his wife. "If Sara isn't upset with Angel, then you shouldn't be, either. Don't make an ass of yourself just because she mentioned the bed-and-breakfast. You need to accept it, remember?"

Before Nick could reply, his wife returned, her eyes red, her face blotchy. "I'm sorry," Angel said again.

"It's fine. You had no way of knowing I wanted to lie low," Sara reassured her again.

"Look," said Rafe, "we're all upset after the fire, but all that matters right now is that nobody was hurt. From this point on, we have to be more careful. Because the fact is, we have no way of knowing *who* the intended target actually was."

He met Sara's gaze, and she nodded in agreement.

It was possible Morley had sent people after Sara, and the accelerant had lit either too soon or too late, and thank God she hadn't been in the booth. But there was the equal possibility that someone had a grudge against Angel or her family and the booth fire had been a warning.

Until they knew who the target was and why, Rafe wanted everyone in his family on alert and being extra careful.

As Nick walked Angel to her car, he thought back to the events of the night. One minute they'd been dancing, getting closer, and she'd obviously panicked. She said she'd needed air, and he'd let her go, giving her space. The next thing he knew, he heard people yelling. He'd nearly had a heart attack when he'd seen the smoke and fire in her booth, not knowing if she'd gone there to be alone.

If he hadn't already been shaken up by Biff's and Todd's interest in his wife, the fire had been an additional wake-up call. He had to fix things before it was too late.

"I'm sorry about the blog. I never intended to hurt Sara," Angel said.

Nick nodded. "I know."

"It's been an awful night and I can't wait to just crawl into bed. Good night," she said softly.

"I'm staying over, remember?"

"I thought you just told my father and Vi you'd stay over so they wouldn't worry. I can't imagine you really want to sleep there," she said of the bed-and-breakfast, the major point of contention in their marriage.

He stepped closer. "Is that what you

think?" His heart slammed inside his chest.

She nodded.

"Well, you're wrong. If the fire had happened earlier in the day, you could have been killed." And he'd have lost any chance he had of making things right.

She leaned against the door and met his gaze. "You panicked. I understand. But that doesn't change the truth about us."

"Which is?"

"It's one thing to dance together and to get along for twenty minutes without arguing. It's another to agree on what fundamentally divides us," Angel said softly.

He grabbed her forearms and pulled her close, kissing her hard on the lips. She stiffened in shock, then slowly but surely relaxed against him, kissing him back. Opening for him. Accepting him and everything he wanted to give but didn't know how to express in words.

He broke the kiss first, leaning his forehead against hers. "Let me come home with you tonight. Let me make sure you're safe." He barely recognized his gruff voice.

She licked her lips, then slowly nodded. "Okay. You can come home with me."

His heart began a race inside his chest once more.

"But nothing can happen between us," she

said, putting the breaks on.

He silently counted to five, unwilling to argue and lose ground. And *that* was a first for him. "I understand."

But him staying over wasn't enough. He needed to be back in her life for good. She still focused on his resentment of the B and B as the source of their problem, but he believed they needed to talk and grieve together. Something she wouldn't do unless pushed.

"What if we see a marriage counselor?" he asked, surprising himself. "That way we can make sure we agree on how to fix what's wrong before we try."

"And before I invest my heart again." She blinked, and tears fell down her cheeks.

He wiped her cheek with his thumb. "Your heart is still invested," he said gruffly. "And so is mine."

As he followed her back to her place, for the first time, Nick felt a glimmer of hope. She'd agreed to see a marriage counselor. Maybe a trained therapist could help her learn to talk about the miscarriage and guide them toward redefining their future.

He didn't know if either of them could make this work. But he loved her enough to try.

Rafe shut the door, locking it behind his brother and sister-in-law. Then he set the burglar alarm. "First thing tomorrow I'm calling the alarm company and having a perimeter alarm installed," Rafe said.

"Isn't that what you have?" Sara asked.

"No. I have one that just hits the main doors and entrances. Truth is, I only installed an alarm at all because I'm rarely here. The crime rate is so minimal, nothing more was necessary."

Sara bit the inside of her cheek. Guilt was already eating away at her. If she had been the target of the fire, she'd caused fear and aggravation for his family, not to mention the cost of the destruction of the booth.

"I don't want you to spend more money on the alarm system because of me. If you didn't need it before, you don't need it now."

"Don't argue. It's necessary. You came here to feel safe, and I intend to make sure you stay that way. Besides, it's never a waste of money to invest in a better alarm system." He shut the light in the kitchen and walked over to where she sat on the couch, sitting down beside her. "What's wrong?"

"I just don't want to cause problems for your whole family. Maybe I should go back to the city."

He raised an eyebrow. "If you do, I'm going with you. Then we'll have to have a state-of-the-art alarm system installed in your apartment and on the main front door, which will only piss off the landlord. So? What's it going to be?"

"Okay, you can upgrade the alarm here." But she'd pay him back, no matter how much he argued.

A satisfied grin settled over his face.

He was sexy when he was worried, sexy when he was happy, sexy when he had a satisfied grin on his handsome face. Boy, she had it bad, Sara thought.

"Earth to Sara?" Rafe waved a hand in front of her face.

"Sorry, I was distracted," she said, shaking her head. "What did you say?"

"I asked if you thought Biff and Todd seemed like possible suspects."

She wasn't surprised he'd asked. He'd disliked them on sight. Besides, they'd begun to make her uncomfortable with the way they were constantly around. "They're odd, but I already discounted them because when they checked in, they said they'd had the reservations way in advance. We could ask Angel, but I have a feeling they're telling the truth."

"Yeah, odd doesn't necessarily make them criminal. But I'm keeping an eye on those two."

Sara nodded. "I think that's a good idea."

"Thanks for going easy on Angel. I think Nick took his cue from you," Rafe said.

"She didn't mean any harm."

"Now do you see what I mean about how hard it is to live here, everybody in everyone else's business? To Angel, telling the Bachelor Blogger about you was just like telling her next-door neighbor."

She curled her legs beneath her, getting more comfortable. "Actually, I think it's kind of nice. Do you realize that in the city we rarely ever see our neighbors? We rarely see our friends unless we make a huge effort! Around here, people *care* about each other."

"You don't mind that Angel turned you in for her own selfish business reasons?" he asked.

"I'd care more if she did it to hurt me, but she had no idea I was hiding out here." She met Rafe's gaze. "I guess I just like the idea of having a place where I feel a part of things, you know?"

"Similar to how I realize I'm coming to

like you hanging out with my family," he admitted, his voice gruff.

She thought back to their earlier conversation about his ex-fiancée and how he hadn't wanted to share her with everyone or expose her to the chaos that came along with his family. He'd drawn an unspoken distinction between her and Sara. She felt herself being pulled deeper into this small community and this loving family, and she didn't know what to make of it — or them.

"I'm tired," she finally said.

"It's been a long day. We should get some sleep."

"I'll be right in," she said, needing time alone to regroup.

And to remind herself that she didn't do long-term relationships or commitment. That as much as she liked his family, she was a visitor passing through and would be returning to her solitary life very soon.

The thought didn't bring as much comfort as it should have.

CHAPTER TWELVE

The next morning dawned bright and sunny, but the mood at the festival was dim. Word spread quickly that the pie-booth fire had been set deliberately, but the culprit was still at large. As a result, everyone was on edge, worried their booth might be next. Some parents kept their children home, and the carnival area was empty. It didn't help that the smell of burnt wood lingered in the air, and red tape surrounded the area to keep people out.

With Rafe by her side, Sara spent the afternoon helping his family run the spice booth. She spent much of the day on a stool behind the booth thanks to the aching pain in her knee, a reminder that she had more to worry about than Morley sending men after her.

"What's on your mind?" Rafe asked, coming up beside her.

She blew out a long breath. "My knee

hurts. Up till now, I've kept busy enough that I haven't had time to dwell on it." She perched her chin in her hands and sighed.

He settled into an empty stool. As usual, he knew when to talk and when to back off, and right now he remained silent, offering support with his mere presence. But the anxiety she'd begun to feel still clawed inside her chest.

"If I don't have my career, who am I?" The thought had occurred to her when she'd reinjured her knee and remained, always there, hovering.

"You're a smart woman who is a lot more than her career. What did you major in?"

She thought back to her days in college. "Criminal justice and sociology."

"All great stepping-stones. And you have great people skills. You could do counseling, be a social worker. . . . You could work within the department and not on the street."

"A desk job?" she asked, horrified.

"When's your next doctor's appointment?" he asked, ignoring her panicked question. No doubt because he couldn't imagine being sidelined, either.

She shrugged. "I have to schedule one when I get back to the city. But I know my body, and it's not healing right. I can feel it." She rubbed her swollen knee, an ever-present reminder that her future might be far different than the one she'd envisioned or planned.

Rafe wrapped an arm around her and pulled her close. "Don't panic until you have to," he suggested. "I know you're scared, but I guarantee you'll find something equally rewarding if you can't return to active duty."

"Rafe!" Aunt Vi's distinctive voice called out. Aunt Vi ran over to them, waving her hands.

"Sorry," Rafe said.

Sara shook her head. "I was about finished with the subject anyway." And she was grateful for the interruption.

Rafe rose, then held out a hand, helping Sara to her feet. "What's going on?" he asked his aunt.

"Pirro has been acting very odd. He's so quiet, which isn't at all like him," Vi said.

Rafe inclined his head. "I noticed the same thing last night. But the fire was enough to upset him, don't you think?"

"Yes, but he's been acting strangely for a while. It's just worse now. And when we should be pulling together as a family, he's more distant." She pulled a tissue from her purse and blew her nose loudly.

"Maybe you're worrying for nothing," Sara said. "I realize it's none of my business, but did you ever think of talking to your husband? I don't know anything about being married, but I know plenty about divorce, and secrets are damaging to any relationship."

"Which is why I asked Rafe to find out what's going on with him!"

"Or you could just ask him outright." Sara tried again to reason with Rafe's aunt.

"I couldn't! What if he is cheating? Do you think he'd tell me? And if he isn't, I'll do irreparable damage to our relationship by questioning his integrity! I need to know what I'm dealing with first," the other woman said firmly.

Rafe grasped her hand in his stronger one. "I already promised to look into it for you, but you have to promise me you'll calm down. Getting worked up like this isn't good for you."

Vi sniffed back tears. "I'll try."

"No, you'll do it, or else I'm not helping you. You know you have to watch your blood pressure," he gently chided.

Sara couldn't contain her smile. Rafe liked to complain about his meddling, overreactive family, but deep down he adored them, and they relied on him for so much. Which was why he preferred living away from here, she realized now. When he was in town, he gave whatever they needed, but he had to leave to regroup, too.

"Okay, I promise." Vi straightened her shoulders. "I'll calm down, but only because I know you're in charge." She drew a deep, visible breath. "Okay. Calm. You see? Now I'm going home to soak in a warm tub. And maybe when Pirro finally gets home, I can entice him into bed," she said with a dreamy sigh.

"Aunt Vi!" Rafe gave an exaggerated shudder.

Ignoring him, the woman walked away, humming.

Rafe groaned. "I swear sometimes I think she'll drive me to drink," he muttered.

Sara laughed. "She's a character. I hope she's wrong about Pirro."

"I do, too. There's nothing I believe in more than fidelity."

Sara reached out and touched his cheek. "Angel told me about your father," she said softly. "It couldn't have been easy for you or your family."

"It wasn't." A muscle ticked in his jaw as he struggled to explain, hating the memories that came back to him. "My mother would pretend to be strong for us during the day, then at night she'd cry herself to sleep. I wanted to hate him," he said of his father. "But when he came home and made things work, I settled for promising myself I'd never be like him."

She grasped his hand, knowing how hard the admissions must be for him.

"Let's walk." She guided him away from the family booth and any prying eyes or ears. She didn't ask questions, either. She waited for him to talk when he was ready.

They strode down Main Street, toward where he'd parked his car hours earlier. "You want to know the ironic thing?" he finally asked.

"What's that?"

"Right before I switched shifts and stopped being your partner, I nearly followed in his footsteps."

"How?"

"By cheating on my fiancée with you."

Sara opened her mouth, then closed it again, shocked by his words. She could still remember the way he had looked at her while he was buried deep inside her body. She'd been so shaken by the wealth of emotions he made her feel, and now this admission. He'd left their partnership to avoid acting on his feelings for her. The thought both thrilled and panicked her at the same time.

She moistened her dry lips. "But we never even came close to kissing. Or to admitting we had chemistry."

"But we wanted to." He met her gaze, a knowing look in his eyes. "And if I'd stuck around, it was only a matter of time before we did."

Sara shook her head, everything in her rebelling at his words. "I'm sorry, but I can't jump to the same conclusion as you. We wouldn't have acted on it."

He stopped in his tracks and turned to face her. "What makes you so sure?"

"Because I know you. You have more honor and integrity than anyone else I know. More self-restraint, too. You'd have to have it in spades to be a hostage negotiator."

"Thanks for the vote of confidence." A grim smile settled over his lips.

"You're welcome. Now, quit being so hard on yourself," she said, trying to change the subject and lighten the mood.

"If you say so."

Sara shivered despite the summer sun beating down on her from overhead.

They climbed into his car and headed back to his house to shower and change for the wine tasting that night. Sara remained silent, deep in thought. She had a new understanding of this man and his feelings for her. Whether she could handle them or not was something else entirely.

The wine tasting was held at a town park, the land donated by a wealthy vineyard owner who'd had a part in organizing this annual event. Tents had been erected and placed around the area to help shade the event-goers from the heat until the sun finally went down well past 8:00 p.m. Hundreds of wine vendors from the Finger Lakes area showcased their wines.

Sara held Rafe's warm hand inside hers as they made their way through the mass of people. She'd managed to avoid any intimacy between them while they were home and was still working on shoring up her defenses. Never before had she felt vulnerable to a man, and though she'd gone into this thing with Rafe knowing it was risky, she'd never imagined that sex could lead to such complications. Not for a woman who prided herself on moving on without looking back.

And she had more important things to concentrate on than emotional attachments. So far neither she nor Rafe had noticed or felt anything out of the ordinary. No odd people watching her, just a lot of strangers milling around.

"Is it my imagination or is it twice as crowded tonight compared to earlier this afternoon?" she asked him.

"It's not your imagination at all. And it'll only get worse as the weekend goes by. Friday midday brings in stragglers who can take the time off from work to get here for the opening festivities. By Friday evening, you've got people who left work early, and by Saturday, things are in full swing," Rafe explained.

She tried unsuccessfully to glance beyond the bodies into the individual booths to see what they were giving away. Frustrated, she gave up. "I'm not really a wine connoisseur, but how do you compare tastes at an event so crowded?"

"You don't. Hang on." He pushed through the mass of people and returned with a plastic cup of white wine. "When the festival first started, it was more about actual wine tasting and comparison. Lately it's become a drinking, partying event."

She laughed. "Works for me." She raised her plastic cup.

"Me, too. So, when in Rome . . ." He lifted his cup. "To . . ." He trailed off, obviously stumped.

"To friends with benefits," she said, touching her cup to his and solidifying what they were to each other by saying it aloud.

She'd been so thrown by his comment about having feelings for her while still engaged, by the way he'd looked at her while he was buried deep inside her body, so frightened by the wealth of emotions he'd made her feel, she had to gather her defenses.

He stared at her, dumbfounded. His eyes, once warm, frosted over. "Thank you for the reminder." He straightened his shoulders, his emotional walls firmly in place.

It was what she wanted, what she needed to do for herself, and yet the sudden chill between them scared her more than the emotions that had swamped her earlier. "Rafe . . ."

"There's a deejay beyond the tent. Let's go listen to music," he said, then clasped her hand and headed out of the crowd and the tents.

The closer they got to the open arena, the louder the music became, geared more toward the young kids, with what Sara recognized as Top 100 music keeping things hopping. And though Rafe remained by her side, there was no warmth between them anymore, no relaxed enjoyment of their time

213

together.

She'd blown that in one selfishly spoken, fear-induced toast.

Sara didn't kid herself, either. If not for his promise to the captain to help keep her safe, Rafe would walk away and leave her behind. But Rafe was a stand-up, honorable guy. And he deserved a lot better than a commitment-phobic woman like her.

The next hour flew by in a blur of people, introductions and wine being passed around by different distributors who wanted people to taste their product. Sara had no time alone with Rafe, and he made it a point of keeping busy talking to his friends and neighbors — and of introducing her as his ex-partner visiting from the city.

Not even as his friend.

Her heart lodged in her throat, pain she herself had caused nearly swallowing her whole. Just when Sara thought she couldn't stand his aloofness anymore, the deejay suddenly began to speak into the microphone, capturing the crowd's attention.

"I'd like to get this party started! I want more people on the dance floor, so if I say *Snowball,* you all know what to do!" The music immediately switched into high gear, and people began to couple up to dance.

Rafe grabbed Sara, keeping his word to

stick close. He held on to her hand, doing the obligatory dance while keeping the pace slow, careful to watch out for her knee.

It was the first chance she'd had to get him alone, and though she wanted to apologize or at least try to explain her thoughtless words earlier, words failed her. She couldn't just launch into a bumbling explanation of how much he meant to her, but she couldn't allow herself to feel more.

"What's Snowball?" she blurted out instead. She'd work her way up to the apology.

Rafe wasn't in the mood to talk, but better to discuss the type of dance than get into a discussion of feelings. She obviously had none.

"Every few minutes, the deejay says *Snowball* and the music stops long enough for everyone to switch partners." Which meant it was probably time for him to get Sara out of here, he thought.

He wasn't looking forward to being alone with her in his house, where anything they did together was a reminder that they were just *friends with benefits.* Even now, the words stung.

He shouldn't have been shocked by her proclamation. Even when they'd made love, he'd known the minute she realized there was more going on between them than sex. That second when they'd locked gazes and *more* passed between them, she'd panicked and attempted to pull back, but even then, she'd asked him to *make love* to her.

And he had.

Afterward, he'd refused to let his mind go anyplace but forward, and her words had been like a bucket of ice water dumped over his head. He ought to thank her for the cold shock of reality before he deluded himself even more.

"Snowball!" the deejay called out.

Shit. Rafe tried to hang on to Sara's hand, but his brother immediately cut in, leaving Rafe with no choice but to switch partners and dance with Angel while keeping an eye on Sara from a distance.

"Uh-oh. You look like you want to kill someone," Angel observed.

He frowned. "Sorry. I was just thinking it's time to get out of here. The crowds are getting to be a little much."

"I don't blame you for being worried about her. Rafe, I really am sorry I let the Bachelor Blogger know where to find her."

"I know that. You didn't mean any harm."

"Thanks." She smiled at him. "Sara's lucky to have you. I hope you know what a good thing you have and don't let her get away," Angel said.

Rafe shook his head, amazed by his sister-in-law. Separated from her husband, Angel had every reason to be bitter and disillusioned about relationships, yet she still believed in romance and forever.

Unlike Sara.

"Go cut in on Nick," Angel suggested.

"In a minute. Is everything okay with you?" They both knew he was referring to Nick.

"Things seem to be looking up, but I take one minute at a time." She smiled as they kept up with the beat.

"Snowball!"

"Bye!" Angel said, twirling away.

Rafe noticed one of her boarders grabbed Angel next, and he intended to get Sara before the other one zeroed in on her. But an old high-school girlfriend swooped in on Rafe first, and because they hadn't talked in a while, she refused to take the hint and free him up.

"Snowball!"

He looked around for Sara and noticed her with a local. A woman who said her name was Joy grabbed hold of him for a few minutes before they were separated by the deejay.

"Snowball!"

This time when Rafe glanced around for Sara, too many other couples blocked his view. Panic consumed him, and he ducked out on the next waiting woman and began a hunt for Sara, pushing past old couples, young couples, people he knew and too many he didn't while he roamed the grassy dance floor. It took what felt like forever for him to locate her, and when he did, she wasn't with a dance partner, either.

Pale and seemingly frantic, her gaze darted around warily, looking for him. "Sara! I'm right here!"

She turned, catching sight of him, and he knew immediately something was wrong. "What happened?"

"Not you! I'm looking for *him!*"

"Who?"

She strained to look past him. He grabbed her shoulders. "Hang on. Take a breath and talk to me."

She nodded. "I was dancing with Nick. Then someone I didn't know, but he could have been my grandfather, and he was sweet, and then Biff, and then another man . . ." She narrowed her gaze. "Young, dark hair, white T-shirt, scruffy like he hadn't shaved."

"That sounds like half the men here."

"It was quick. The quickest dance of the

night. Unmemorable except for what he said. *Anywhere, anytime. I told you so.*" She shook her head. "That's exactly what was in the note left at my apartment. *We can get to you anywhere, anytime.*"

"We're getting out of here," Rafe said.

Sara didn't argue.

Their personal problems took a backseat to the real and present danger. The Snowball dance and the partner switch had been a nice break from the intensity of being with Rafe, and Sara had even managed to put the danger factor aside for a little while. Until the stranger had whispered in her ear.

She shivered at the memory.

It dawned on her, as it had after the crisis on the roof, that being a cop in charge of keeping someone else safe was a whole lot different than being the one directly threatened. Once the adrenaline of the chase had disappeared and she'd lost the man in the crowd, panic had set in, but now, back at Rafe's, she wasn't scared: she was angry.

She changed into her pajamas and climbed under the covers. Outside Rafe's bedroom, she heard noises from the kitchen. She wondered if he'd sleep in here again or if he was angry enough at her to use the spare room. She wouldn't blame him if he did, but she'd like it a lot more if he put his feelings aside and came in, if for no other reason than to keep her company. His big bed was cold and lonely without him.

She turned over to shut off the lamp on the nightstand when she heard a knock at the door.

She turned back around, turning the light on. "Come in."

Rafe stepped into the room. "I wanted to check on you before I turned in."

"I'm fine," she said.

Although looking at him all sexy and disheveled in his unbuttoned jeans and faded T-shirt, she was anything but. She was needy and aching for him to hold her.

She bit the inside of her cheek. "Are you really going to sleep in the other room because of what I said earlier?"

"Friends with benefits might suit your lifestyle, but I don't do meaningless sex, and I'm not going to pretend otherwise just to make you feel better. So, yes, I'm going to sleep in the other room," he said, meeting her gaze with a cold one of his own.

Too bad she knew him so well. Rafe wasn't as cool as he pretended. Fire burned in his gaze, anger warring with desire.

He wanted her. And he hated himself for it.

"We agreed on no strings," she said, the words sounding weak and pathetic, even to her.

Rafe shook his head. "We didn't agree on anything except that we wanted each other." He'd never agreed to keep his feelings out of the mix.

He'd known going in that would be an impossible proposition.

Alone in his large bed, wearing nothing but one of those flimsy, barely there outfits she preferred, she appeared soft and vulnerable. He knew better. The woman had a heart of steel to be able to deny there was anything more going on between them.

Not that it mattered. Even now, when he was so angry he wanted to shake her, he was still drawn to her in every way imaginable.

"The alarm company is coming first thing Monday to upgrade the system. But for now at least it's set, so you can sleep soundly," he said, changing the subject.

"We need to talk about what happened tonight and what we're going to do about it."

"We have all day tomorrow. Between the fire and the warning you received tonight, there's no way we're going back to the festival tomorrow. We need to wait until all

221

the visitors leave and things get back to normal. Then we'll be able to spot someone who doesn't belong here."

She nodded. "True. And I guess that's a plan in and of itself."

"I guess it is." He gripped the doorknob.

It was time for him to leave before he did something stupid, like climb into bed with her and allow her to pretend he meant nothing to her at all.

"Good night, Sara."

She met his gaze with a silent, imploring look.

It took all his strength to turn around and walk away.

CHAPTER THIRTEEN

The sound of Sara's voice drew Rafe out of his room early Sunday morning. He hadn't slept the night before, tossing and turning for more reasons than he cared to think about now. Needing coffee, he headed for the kitchen and found her sitting on a kitchen chair, fully dressed for the day in white jeans, a loose purple tank top and bare feet.

She held the telephone to her ear.

He didn't have to make coffee since a fresh pot sat on the counter. A warm, fuzzy feeling crept into his chest before he ruthlessly squelched it. She didn't belong here. She wasn't making herself at home and enjoying his place; she merely needed his protection, and he'd offered her a safe place to stay. End of story.

He poured himself a cup of coffee and left it black, needing the hard jolt of caffeine, before settling into a chair at the table.

"I'm fine. What has the blogger said now?" Sara asked whoever was on the other end. "Break it to me gently."

As she listened to the reply, her eyes widened and her mouth opened in a perfect circle. "That's so wrong! It's an invasion of privacy, that's what it is." She sighed and waited a beat. "No, you're right. I can't get worked up about what I can't control."

Rafe drew a long sip of the coffee. At least she'd made it strong, just the way he liked it.

"I'll keep in touch. Bye, Dad." She disconnected the call and hung up the phone, turning to face him. "My father," she said needlessly.

"Everything okay at home?"

She nodded, glancing at him warily, obviously trying to judge his morning mood.

He wasn't in the *mood* to give his feelings away. "What'd the blogger say that had you so upset?"

"Something about how smart we are using a festival to cover for our secret rendezvous," she said vaguely.

He narrowed his gaze. "And? There had to be more considering how upset you got."

She sighed. "Fine." Rising, she picked up her coffee cup and walked to the sink to rinse it out. "The blogger said from the looks of things at the dance the other night, we'd found love, and she highly recommends the upstate New York air to whoever is looking for the same." She slammed the water faucet off and dried her hands, not turning to face him as she spoke.

"I guess the blogger doesn't know everything," he said and let out a dry laugh.

"I guess someone at the dance reported in." She ignored his sarcastic comment.

"Probably. I'm sure Angel wouldn't have done it again."

Sara nodded. "I agree. My father said he'd keep me updated with any new blog posts."

"Good."

Silence descended.

Not the comfortable, relaxing silence they normally shared, but an awkward, tense quiet.

They had at least twenty-four hours before the town emptied out and they could go out knowing he'd recognize someone who didn't belong, and Rafe couldn't stand being cooped up in the house with this kind of tension.

"What's your father like?" he asked, curious about the man she'd been speaking to. The single father who'd raised her to be so afraid of commitment.

She relaxed her shoulders at his neutral

question, and a soft smile curved her lips. "He's big and gruff, and on the outside he looks like your typical old-time, don't-mess-with-me kind of cop. But on the inside he's a big softie."

They obviously had a good relationship. "You said he raised you after your mother left?"

She settled back into a chair at the table. "He did. The house went from constant yelling and battles to easy silence. Dad isn't a big talker, but when he has something to say, it's usually important." She leaned her elbow on the table, relaxing as she gathered her thoughts. "I think he taught me the value of silence," she mused.

"It's an important asset for a cop."

She nodded. "Of course I was the opposite. I chattered nonstop, talking about anything and everything. I'd come home from school and tell him about my day, from schoolwork to girl issues and then boys. He learned pretty quick that he had to pay attention or I'd call him on it." She laughed. "Eventually we began to balance each other out." She stared into space, obviously thinking, remembering.

Wanting to hear more, he took his cues from her and kept quiet.

"I'd have thought my father would have

been sad after my mom left, but he wasn't. He was happier, came out of his shell more. And I think, by seeing that, I came to associate being alone with being happy." She blinked hard and suddenly focused on him, looking a little wary, as if she'd revealed too much.

He wanted more. "What about relationships? Did your father date?"

She nodded. "He'd get involved with someone, I'd hear her name for a while, then suddenly he'd stop mentioning them. I'd ask, and he'd say it had been time to move on." She shrugged, as if things had been that simple. "Eventually he'd find someone else, and things would follow the same pattern. His women never interfered in my life, never even made a dent in our everyday pattern of living. To me, it seemed like an ideal life for a cop."

To Rafe, it sounded lonely as hell. Never allowing for intimacy or feelings to come into play, always moving on before you got too close.

She'd dug deep and shared her memories, giving him more insight than he'd hoped for. He now understood how Sara's views on marriage and relationships had been formed. Grounded in her childhood experience, marriage equaled misery; short and sweet relationships sufficed.

He could no longer blame her for wanting to keep things simple between them and, when she started to feel things, panicking and building walls. But instead of discouraging him, the fact that she was feeling things gave him hope. If they were back in New York, she could break things off, return to her apartment and her solitary life. But she was stuck here until the threat was over or it was time to testify at the trial. Which meant she had nowhere to run and hide from her feelings.

Rafe had one shot to get through to her. He needed to make her feel things over and over until it was time for her to leave.

Then, when she returned home to her life in New York, he had to pray the loneliness sent her running back into his arms.

Good luck, he thought wryly.

Rafe had spent many hours alone in his house, enjoying the peace and quiet that came with the cabin. But Sunday was the longest day of his life, thanks to Sara's mere presence. She curled up on the couch with a book, pulled a light blanket over her legs, and read silently. She shouldn't have been a distraction, but she was.

She'd showered and smelled like a combination of Sara and his shampoo, so every inhale left him more aware. Each time she shifted positions, he looked up from the newspaper he was trying to read. He then ended up staring at the way the light from the windows bounced off her blond hair, which led to thoughts of running his fingers through the strands, and of course taking her to bed.

By the time the phone rang and his mother reminded him they were expected at Sunday night dinner, he almost viewed the obligation as a relief.

"Let me talk to Sara and get back to you," he said to his mother and hung up before she could cite all the reasons Sara would want to share a meal with his family.

Mostly because his mother would probably be right. Sara had taken a liking to his family that surpassed being polite. She enjoyed each and every one of them, from his mother and father, who had surprisingly given her space and not pressured her about her relationship with their son, to his sisters, whom he'd seen her talking to during the festival the other day. He supposed it was easy for an outsider to view his large family as a novelty to enjoy. Although he had to admit, he wasn't as bothered by them as much as he used to be.

With age came understanding, he thought wryly.

"Talk to me about what?" Sara asked, placing her book on her lap.

"Mom called to invite us to dinner."

Her eyes lit up. "Ooh, I'd love to go. Do you think it's safe?"

"Whoever's after you just wants you not to testify. I don't think there's a problem going to a family dinner where we know everyone."

She nodded. "I agree. So, what can I bring?"

"Yourself. My mother doesn't expect you to show up with anything."

Sara flung the blanket off her legs and stood up. Rafe hadn't realized she was wearing shorts.

Short shorts. Cutoff, fringed, fuck-me shorts.

And he wanted to do just that.

"After I showed up uninvited last time, I want to bring something. Mind if I go through your kitchen cabinets?" she asked.

"Knock yourself out. What are you looking for?"

"Basic cake-making supplies," she said, already poking around the cabinets, pulling out assorted things like flour and sugar before moving on to the refrigerator for milk and eggs. "You have everything I need." She sounded surprised.

"My mother keeps this place stocked, and if I tell her I'm coming, she brings in the perishable things, too."

"Lucky you!"

She opened another cabinet and shut it again, then repeated the process a few more times, obviously not finding what she was searching for.

"What are you looking for?"

"I need cake tins." She called over her shoulder.

He raised an eyebrow. "Umm . . . I have disposable tins like these." He opened a high cabinet and pulled out aluminum pans he used when he marinated steak to make on the outdoor barbeque.

"That'll do. Thanks!"

If he thought he was distracted before, he was nearly crazed by the time she was finished baking a cake in his kitchen, making herself at home with his things, humming as if she'd done this a hundred times before.

"I know you were helping Angel make pies, but I didn't know you baked on your own, too."

She met his gaze with a humorous one of her own. "There's a lot you don't know about me. My father wasn't good in the kitchen, so I took over. And since he rarely remembered to buy birthday cakes, I used to bake them myself, and it became our tradition. Of course, this one's going to be unfrosted."

She perched her hands on her hips and frowned at the cake in the oven. "Unless we pick some up at the store on the way."

He shook his head and laughed. "Not a problem."

"Good. Thanks." Sara turned and began cleaning up the kitchen, needing the distraction from Rafe's constant presence.

The cake had been an inspired idea and had kept her busy, unlike the book, which she'd tried unsuccessfully to read for hours. She kept realizing she couldn't remember a thing and had to turn back to where she'd started. All because Rafe had been sitting in the same room, restlessly moving around, alternately reading the paper and watching her when he thought she wasn't looking.

Ever since their talk this morning, his mood had changed. No longer angry, he seemed more contemplative. It was as if he was looking for something that would explain her to him.

She couldn't figure herself out. How did he expect to?

She rinsed the items she'd used to cook and loaded them into the dishwasher, then cleaned off the countertops. The cake needed another half an hour, and she set the timer to remind her.

Finally finished, she let out a satisfied sigh. She turned, surprised to find Rafe standing right there.

In her breathing space.

His gaze was deep and dark, his expression giving nothing away.

"What's wrong?" she asked.

"Everything. You, me, being in the same house, the same room, pretending we're not looking at each other. Wanting each other."

Her mouth grew dry. "Oh."

"Exactly."

"I wasn't the one who pulled away," she reminded him.

He scowled. "Not physically, but you sure as hell put on the brakes when you made that toast."

She opened her mouth, then closed it again. She couldn't argue with the truth. But he wanted more than she was capable of giving.

"I want to propose an idea." He ran his hand down her nose. "Flour again," he said, holding up his finger.

She shivered under his touch, her breasts

growing heavy, her nipples taut. "What was your idea?" she managed to ask.

"I suggest we go back to the way things were *without* any discussion that's bound to throw things off balance."

Hmm. That stumped her. Sex with no discussion about what it meant. Sex without strings. That's the way they'd started out, and she'd really been enjoying it, but ever since she said those words out loud, *friends with benefits,* she'd had a knot in her stomach larger than her fist. And now that he'd actually stated he'd go along with her request, something inside her wanted to cry.

Then he kissed her, and she only wanted *him.*

The kiss started in the kitchen, and she didn't care if they finished there. She wound her arms around his neck, pulling him closer. She opened her mouth, and he slid his tongue deep inside, swirling around and around until her knees went weak. He took her hand and pulled her to the couch. They shed their clothes along the way.

He lay down and pulled her over him, and soon he was entering her, sliding high, far and deep. She gasped, feeling him connect with her completely. Every roll of his hips, each thrust as he penetrated deeper, took her higher, until climax was just moments away.

And then he slowed down, kissing her endlessly, focusing on her mouth, making love to it with his tongue, mimicking what his body had been doing to hers seconds before. Her body was on heightened alert, ready to go off, and now the tension eased, still beautiful, still there, waiting for him to start again.

He slid his hands between them and cupped her breasts, massaged her nipples with his palms.

She moaned. The friction felt so good she began to move her hips in circles, seeking harder contact again. She wanted him to thrust harder. Needed to feel him pulse inside her and make her come.

He gripped the back of her hair with one hand and wrapped the other around her back, and did just that. He drove into her, faster, harder, and she accepted each deep plunge until he took her up and over into spiraling oblivion.

Rafe knew the moment she came, freeing him to let go, and he did, gliding in and out of hers, pumping his hips against her body until he couldn't think or hear, only *feel* as, skin to skin, he came inside her.

He barely remembered collapsing beneath

her on the couch, or her falling over him. As awareness came back, he heard her ragged breaths, the sound like music in his ears.

"I must be heavy," she finally said.

"Couldn't tell you. I can't feel anything."

She jumped off him, and he laughed, reaching for her but missing. "I'm kidding. Get back here."

She shook her head. "Shower. And then I have to get ready for dinner at your mother's."

"I'll be right in." He laid his hand over his head and groaned.

Every time he thought he had a solution to his problems with Sara, he only ended up sucking himself in deeper. Because *that* hadn't been sex.

Because *he loved her.*

The truth hadn't snuck up on him, and he wasn't surprised. That special kernel of feeling had been planted a long time ago, back when they were partners. It had merely grown since then, often slowly. Sometimes it had even gone into hibernation, but it had been there all along.

Unfortunately, whether it went anywhere was out of his control.

Apparently dinner at Rafe's parents' house

was always a big event. Any family member who wanted to come over was welcome. Today's group included Pirro, Aunt Vi and, to everyone's surprise, Nick and Angel. Everyone was so happy to see them together, nobody asked any questions, afraid of bringing up a subject that might cause trouble between them.

Sara's homemade cake had been a success. Later, after everyone had finished coffee and dessert, different groups gathered in various rooms to talk.

Sara pulled Angel aside, wanting to catch up with the other woman. She started by reassuring her again that she wasn't angry about the Bachelor Blog incident.

Toni bounced into the kitchen, her ponytail bobbing in time to her walk. "Sara, guess what?"

"What?" she asked the teen.

"I have a boyfriend!" she said in a squeal. "Pete asked me out, and I said yes! Thank you for your advice!" She wrapped her arms around Sara's waist and hugged her tight.

A warm — dare-she-think-maternal — feeling filled her at the young girl's gratitude and easy hug. "I'm happy I could help," she said, her voice thick.

The chirping of a cell phone interrupted them. "It's *him!*" Toni said. "Gotta go somewhere private and take it." She bounced out of the room, leaving Sara a little overwhelmed, in a good way.

"What does *asking someone out* mean these days?" Sara asked Angel.

"From what I hear, it means they're going steady, rarely talk in person, text on the phone, and break up within a week or so." Angel shook her head, laughing.

Sara chuckled. "Glad I don't have to deal with a teenage girl." Realizing what she'd just said, Sara's hands flew to her mouth, horrified. "I'm sorry. I mean — You can't — I didn't mean —"

"Relax, I know you didn't! I told you, I've moved on and accepted," Angel reassured her.

Sara wasn't convinced, but she wanted to put her foot-in-mouth moment behind her. "Looks like you two are getting along," she said, changing the subject.

Angel nodded. "I'm cautiously optimistic."

"And I'm happy for you!"

"Thanks." Angel glanced around to make sure they were alone. "He agreed to go for marriage counseling."

Sara nodded. "I think that shows you how much he wants to make things work. I hope that means you'll meet him halfway?"

Angel shrugged. "We both agreed to try.

I'll call tomorrow for an appointment, and then we'll see. So, what's going on with you?" she asked, deliberately changing the subject again. "The fire department investigators told me they have no leads. Did you find out anything more?" Angel's big eyes were filled with concern.

"Nothing new. My captain hasn't heard anything, either, so for now I just have to be cautious."

"Maybe it *was* just a random act, kids playing with fire. Stupid and dangerous, but random."

"Maybe," Sara hedged. It was better for Angel to believe her own words.

"So . . . where do things stand with the two of you?" Angel tipped her head toward Rafe, who was sitting beside his mother, talking.

As if he realized they were talking about him, he glanced over and treated Sara to a sexy wink before turning his attention back to his mother.

She swallowed hard. "We're fine." If she considered the wall between them fine.

Except this time the wall hadn't come from Rafe; it came from Sara herself, who was confused as to why getting what she wanted didn't feel as good as it should.

"Vague and unacceptable." Angel grinned. "Spill."

Sara drew a deep breath. "The truth is, I don't do relationships. I never have. I don't believe in happily ever after without a whole lot of work and aggravation, and when you factor in the stress of us both being cops . . ." She trailed off. "Look, the majority of relationships don't work. My entire family tree is a prime example. Rafe and I don't see life the same way. We don't want the same things."

"What is it you want?" Angel asked without judgment, and Sara was grateful for her understanding. Obviously, Angel knew firsthand that the work-and-aggravation part were true in an ordinary marriage.

"You know, I never really gave it much thought except to know I always wanted to be a cop. It's in my genes. But my bad knee might make the one thing I always took for granted impossible."

"Which means you may have to reevaluate your future." A sympathetic expression settled over Angel's face. "I know I did when I lost the baby." She lowered her voice. "Actually, I've had two miscarriages, but the family only knows about the one. The first one happened so early, we hadn't even told them I was pregnant yet."

"I'm so sorry."

"Thanks. But my point is that I always thought I'd be a mom. I can imagine how that sounds to you, but that was *my* dream. And then one day it was gone. The doctor said I probably couldn't carry to term, and suddenly my future looked empty. Sound familiar?" she asked.

Suddenly the notion of not being able to return to active duty seemed trivial compared to the end of Angel's dream.

Sara glanced down at her feet, embarrassed. "You must think I'm ridiculous. Here I am mourning the potential loss of a job, when you can't have children." Sara pressed her hands to her burning cheeks. "I'm so sorry."

"Don't you dare be sorry!" Angel said, clearly affronted. "Nobody's dreams are any more or less important than anyone else's. I'm just trying to tell you that when things look their darkest, you *can* find opportunity and even end up happy again."

"Thank you," Sara said, touched that Angel would dig into her deepest pain to help her. "You and I talked just now, right? So maybe you could do the same with Nick?" she asked tentatively.

"It's different talking to someone who doesn't share the grief." Angel cleared her throat, obviously emotional.

"Say no more. I understand." Sara quickly let the other woman off the hook.

Angel reached out her hand. "I don't know about you, but I need a good hug."

Sara smiled and pulled the other woman into a sisterly embrace.

To her surprise, the simple human connection made her feel better.

A little while later, Sara and Angel were helping Rafe's mother clean up in the kitchen when Rafe poked his head into the room.

"Can I talk to you for a minute?" he asked.

Sara glanced at Mariana, not wanting to leave her alone to dry the pots and pans.

"Go," the other woman said. "I'll finish up in here." She waved Sara away. "You, too, Angel. Go find Nick," she said pointedly.

Angel rolled her eyes, but did as her mother-in-law suggested.

Sara followed Rafe into a small hallway. "What's going on?"

"Pirro announced he's going to play poker, and Aunt Vi wants me to follow him." He groaned, telling Sara what he thought of that idea.

"Is there any chance he really is playing poker?"

Rafe cocked his head to one side and nodded. "There's every chance. But until we do this a few times and reassure her, this will never end."

"Okay, so what's the plan?"

"When Pirro leaves, I'll say it's time for us to go, too. I can't follow him directly — he knows my car, and it'll be too obvious, but I know all the men in his poker game. We'll wait a few minutes and drive by each house until we find his car, snap a picture on my cell and be done with it." He sounded more amused than annoyed by the plan.

"Works for me." In fact, Aunt Vi's drama was just the excitement and distraction she needed from the chaos of her own life.

Pirro was in no mood for poker or his friends, but the only way he could spread news was through their game. Jonah Frye had the perfect location for poker in the summertime, a barn in his backyard that he'd converted into a hangout for the boys. The fact that they hadn't been boys in years didn't seem to bother any of them as they gathered together to eat, drink and play.

Pirro waited until they'd played a few hands and everyone was relaxed to make his announcement. "My supply's going to decrease for a while."

Ernie slapped his cards onto the table. "That's unacceptable. I've been courting Mary Braunstein. It's been a year since Sydney passed on, and she's almost ready for that next step. I can't have my pecker at half-staff!"

Ernie just loved using the word *pecker,* Pirro thought. "What happened to the last batch of pills I gave you?"

Ernie flushed red in the face. "Gone. I had to take 'em every time we went out for dinner. You know, just in case she decided it was time to open the door."

"Well, you're just going to have to stall her." Because Pirro wasn't meeting with his supplier as scheduled.

"Why can't you get us the pills?" another of his friends asked.

Pirro groaned. Lies upon lies. "Because my supplier's out of them," he lied. "As soon as I can get my hands on some more, I'll let you know."

"Fine," Ernie said, and the rest of the men grumbled.

Pirro had a hunch not all of them needed the pill; it had just become an insurance policy for all of them, so they could get it up no matter what. Well, they'd have to make do.

Meanwhile, he needed to lie low and keep stalling those nasty men. He couldn't even think the words *drug dealers* without wanting to gag. They'd bought his quick-thinking excuse, but he still needed to figure a way out of this mess.

He'd contemplated talking to Rafe. The cop had dealt with men and situations like this before, but Pirro wasn't blameless. He'd known what he was doing wasn't totally aboveboard. But he wasn't a bad man. He'd made sure all his friends had taken a physical and had their tickers checked out before giving them the meds. Now he was forced to look at how Rafe might view his dealings, and he was embarrassed by what he found.

"Pirro, it's your turn," Ernie yelled. "You going deaf?"

No, but he might be going to jail.

As a cop, Rafe might have no choice but to arrest him, a thought that made Pirro panic. He was getting on in years. He was soft. He couldn't possibly go to the slammer.

He played his hand in a fog, hoping he could come up with a plan to save them all.

CHAPTER FOURTEEN

No great surprise to Rafe: Pirro was in fact playing poker. Rafe snapped a photo of Pirro's car outside Jonah Frye's house to show his aunt as proof. But he also wanted to talk to him and convince him to set things straight with his wife so Rafe wouldn't have to get involved playing private investigator again.

He cast a sideways glance at Sara. She sat beside him, patiently resting her head against the window, as they waited for Pirro to come out of the barn.

"Did you ever consider private-investigation work?" Rafe asked her.

She turned toward him. "No, but until today I haven't really been willing to consider any alternatives."

"What changed your mind today?" he asked, surprised.

She still stared out onto the street. "I realized how self-absorbed and selfish I've been, thinking my whole life is over because I can't do a job I love."

Hmm. "Why the change of attitude?" *And what else might it apply to?* he silently wondered.

"Angel. Imagine being told you could never have children."

He narrowed his gaze and ignored the kick start in his heart at her mention of children. "You want kids?" he asked, surprised.

After all, kids were usually the result of a long-term relationship, something Sara emphatically did not *do.*

"Not me — Angel. We were talking about what I wanted out of life, and I said I never had to give it much thought. That I always wanted to be a cop, but, thanks to my knee injury, that might not be possible. She said she knew a lot about reevaluating life because she'd always wanted to be a mom. And then she found out she couldn't." Sara inhaled deeply, then breathed out, almost a sigh.

"Sara . . ."

She shook her head. "I just feel so selfish, pitying myself because I might not be able to be a cop. She can never have *children.* That's a much bigger blow, and look how she's bounced back! She's even happy. So that's why I think it's time I look at what other options are open to me in the future."

She was clearly struggling with her issues, and a mixture of pride, pleasure and a little bit of pain rushed through Rafe, all at the same time.

"You should never compare yourself to someone else," he said in an attempt to comfort her and give her a good dose of reality. Everyone's problems were equally real to them.

"Angel said the same thing. But if there are lessons to be learned, I'm not averse to learning them. If she can overcome her tragedy, I can pull myself together and find another purpose."

"Yeah, you can," he said gruffly.

He knew better than to point out that there was suddenly a bit of optimism in her attitude. Or that if she could reevaluate what she wanted out of her career, maybe her personal life wasn't all that different. He'd put a new rule into effect: no discussing anything that would throw either of them off balance.

Whatever conclusions she drew, she'd have to come to them on her own.

They returned to silence until finally Pirro walked out from behind the house.

"I'll be right back." Rafe jumped out of the car and caught up with his uncle at the end of the driveway.

Sara waited in the car.

"Rafe, what's wrong?" Pirro asked.

"Don't panic. We just need to talk." He paused, wondering how to phrase things without really telling the man his wife had asked Rafe to follow him and make sure he was telling the truth. "Is everything okay at home?"

Pirro narrowed his gaze. "Why wouldn't it be?"

"Aunt Vi is upset. She's worried that you haven't been acting like yourself, and you're going out more often. And I've noticed you've been very quiet lately."

He waved Rafe away with one hand. "I'm fine. Everything's fine."

"Then why does Aunt Vi think there's someone else?" he said, awkwardly but as delicately as he could.

Pirro's eyes opened wide. "She said that? And sent you to ask me?"

Rafe dipped his head. "Sort of. Look, you're here where you're supposed to be, which is exactly what I figured. But she said there are times when you leave at odd hours, telling her you're going to play poker when there's really no game, and you know Aunt Vi. She's imagining the worst and spinning all sorts of weird scenarios." Rafe refused to elaborate on those. "So, what's going on? And how can I help?"

"Nothing." Pirro shuffled his feet and glanced at the blacktop driveway.

Clearly he was lying. "Come on. Man-to-man. If there's something you want to tell me, I'm here to listen."

Pirro paused. In the silence that followed, Rafe believed he was considering confiding in him.

"There's nothing."

Damn. Still, Rafe decided to give it one last shot. "I know she's not an easy woman to live with, but you love her, right?"

Pirro raised his hand to his chest. "With all my heart!"

"Good. Then do us both a favor? Go home to your wife. Convince her everything's fine and you're not . . . seeking comfort with someone else." That way Rafe would never have to humiliate himself like this again.

"Of course I'm not seeking comfort with someone else! There's no other woman for me."

Rafe stepped forward and put an arm around the older man's shoulders. "Then where are you going when there's no poker game going on?"

Pirro shook his head and puffed out his

shoulders. His face turned red with anger. "Can't a man have any privacy anymore?" Pirro asked. "I need time and space to myself, that's all."

He was lying.

Rafe had interrogated too many suspects who became defiant when they didn't want to answer a question not to recognize Pirro's deflective behavior. "Fine. If you ever want to talk, I'm here. But for now, go home to your wife and calm her down, okay?"

The man nodded and headed for his car, leaving Rafe with no answers and an uneasy feeling that something was very wrong.

Angel's Bed-and-Breakfast was a four-bedroom house with three bedrooms available to boarders. Two of those bedrooms were occupied by the ever-present Biff and Todd, leaving one couple from Connecticut in the remaining room. The couple left late Sunday afternoon after the wine festival had officially come to an end. Only Biff and Todd remained. Their stay was indefinite, as they claimed to be on a working vacation, and now that the business part of their trip had ended with the festival, they planned to stay on.

Which meant Nick wasn't going anywhere anytime soon. He had been staying at

Angel's since the fire Friday night. He wouldn't call the pullout couch in the small den comfortable, but at least he was able to keep an eye on her. The unsolved arson case weighed heavily on his mind, as did the idea of the two men staying under the same roof as his wife.

He appreciated the chance to wake up and see Angel first thing in the morning. She prepared an elaborate breakfast for her guests, clearly enjoying her new role, and she'd invited him to join them all for breakfast.

He'd agreed and was certain that the meal was the best thing he'd eaten in the six months since he'd moved out. Man, he'd missed her home cooking.

But not as much as he'd missed her.

He reminded himself that this didn't have to end. She'd offered him the possibility of reconciliation, but their getting back together hinged on coming to terms with the things that divided them. He'd have to get over his aversion to Angel's business if he was going to fix his marriage. But accepting her B and B was easy now that he'd allowed himself to really *see* Angel and how much she enjoyed operating the business and interacting with her customers. She deserved some happiness after what they'd been through, and he'd never take that joy away from her. But until she faced their loss, until she talked it through with him and they grieved together, not separately, he couldn't just accept it and go on as if nothing tragic had happened.

Lunchtime Monday, Rafe and Sara walked into Moe's, the main restaurant in town. When Nick had called and asked Rafe to meet him, he'd agreed on lunch, wanting to wait until the alarm company was settled in doing the install. Going to town later in the morning also gave the remaining stragglers from the festival a chance to get out of town. If Rafe was going to bring Sara out in the open, he wanted to see as few strangers as possible.

The counter was full of regulars, including his uncle Pirro and the bookkeeper who was new to the business but not to the town. The booths were also filling up, but Moe's wife, Nadeen, pointed to a table where Nick was waiting. All in all, everything looked and felt normal.

Rafe was about to head to his brother, when Sara tugged on his hand, stopping him.

"What's wrong?" he asked.

"Nick wanted to talk to you. Maybe I

should wait up front," she offered.

"No." Rafe was not leaving her alone. "Come sit with us. Besides, you have to eat lunch." Grasping her hand tighter in his, he pulled her toward the table.

Nick rose to greet them. "Hey. Thanks for coming."

"No problem." Rafe stepped aside to let Sara slide into the booth first before easing in next to her.

She'd been edgy since getting off the phone with the captain this morning. The Bachelor Blog, though spotlighting a guy in the city, still made sure to hit on the Sara-Rafe romance daily, reminding the city that they were huddled together in Rafe's hometown, Sara getting to know his family and Rafe getting to know Sara even better.

The captain had tried placing a call to the editor of the *Daily Post,* asking them to lay off publishing information on Sara's whereabouts, but citing the Bachelor Blogger's First Amendment right to free speech, the editor had respectfully declined. Sara felt like a walking target.

Which was why Rafe was sticking by her side.

Aida, the waitress, stopped by their table for chit-chat and to take their orders. When another table waved to get her attention, she finally left them alone to talk.

"So, what's up?" Rafe asked Nick.

"That's what I wanted to know. Did you hear anything on who set the fire?"

Rafe shook his head. He'd made some calls this morning. "The fire inspector can only confirm arson. The state police in charge of the investigation questioned people, but nobody saw anything definitive. Basically, they know nothing."

Nick frowned. "What about you, Sara?" he asked, lowering his voice. "Any news from New York?"

She shook her head. "According to our captain, the guy I'm supposed to testify against is smugly asserting he'll get off. The D.A. takes that to mean I should watch my back. But it's all inconclusive."

"And we're on the lookout for anyone suspicious now that most of the tourists are gone," Rafe said. "Anyone come to mind?"

To Rafe's surprise, Nick nodded. "Guess who didn't leave town?"

Rafe narrowed his gaze.

"Biff and Todd," Nick said before either Rafe or Sara could reply.

"What are those two still doing here?" Rafe asked.

"They said they were in the wine business, so I would have thought they'd be gone with the rest of the festival people," Sara said.

"Lunch is ready!" Aida arrived with her hands full of plates. She served them all quickly. "Anything else I can get you?"

"Ketchup for the burger," Nick said.

"Some more coffee would be great, please." Sara lifted her empty cup.

"I'm good," Rafe said.

"Back in a jiffy!" Aida promised, rushing off to fill their requests.

"I'm going to have the captain run a check on those two," Rafe said of Biff and Todd. "Can you get me their full names from Angel?" he asked his brother.

"Will do."

Rafe took a bite of his turkey club sandwich.

Beside him, Sara picked at her salad, her wary gaze darting around the room. Obviously, she was more interested in the customers than the food.

Knowing nothing he could say would distract her, Rafe made small talk with his brother as they all finished their meals. Soon they had paid and were back outside in the hot, humid summer air. Compared to the weekend, when the festival had been in full swing, the streets were empty, people preferring to be inside where the air conditioners kept them comfortable.

"Nick! Sara! Rafe!" Angel called their names and came running toward them. "You won't believe it! I can't believe it!"

"What's going on?" Nick asked first.

"I just had a phone call from the features editor at the *Daily Post* in Manhattan! She's going to include my bed-and-breakfast in a story about great summer getaways!" Angel practically shook with excitement.

"That's the same paper that prints the Bachelor Blog," Rafe said, immediately wary.

"That's how they heard about my B and B," Angel said, her tone more tempered now that the conflict of interest overtook her excitement. "Look, I know I was wrong to let the Bachelor Blogger know about you being here, but can't I be excited that it led to this kind of exposure?"

"Of course you can," Nick said, surprising everyone.

"Right," Rafe agreed. "It's just that the less exposure this little town has, the better as far as I'm concerned. At least until it's time for Sara to go back to the city." He shot a worried glance her way, but he couldn't read her feelings from her expression.

"Amanda Stevens, that's the editor, is

coming here tomorrow for a firsthand look. She's going to do an interview and bring a photographer to take pictures. And the timing is perfect, because just this morning, Biff and Todd decided to move into the Hilton for the rest of their vacation, so I have rooms available."

"Biff and Todd moved out?" Sara asked, obviously as surprised as Rafe.

"They said they'll be around town," Angel replied, "but they wanted a pool and a gym, all the amenities a full-service hotel offered."

Those two were odd ducks, Rafe thought.

"You all have a funny look in your eyes." Angel's gaze darted from Rafe to Sara. "Did I step in it again?" she asked, confused.

Rafe didn't want to upset her. She was an innocent bystander in all this drama, and she deserved success.

"You did nothing wrong, and of course it's okay to be excited," Sara said. "I'm thrilled for you!"

Angel smiled. "I have to go clean up for my guests. And I need to cook!" She started back down the street, when suddenly she turned. "Nick?"

"Yeah?"

"Come help me?"

Nick paused, obviously surprised by the

request.

Rafe nudged his mute brother in the side. "Go."

"I have to work."

"Call in sick," Rafe said wryly.

Nick nodded, his brain seeming to catch up. "Right. Coming!" he called out to his wife. "See you later, bro."

Rafe inclined his head, grinning.

Nick raised one hand in a wave and walked away.

Alone at last, Rafe turned to Sara. "Do you want a break from all this? We can figure out what to do about the features editor later."

Her eyes lit up. "Always. What do you have in mind?"

"Going out on my boat. Away from people, places and things." His favorite place on earth that he wanted to share with her. "Are you game?"

She nodded. "Sounds like heaven."

He could not agree more.

Sara stood holding on to the rail in front of her as Rafe propelled the small speedboat across the lake. There was not another boat in sight; the peace and solitude was all-encompassing. The wind blew her hair, and the sun baked down on her body, freeing her mind and her spirit.

"This is fabulous!" she called to him.

"I'm glad you like it."

She liked the view more. Not the beautiful trees and shoreline landscape, but the sight of shirtless Rafe in bathing trunks that hung low on his hips and revealed his tanned body and hard abs. Then there was the scar, which was a constant reminder that he'd taken one for the team.

For her.

Sunglasses covered his eyes, and the wind blew his dark hair off his forehead, giving him a sexy, rakish look.

She appreciated the fact that he'd sensed her tension and brought her here to ease it. He always knew just what to say or do to fix things in her small part of the world.

"Have you ever been on a boat before?" he asked, slowing the motor and letting them bob on the calm surface of the water.

She pulled her hair off her face. "Does the ferry to the Statue of Liberty count?"

He grinned. "Not really."

"Then, no."

She eased herself down on one of the padded benches that stretched across the width of the deck and leaned back, resting on her hands.

"I take it you grew up on a boat?" she

asked him.

He nodded. "My dad would take us out. The boys one time, the girls another. Sometimes we'd get alone-time with him, and that was usually the best day," he said, obviously remembering good times.

She smiled. "Sounds great."

"It was. I always told myself I'd take my own kids one day."

The notion, once spoken, was out there between them, and she couldn't help but imagine Rafe and his son or daughter spending time together on this boat. The image stuck with her, making her melancholy and sad, knowing that meant she'd be long gone out of his life.

She shook her head hard. She usually wasn't so wistful in her thinking, but lately that seemed all she was able to be. Well, no more. When would she ever have the opportunity to enjoy summertime on a boat on a lake again?

She cleared her throat. "Did you ever bring a girlfriend out on the lake?" she asked.

He lifted his glasses and met her gaze, obviously surprised by the question. "Back in high school, if I could convince my father to lend me the boat, and then only if I could smooth talk a girl into trusting me alone on

261

the lake." He treated her to a wink.

"Were you a bad boy?" She was curious about what kind of reputation he'd had.

"Hang on one second." He turned to drop anchor, so they could hang out for a while.

He stepped toward her, settling down on the bench beside her, leaving no doubt in her mind he was every inch the bad boy.

"Now, where were we? Oh, yeah, was I a bad boy? Hmm. I was the guy everyone knew wanted to leave the small town behind as soon as possible. That made me a risky proposition."

"I can imagine."

He grinned. "I bet I could have sweet-talked you onto my boat."

She shook her head and laughed. "You just did."

"So . . . What kind of kid were *you?*"

She figured turnabout was fair play. "Considering most of my family was on the force? I had a pretty solid good-girl thing going." She made a face at the reminder. "But at the same time, I was pretty stubborn, had my opinions and wanted things my way, which made the guys steer clear. Needless to say, I caught on and became much more male-gender friendly."

"Do tell." He traced the outline of her bathing suit with one finger.

She trembled as the heated touch set off sparks inside her belly, between her legs and everywhere else. She licked her dry lips. "Have you ever had sex on a boat?"

His eyes darkened with need. "No."

She glanced around the sparkling lake. "Do you think anyone will pass by and see us?" she asked nervously.

He laughed. "Is the big bad police officer scared of getting caught?"

"More like being exposed."

He rose and took a good look around. "Not if we hurry."

Her heart skipped a beat. "Then what are you waiting for?" She barely recognized her husky voice.

He leaned close and pressed his lips to hers, seducing her with his hot mouth. He followed as she lay down on the bench, coming down over her until his erection pulsed, hard against her stomach. She gripped the back of his head as her tongue dueled and tangled with his, mimicking sex, making her burn. The kiss was as hot as the sun overhead, consuming her just as he wanted to be consumed. A trickle of moisture settled between her legs, and her desire to have him inside her grew.

His lips moved from her lips to her jaw, trailing moist kisses down her neck to her collarbone, traveling lower until he settled between her breasts. He paused there, drawing lazy circles over her skin. She moaned and arched beneath him, the sensations arousing but not nearly enough.

With an easy pull on the string, he released her bathing-suit top. He yanked, and the bikini came off in his hands. Then he cupped each mound.

"No matter how many times I see you like this, you take my breath away." Intent on his task, he slid his hands down her waist and over her stomach.

She quivered at his touch. And once more he pulled and released her bathing suit, tossing the bottoms to the floor. She bent her knees, and without missing a beat, he thrust deep inside.

She exhaled hard, accepting all of him, and together they soared to completion.

A short time later, they were dressed and heading to shore. She stood beside him, wind blowing her hair, his arm looped around hers as he steered them home.

Home.

She really needed to get out of here before she became too comfortable with the word.

CHAPTER FIFTEEN

Pirro both liked and respected Rafe, and he took his advice to heart. After his poker game last night, he'd headed home, intent on reassuring his wife that there were no other women in the world for him, but she'd been fast asleep, a box of tissues by her side.

She was still sleeping when he woke up and left for work this next morning. He headed to the office, which was built on the same land where the spices grew in green houses that regulated the temperatures to ensure healthy plant growth all year round. He had a full day of meetings, and he worked through lunch. By five o'clock, he was ready to call it quits for the day.

He stopped in town for flowers and walked out of the florist, hopeful he'd make Vivian understand his stress had nothing to do with his feelings for her. In his hands, he held a dozen red roses in a crystal vase so large that it blocked his view. He bumped into someone on the sidewalk.

"I'm sorry!" he said, righting himself before he stumbled.

"No worries. We were waiting for you anyway."

Pirro dropped the flowers, and the glass shattered. Whatever they wanted, it couldn't be good.

Rafe took a quick shower while Sara checked in with the captain in the city. While she showered, he put marinated steaks on the outdoor grill. *Thank you, Mom,* he thought silently. He'd snuck in a phone call earlier, asking her to check on the alarm company and stock the fridge. She'd taken over everything while he was out for the day. The alarm upgrade was complete, and now he placed a chilled bottle of wine, grilled steak and corn on the cob on the picnic table outside.

Sara walked out of the house. Her damp hair hung loose around her shoulders, ripped denim shorts showed off her long legs and bare feet, and a large V-neck T-shirt still somehow looked sexy.

"What's all this?" she asked, her gaze sweeping over the set table.

"Dinner is served. Have a seat."

"Well, well. This is a nice surprise!"

He shrugged. "It's basic enough that I can handle it."

She laughed and dug into her meal. "Delicious," she said when she'd finished her first taste.

"I'll tell Mom you like her marinating," he said with a grin.

"You are a bad boy." She waved her fork at him in a chiding manner, laughing along with him.

"Don't I get points for coming up with the idea?"

"That you do." How could she resist that dimpled grin? Sara wondered.

They finished their meal in silence and, with their wineglasses, moved to the porch swing. She curled her legs beneath her and sipped from her glass, not-so-covertly watching Rafe.

He stretched an arm along the back of the seat, his fingertips grazing her shoulder. "So, tell me about your family."

She wrinkled her nose. "Really? Why?"

He rolled his eyes. "Why do you always question me when I want to get to know you better?"

She paused, taking another sip of her wine. "It's just that nobody has asked before."

"Ahh. Want to know why?"

She nodded.

"Because before me, you've only dated men interested in one thing," he said pointedly. "So, tell me about your family. You said they're all cops?"

On the job, she admired his interrogation tactics. Off the job, she could do without them. "They're all cops. My grandfather, my dad, an uncle . . ." She paused in thought. "My aunt was the first female cop in the family," she said with pride.

"All divorced?"

She should have known he'd get around to that point eventually. "Yes, all divorced. Well, all but one," she amended, thinking of her cousin.

"Then I definitely want to hear about him."

"Her."

His eyes opened wide. "Really, now."

Sara let out a sigh. "Yes, really. My cousin Renata. She lives in Hoboken."

"New Jersey."

"Yeah. Reni said it's easier to maintain her family life outside of Manhattan," she said wistfully. She missed having her cousin close by. "When she lived in the city and Reni was single, we'd hang out a lot."

"And now?"

She shrugged. "Not so much. Different

cities, different lives with her married, me single. But when we were kids, we were like this." She crossed two of her fingers together.

"And you miss hanging out with her, don't you?" he said, his tone sympathetic.

He read her so well. "How did you know?"

"It might have something to do with how much you enjoy my crazy family."

She couldn't suppress a smile. "Well, I do."

"Then why don't you make an effort to spend more time with Renata?"

Because every time she saw her cousin with her husband and kids, Sara left depressed. In the past, she was never quite sure where the melancholy came from. But now, she realized, her sadness stemmed from watching her cousin's happiness and the family life Sara would never have because of the choices she deliberately made.

Choices that made sense, she reminded herself.

"You're right. I should spend more time with her," Sara said to Rafe.

Finished with the subject, she rose and headed inside.

Rafe let Sara go. For whatever reason, the subject of her happily married cousin rattled her. He never meant to upset her, but he couldn't deny being pleased that here was a chink in the armor she used to defend against happily ever after.

His cell phone rang. He pulled it out of his pocket, looked at the caller and groaned. "Hi, Aunt Vi," he said through gritted teeth.

"Hi, honey. Rafe, he's on the run again!"

He didn't have to ask whom she was talking about. His head began to pound, and he pinched the bridge of his nose in frustration.

"Aunt Vi, I e-mailed you the picture of his car outside Jonah's house last night. And I told him to go home and make peace with you. Didn't he do that?"

She sniffed loudly into the phone. "I was asleep last night and this morning. But he came home from work in a mood, barely said a word through dinner. He barely ate my manicotti! And then he said he had to go out. He wouldn't say where. He just left!"

That's it. Rafe had had enough of Pirro's games. "I'll take care of it, Aunt Vi."

A few minutes later, he and Sara were once again driving around town looking for Pirro's car.

"Do you think he's playing cards?" Sara asked.

"I don't know what he's doing, but he's

obviously hiding something, and I'm going to get to the bottom of whatever it is."

Except this time there was no sign of Pirro's car by any of his poker cronies' houses, and a distinct feeling of unease settled over Rafe.

"What do you want to do now?" Sara asked.

Rafe made a U-turn and headed back toward Aunt Vi's house. "Now we wait for him to come home and find out what's going on once and for all."

Thankfully, they didn't have to wait long. Pirro's car turned into the driveway a short time later. It wasn't late at night, still early enough for Pirro to run any normal errand, but he'd tell his wife about one of those.

Rafe opened his car door and gestured for Sara to come along. "Last time I appealed to him man-to-man. This time we can both interrogate him," Rafe muttered.

"Pirro!" Rafe called to the man before he could disappear into his home.

"Rafe! You startled me." The older man's hand flew to his chest. "What are you doing here?"

"We're going to have a talk, and this time you aren't going to stonewall me."

Rafe waited for Pirro to hem and haw, or stutter while he struggled to find a believ-

271

able excuse.

"You're right," Pirro said instead. "I can't do this alone."

Startled, Rafe glanced from Pirro to Sara.

She shrugged, as if to say she was equally surprised. "Do you want to go inside?" she asked, her voice gentle.

Good cop, bad cop. They played the old cliché well.

"You're such a nice girl," Pirro said, then turned to Rafe. "She's such a nice girl. You hang on to that one."

Rafe shook his head, knowing the older man would get off track if he let him. "Do you want to go inside to talk?"

"No!" Pirro waved a hand in the air. "I don't want Vivian to hear any of this. She's upset enough, and this will only send her over the edge." He inhaled a long, tortured breath.

A look at his tired, wan face told Rafe his suffering was real. "What's going on? Talk to us."

"Maybe we can help," Sara said.

"I hope so, because I'm at my wit's end. How could such a simple act of kindness lead to this kind of thing?"

Rafe placed a hand on Pirro's shoulder. "Why don't you start at the beginning." Maybe then he could make sense of the problem.

"Right. Okay. You see, when I married your aunt, I discovered she was . . . how do I say this delicately?"

Rafe winced, knowing exactly where this conversation was headed. "Just say it fast and keep going."

"My Vivian is insatiable. It takes a real man to keep up with her. I was afraid I would disappoint her, and so I spoke to my doctor, who gave me a few samples of Viagra."

Rafe's cheeks burned. He really did not want to have this conversation with his aunt's husband.

"Go on," Sara said, encouraging him and ignoring the embarrassment factor.

"It worked, but I couldn't fill an actual prescription. I mean, can you imagine if Gertrude at the pharmacy got hold of that kind of information?" The older man shuddered. "A friend told me about a friend who had a friend that had access to an unlimited supply in Canada. He hooked me up, and soon I was . . . in the groove whenever I needed to be."

Rafe remembered the comments outside the barber shop and realized he'd been right about Pirro taking Viagra. "But what does this have to do with you sneaking around town at odd hours?" Rafe asked, frustration building along with the accumulation of useless information. He wished Pirro would make his point.

"I'm getting there!"

"Take your time," Sara said, shooting Rafe a warning glare.

"I shared my little secret with my friends at poker, and they asked me to get them some, too. So I contacted the guy, and soon we had a regular thing going. I'd meet him to place orders and pick up the pills."

Rafe raised an eyebrow. "And that's where you go when you're ducking out on your wife?"

Pirro nodded. "That, and sometimes the guys want to meet privately to place or pick up their orders. Either they don't want the other guys to know they're using, too, or they're afraid of being overheard at home. Plus, they shared the news and my customer base grew."

"You're dealing in Canadian Viagra. And that's what has you so upset?" Rafe asked, appalled.

"That's not all." Pirro shoved his hands into his pockets and shifted from foot to foot.

"You've come this far," Sara said, her voice soothing. "You can tell us the rest."

"Two men approached me at the festival and told me they wanted access to my supplier so they could traffic real drugs from here to Manhattan in the Spicy Secret's delivery trucks," Pirro said, his voice cracking. "I said no, of course. I'm not a drug dealer!"

Rafe figured now wasn't the time to argue semantics. "So . . ."

"First my Angel's pie stand burned down, and they made it clear they could get to my family if I didn't cooperate, so I agreed. I bought myself some time, though. I told them I couldn't reach my supplier until our scheduled meeting, which was a lie. They came to me and said I had until Friday to put the deal in motion. Or else."

Rafe wondered how in the world this simple man had gotten himself involved with something so dangerous.

"You did the right thing telling us," Sara reassured him. "Rafe and I will figure out a plan."

"They said it would be a pity to hurt her . . . but I don't think getting your brother out of the way would bother Biff and Todd so much. I'm so sorry!" Pirro trembled as he spoke.

"Biff and Todd are drug dealers?" Sara's voice rose into the night.

"Shh!" Rafe reminded her. "Boy, you really stepped in it," he said to his uncle.

Pirro, looking like an old, beaten man, met Rafe's angry gaze. "I said I'm sorry!"

"You should have come to me immediately."

"And have you look at me like you are now? At first I thought I could say no and they'd go away."

Man, he was naive, Rafe thought.

"And then I thought I could stall them long enough to think of something. But most of all I was afraid you'd send me to jail, and how long do you think I'd last with a cell mate named Big Al?"

Rafe glanced at the starry night sky, praying for strength. "I'm glad you told me." Now he had to come up with a plan. "Today is Tuesday. We have four days."

Sara placed a hand on Pirro's shoulder. "There's nothing more you can do now. Why don't you go inside and get some rest?"

"And reassure Aunt Vi, while you're at it," Rafe said. "We'll be in touch."

"Thank you!" Without warning, Pirro launched himself into Rafe's arms.

Rafe awkwardly patted the man on the back. "We'll figure out a plan," he promised him.

He and Sara locked glances. She inclined

her head, her subtle way of letting him know she had an idea. He wasn't surprised she'd thought of something so quickly, and, not for the first time, he was damned glad she was here.

Back at Rafe's house, Sara put a call in to her uncle Jack, who really wasn't her uncle but was a good friend of her father's from his police academy days. Uncle Jack was a retired DEA agent and still had contacts in the Drug Enforcement Administration and would tell her who to contact for help.

She hung up Rafe's cell phone and walked back into the kitchen to find Rafe pouring himself a tumbler with Scotch.

She didn't blame him.

"Are you okay?" she asked.

He nodded. "I just can't believe Pirro's been supplying Viagra to the old men in this town." He shook his head in disbelief.

Sara laughed. "He's a character, but I truly believe he meant well."

"Did you reach your father's friend?"

"I left Uncle Jack a message and said it was urgent. He'll call your cell as soon as he gets it."

"Thanks. Now that that's in motion, let's check my machine." Rafe hit the play button on the answering machine on the kitchen counter. "Sara, it's Coop. You left this number with me in case of emergency. It's an emergency. Call me ASAP."

Beep.

Another message immediately began to play. "It's Captain Hodges. Call me back," he growled.

Sara groaned. Rafe agreed. The way today was going, neither message could be good news.

CHAPTER SIXTEEN

Using Rafe's cell, Sara dialed the number and reached the older man immediately. "What's wrong, Captain?"

"Your apartment was hit."

A shiver rippled through her. "Was anything taken?" she asked. She covered the phone with her hand and mouthed the word *burglary* to Rafe.

"Nothing taken. Just a note lipsticked on a mirror that said *stay away.*"

She frowned at the warning. "Not very original."

"No evidence it's Morley, but who else would bother? Sounds like he's more concerned with keeping you too afraid to testify than he is with hurting you, but you still need to be careful," the older man said, his voice gravelly from too many cigarettes.

"I will," she promised him. "Listen, Captain, Rafe and I have run into a . . . situation here. Can you do me a favor and run a history on two drug dealers who go by the name Biff and Todd?" She gave him a brief description of the situation and their attempt to get in touch with the DEA, and followed up with a sketch of Biff and Todd, knowing that they could have altered their appearance and/or their names.

The captain let out a long groan. "What part of keep a low profile don't you understand, Rios?" She could imagine him running his hand over his bald head in frustration.

"I don't find trouble, Captain. It's been finding me." She glanced at Rafe and grinned.

"Keep telling yourself that," he muttered. "I'll let you know what I find out. In the meantime, be careful and keep in touch." After giving the order, he disconnected the line.

Sara hung up and met Rafe's gaze. "He's pissed."

"I'm sure he is. Do they know who broke into your place?"

She shrugged. "Not who specifically, but they left me a message on my bathroom mirror, and it sounds like it was just another threat to scare me from testifying."

"So either Morley's guy from the dance has left Hidden Falls or he's got more than one boy doing his bidding." Rafe strode over to the keypad on the wall by the front door and input the new alarm code. "Since we're in for the night, might as well keep it set."

She nodded.

"Are you okay?" he asked.

She nodded. "I'm certainly not going to let threats and warnings stop me from doing my job. Besides, I'll have protection going to and from the trial. It's just a matter of getting through these next few weeks. And I have your uncle's problems to keep my mind occupied."

Rafe groaned. "You just had to remind me."

Sara strode over and wrapped her arms around his neck. "Pirro's lucky to have you," she said, staring into his sexy eyes.

He returned her gaze. "And I'm lucky to have *you*." He pressed a light kiss on her lips and stepped back.

"I need to check in with Coop and see what was so urgent." She used Rafe's cell to make the next phone call. "No answer at home." She left Coop a message and then dialed his cell. "And no luck there, either." She left another message on his voice mail.

"At this point there's nothing more we can do on any front but wait for everyone to get in touch with us."

Sara frowned. "I know you're right, but I hate waiting. And I hate being idle when there are two live situations going on."

Rafe sidled up beside her. "Then it's a good thing I know exactly how to keep you busy passing time," he said in a voice designed for seduction.

One she couldn't resist.

The ringing of the doorbell woke Sara out of a sound sleep. She jumped out of bed. A cool chill immediately reminded her she was stark naked. Rafe was nowhere to be found, and she hoped he was answering the door.

By the time she pulled on a pair of sweats and a T-shirt and ran out of the room, she found Rafe and Coop sitting and talking in the den.

"What are you doing here?" Sara asked, shocked to realize he'd come all this way. "Who died?" she immediately asked.

"Ever the pessimist," Rafe said.

Coop shook his head and laughed. "I see *that* hasn't changed."

"Then why are you here? I'm glad to see you, but nobody takes a five-hour ride just to say hello." Her heart still beat hard in her chest from being woken from a deep sleep, and now, seeing Coop . . .

"Everything's fine," he assured her.

"Lexie?" she asked of his fiancée.

"Great. I swear. With the Bachelor Blogger publishing your whereabouts, I wanted to check on you."

"And?" She pushed him, knowing there had to be more.

"I wanted to talk to you both."

Rafe nodded. "Let's go into the kitchen and sit down. I know Sara and I could use some coffee. What about you?" he asked Coop. "Besides coffee there's soda, orange juice, water and maybe some iced tea."

"Coffee sounds good. The drive drained me."

They shifted to the kitchen, a room with light wood and new appliances. Sara had enjoyed puttering around in here the other day. Now the sun shone through the windows, casting a cheery glow around the room.

Rafe must have been up when the doorbell rang, because the coffee was already freshly brewed and smelled delicious. Sara insisted on pouring everyone coffee and getting the milk.

When they were all settled around the table, she couldn't stand the suspense any longer. "Okay, what's going on?" she asked Coop.

He exhaled a long breath. "Okay. I assume

you know your apartment was broken into?"

Sara nodded. "The captain says it was related to the upcoming trial."

"Do you know how the Bachelor Blog found out you were here?" he asked, switching subjects.

"My sister-in-law." Rafe explained about Angel's B and B and her reasons for calling the blog.

"Ahh." Coop nodded in understanding. "That might help confirm my hunch," he said, more to himself than to either Sara or Rafe.

"I don't understand," Sara said.

"Me, neither."

"Okay, look, Amanda Stevens is the features editor at the paper where I work."

"That's who Angel said is coming here to interview her and feature the bed-and-breakfast," Sara said.

Coop tilted his head in acknowledgment. "And don't you think it's a little odd, that first the unknown, anonymous blogger was contacted by Angel, then the blogger wrote about you staying at Angel's B and B, and then suddenly *Amanda* is interested in featuring Angel's?" Coop asked.

Sara shook her head. "I'm sorry. I'm still not getting it."

"I think Amanda is the Bachelor Blogger,"

Coop said, surprising her.

"Couldn't it just be that Amanda was following up on something she read in the blog when she decided to interview Angel?" Rafe asked.

Coop spread his hands in front of him. "Possible, but I know Amanda, and I wouldn't be surprised if she was the one spotlighting men and matchmaking all over the city."

"How well do you know her?" Sara teased.

Coop shot her a look, warning her not to go there.

Sara laughed. "Okay, so you know her *that* well."

Rafe cleared his throat. "You said you need to talk to us. So, what brings you here?"

Coop clasped his hand around the coffee mug. "Well, as Sara knows, I've been toying with the idea of leaving the newspaper and tackling my writing full-time. Lexie loves to travel, and I've saved enough to give myself a year to see whether doing it full-time can turn it into more of a career than a hobby."

Which Sara knew was his dream. "But you also love reporting, so you're torn."

"I used to love reporting. Lately it's become more of a depressing grind than anything else. And with this Bachelor Blog being the major focus of the newspaper right now, it feels more like a tawdry rag than a weighty newspaper. Not to mention that the damned blog is screwing with a police witness." He pointedly looked at Sara.

"We're in agreement there," Rafe said.

"All to keep the paper in the black. Look, I understand the economic realities for newspapers today, but profit at the expense of even one person's public safety rubs me the wrong way. And if Amanda, who already worked at the paper, is also that blogger . . ." Coop shrugged. "It would change the blog from an acquired moneymaker into a deliberate ploy to take the paper toward the sensational just to make a buck. Either way, I want out. But I need to know first."

"A reporter till the end, right?" Sara asked her friend.

Coop merely laughed. "Lexie's agreed to let me write her grandmother's story if I change the names to protect the *innocent.* That'll give my next book a real-life edge."

"Good for you!" Sara said, excited for him.

"So if this Amanda is the Bachelor Blogger, are you going to expose her?" Rafe asked.

Coop shook his head. "It's something *I* need to know. I'm not out to ruin Amanda or her career, but it'll definitely solidify my decision to leave now rather than later."

"Makes sense to come up here to check it out, then," Rafe said.

"Besides, it gave me a chance to make sure Sara was doing okay."

"I'm a big girl," she reminded her friend. "And I have protection."

Coop's inquiring stare shifted between Sara and Rafe.

No doubt he was wondering just what kind of protection Rafe was supplying, something Sara had no intention of getting into now.

"What's your plan to uncover the truth about the blogger?" Rafe asked.

"It's simple. Right now the blogs are vague tidbits of information. Things like, *Our favorite duo are holed up alone in Rafe's secluded abode. Will they grow tired of each other or will the proximity bring them closer? Could a proposal be next?*" Coop mimicked the blog in a *Masterpiece Theater*-type tone.

Rafe laughed at the imitation.

"I want you two to display some extravisible PDA around town, or at least around Amanda, and see if the blog posts turn more . . . specific and personal." Coop leaned back in his seat. "Ingenious plan, if you ask me. So, can I count on you?" Coop asked them.

Sara glanced at Rafe, wondering how he'd feel about upping their romance quotient in public.

He rose from his seat and walked around to Sara, leaned down and pressed a long, lingering kiss on her cheek. His breath was warm, his lips hot, and her entire body reacted to the simple gesture. She hoped neither man noticed that her nipples puckered beneath her thin T-shirt.

"I'll take that as a yes," Coop said, his eyes taking in the implications of that kiss. "So, want to take me over and introduce me to your sister-in-law, Angel?"

"Sure," Rafe said. "I'll give my brother a call and see if he can meet us there. I need to talk to him anyway."

"Isn't he at work?" Sara asked.

Rafe nodded. "But with Biff and Todd out of the B and B, Angel told him she didn't need a bodyguard and is trying to get him to leave, too. I'm sure he'll jump at the chance to see her."

Before he could call his brother, Rafe's cell phone rang.

He glanced at the number and tossed it to Sara. "I don't recognize the number. It must be for you."

Uncle Jack, she hoped. She glanced at the

incoming number and nodded. Apparently, the fun was about to begin, and she hit Send.

"Uncle Jack!" As she spoke, she walked away from Rafe and Coop to give herself some privacy to explain the situation to her uncle.

"Hello, princess! How are you?" His big voice boomed in her ear, reminding her how much she'd looked forward to his visits when she was younger. He'd bring her things from around the world, and Sara used to think he was just a world traveler — until she was old enough to understand what a DEA agent did for a living.

She turned her attention back to the call. "I'm great, thanks. How are you?"

"Say that louder. My hearing-aid battery's dead, and I can't hear a damned thing," Uncle Jack yelled into Sara's ear although she'd had no problem hearing him before.

She shook her head and laughed. Extreme hearing loss caused by an explosion had forced Uncle Jack into retirement. He hated the hearing aids and always claimed the damned things were broken or the batteries dead as an excuse not to wear them. Uncle Jack was vain and thought the device killed his chances with the ladies.

And forcing them to yell at him wouldn't?

Sara thought wryly. "I said, I'm great, thanks!" she shouted into the phone.

"Don't lie to me, princess. Your father told me you have a busted knee. But we'll discuss your future another time. Your message said you needed my help."

"I do. I mean, I do!" She remembered to speak louder.

She had to raise her voice and repeat herself until Uncle Jack heard her, but eventually, she'd explained Pirro's situation and the sting idea she and Rafe had come up with as a solution.

Uncle Jack promised to have a DEA agent contact her as soon as possible, and in return she promised to visit him when she returned to the city so they could catch up.

She disconnected the call and returned to the two men in the family room.

"He's on it," Sara said to Rafe.

Coop stepped toward her. "Let me get this straight. Rafe's uncle is being threatened by drug dealers, and you two plan to get a DEA agent in here to pretend to sell them drugs?" he asked excitedly as his reporter's instincts took over and he smelled a big story.

He'd miss this when he retired. She hoped he could find another way to get the excitement and adrenaline rush when he left his job behind. Almost immediately, she realized she might as well be talking about herself.

She shivered and pushed the thought away. She had more important things to concentrate on now.

"That's right," Sara told Coop. "And as far as you're concerned, it's *off the record*," she informed him, wagging her finger in front of his face for emphasis.

Coop folded his arms across his chest. "Come on, Sara. That's a huge story you're asking me to suppress. Give me some incentive beyond our friendship to keep quiet."

Sara knew he was only partially kidding. The journalist who knew a good scoop when he heard one wanted in.

She glanced at Rafe, whose expression had darkened. He looked ready to strangle Sara's best friend. She placed a calming hand on Rafe's arm, silently asking him to relax. From the minute she'd had to start yelling in order for her uncle to hear, she'd known she would be letting Coop in on what was going down. But Sara would trust Coop with her life. Or in this case, Rafe's uncle's life.

She felt certain the feds would give Pirro immunity in exchange for his help capturing the higher-ups in a New York City drug ring, but they hadn't even met with the DEA yet. There were no guarantees. And Rafe didn't want his uncle's dealing in drugs exposed to the world.

She pivoted and faced Coop. "When the sting is over, we'll give you an exclusive. You'll be the first to run the story that includes interviews with all parties, and you'll see that Pirro is just a man who tried to help out his friends and ended up caught in an impossible situation."

Coop narrowed his gaze. "I tell the truth in my reporting," he warned Sara.

"I knew this was a bad idea as soon as you said it," Rafe muttered.

Sara shook her head. "No, it's fine. Because when Pirro tells his story to Coop, he'll get that truth."

"I still don't know about this," Rafe said, his defenses understandably high.

"Well, I do."

Rafe didn't know Coop as well as she did. "Trust me, this is a win-win situation for all of us. Coop gets the exclusive and puts out the information by which all other reporters will get their content. It will work in Pirro's favor, I promise."

Rafe turned toward Coop. "If you meet Pirro and agree with how naive he really is, do you promise not to portray him as some upstate drug dealer with no conscience? I admit I'm biased, but I'm also a cop, and the man was supplying Viagra to his friends so they could enjoy their . . . uh . . . l-love lives," Rafe stammered, searching a tasteful way to explain.

Sara willed Coop to agree. "Well?"

He strode over to Rafe. "Deal," he said, extending his hand.

Rafe's gaze darted from Coop to Sara, and though she knew Rafe was wary, he finally inclined his head and grasped Coop's hand. "Deal."

A wary truce had been declared.

By giving Coop a dream story, Sara had gotten them a modicum of control over how Pirro was portrayed in the news. Something they'd lose if another paper reported the story first. And she knew as well as Rafe did that a drug bust like this would be big news.

Now all that remained was for them to meet the DEA agent sent by her uncle Jack and hope all went as smoothly with the government agent.

It would also help their cause if Pirro proved capable of handling an undercover sting operation without panicking, or they were all in deep trouble.

Rafe drove to Angel's. He didn't know

much about the man in the backseat except that Sam Cooper was involved with a woman Sara liked a lot, and that Sara trusted him implicitly.

Sara didn't extend her faith in people easily, so if she believed in him, Rafe would do his best to do the same. He had no choice. His uncle's future — his entire family's future — was at stake.

"So, Coop, where are you staying?"

"I was hoping to get a room at Angel's."

Sara turned and faced Coop in the back. "Those rooms will be occupied by Amanda Stevens and her photographer. But if you could get a room at the Hilton where Biff and Todd are staying, maybe you could keep a subtle eye on them?"

"Works for me." Coop pulled out his phone, called information and was soon confirming a reservation with the concierge at the hotel. "All set," Coop said as he disconnected the call.

Rafe nodded. "Good. After we're finished at Angel's, I'll take you back to my place for your car and you can follow me to the hotel."

"Thanks," Coop said.

"This is it." Rafe parked on the street in front of the bed-and-breakfast and they all climbed out.

Nick's car was in the driveway.

They reached the front door, which as usual during the day was unlocked. Rafe rang the bell and let them all inside. He was about to call for Angel when he heard arguing in the kitchen.

He met Sara's concerned gaze. "You and Coop stay here. I'll let them know we have company."

Rafe headed for the kitchen and entered without knocking first. "Hey, are you two looking to scare away guests?"

Angel turned his way, hands perched on her hips, fire in her dark eyes. "Would you please tell your brother that he no longer needs to stay here? Biff and Todd have moved into a hotel, and the only guests here will be from the newspaper in New York. Not someone who was here during the festival. I'm perfectly safe."

Nick shot Rafe a pleading look. Luckily for his brother, Rafe had no choice but to take his side. "Angel, Nick does need to be here."

"Why?"

Rafe thought of and discarded a bunch of reasons that didn't involve him revealing her father was involved with drug dealers.

He finally settled on the one he thought she'd find the most believable. "They haven't caught whoever's after Sara yet, which means whoever she's close to is in potential danger. Look at what happened to your booth. You don't want to risk someone breaking in here to send a message to Sara and you being alone and caught off guard."

She opened her mouth to argue, then closed it again.

Nick wisely remained silent.

"Fine. He can stay." She turned around and walked up the back stairs that led to the upstairs bedrooms.

"What's got her so worked up?" Rafe asked.

Nick groaned. "Our first marriage-counselor appointment is in a couple of hours. I think it's clicking that she's going to need to talk and open up. And she resents me for putting her in that position."

"Well, then. I'd say you're making progress." Rafe slapped his brother on the back. "Good luck."

"Thanks," Nick said wryly.

"I take it the newspeople aren't here yet?"

He shook his head. "Angel got a call saying they'd arrive around dinnertime."

"Okay. Well, I had someone from the city I wanted her to meet, but all things considered, I think it can wait."

"Who?"

"Another news guy. He's Sara's neighbor, and he's here playing a hunch."

Nick rolled his shoulders. "Whatever that means. Look, I'm going to see if Angel's okay and make sure she's calm before this appointment."

Rafe nodded. "Stay close to her," he warned his brother.

"I will," Nick said, but Rafe caught the curious look aimed his way.

Rafe wasn't about to get into details about Angel's father, Viagra, drug deals and the DEA. Even if he wanted to fill his brother in, there was every chance Nick might not believe the story, anyway.

"Good luck at the marriage counselor's," Rafe said, heading back to where Sara and Coop waited in the front hall.

"And good luck to you with whatever you're involved in," Nick shot back.

"Thanks." Because they would definitely need all the luck they could get.

CHAPTER SEVENTEEN

Later that night, Mark Lopez, the DEA agent from the Buffalo field office and a member of the local task force, arrived at Rafe's house. Agent Lopez appeared more boyish than the youngest beat cop back in New York City. Rafe knew looks could be deceiving and hoped the man was up to the job.

Because nobody knew if Pirro would be.

Over the next twenty-four hours, Agent Lopez arranged the sting. He'd instructed Pirro to set up a meeting between Biff, Todd and Pirro's *distributor*. It had taken a while for Pirro, in his agitated, panicked state, to understand he didn't really have to get in touch with his Canadian contact. Agent Lopez would play that role.

The sting operation was set for ten o'clock. All Pirro had to do was get wired, show up, meet the men, make the introductions and let Biff and Todd incriminate themselves.

Rafe and Sara wouldn't participate in the actual bust; they'd be monitoring the situation from a nearby truck set up with surveillance equipment. Once money exchanged hands, Agent Lopez would arrest Biff and Todd, and, with a little luck, they'd roll over on their ringleader in exchange for some kind of deal.

The sting was set for later tonight. Pirro was under strict instructions to keep his mouth shut and get through the day. He only had to lie to his wife one more time, and this would all be over.

Unfortunately, before the bust, they were all invited to a get together at Angel's Bed-and-Breakfast. She wanted to impress the people from the *Daily Post* visiting from New York. And Coop wanted to tag along with them and surprise Amanda, his co-worker, so he could observe her reaction to Rafe and Sara's lovey-dovey performance. Any way Rafe looked at it, it was bound to be a long evening.

"How are you doing?"

He jerked at Sara's touch on his shoulder. Sitting on his front porch, he'd been so preoccupied he hadn't heard her open the door and step outside.

"I didn't mean to startle you." She sat

down beside him. "Nervous?"

He shrugged. "I do this for a living, but Pirro doesn't. He's fragile."

"And well coached. He knows what's at stake. He can handle it," she reassured him.

"You don't think he's in over his head?" The thought had kept Rafe tossing and turning all night long.

"I think he'll be fine," she insisted.

He appreciated her certainty — even if she was agreeing with him and lying in order to keep him calm. It was working. Rafe leaned back and, with his foot, kicked the swing into slow motion. He enjoyed sitting out here with her, talking about things that mattered.

"Agent Lopez called while you were out here."

"What's up?" Rafe asked.

"First, we're both cleared for backup tonight. Medical leaves waived by special dispensation," she explained.

Rafe nodded. "One issue down. Besides, it shouldn't require much from either one of us to cover Lopez and Pirro."

"Agreed. Even I should be able to handle it." She leaned down and patted her bad knee.

Rafe knew her wry tone covered serious concern, but she was right. Tonight should be a routine cover. Anything more, and he'd be healthy enough to handle it.

"You said *first.* What else did Agent Lopez have to say?"

"Right. He said he ran the name of Pirro's Canadian supplier by the task force east of here working on closing distribution lines between the U.S. and Canada. Turns out he's someone they've been after for a while. They don't want us stepping on their investigation, so they'll handle him . . ." She trailed off.

"But?" Rafe asked, sensing there was more.

"But they may call on Pirro down the road for information or to identify him in person." Her eyes conveyed her regret about that.

But Rafe nodded in understanding. "One thing at a time. Let's get through tonight's sting first."

She nodded. "We're almost there."

"We just have to survive Angel's get-together first."

"Speaking of Angel's, did you reach Nick and find out how the marriage-counseling session went?" she asked, hope in her voice.

"In other words, are we in for a nice time or a war zone?" Rafe asked wryly. "I wish I knew. Nick's not returning my calls."

"Which means we'll find out in . . ." She glanced at the stainless-steel watch on her wrist. "Half an hour."

Rafe said a silent prayer that both of the night's events would go off without a hitch.

Once inside Angel's, Rafe singled out his brother and pulled him outside for a talk. Rafe might be overwhelmed with Pirro's situation and Sara's safety, but he was still worried about his brother and his marriage, and Rafe wanted to know how the counseling session had gone.

"Well?" Rafe asked Nick once they were alone outside. "How'd it go?"

"I am so not a talker," Nick muttered. "But I still picked up the slack for both of us."

"I know it's too soon to ask if you made progress, but do you think you're on the right track?"

Nick leaned against the side of the house. "She listened. She heard me say I missed my wife. She heard me say that without facing the loss, there was no foundation on which to go forward. And she heard the doctor agree. Next time, I'm going to sit in silence even if it kills me, and hope she joins in." He shrugged. "Otherwise, I've done all I can do."

Rafe nodded. "I have faith. She's loved you for too long to throw it all away."

"I hope you're right, but she seems pretty fulfilled with what she has now." He inclined his head toward the house — the B and B — and the source of their friction.

"She doesn't want to lose you. Keep the faith."

"Are you doing the same?" Nick tossed back at Rafe.

They both knew Nick was talking about his relationship with Sara and whether it would sustain itself beyond this short summer fling.

Rafe shrugged. "Beats me. We don't have the same foundation you and Angel have." And Sara didn't have the faith Rafe did, either.

"Everyone comes at a relationship from a different place. It's all a question of how hard both parties are willing to work for it."

Rafe shook his head and laughed. "Every once in a while you surprise me," he said to his brother. "I never pictured you as philosophical."

"What can I say? Separation does funny things to a person. And unfortunately, I have plenty of experience with the notion to know it can make — or break — the best of relationships."

And on that warning note, Nick turned and headed inside, leaving Rafe to wonder if the foundation he and Sara had started creating this summer would be enough to sustain them when this forced proximity came to an end.

Angel held the gathering in her foyer. Sara had noticed on entering that the house smelled warm and welcoming, like apple pie and family, making her smile.

Rafe had immediately caught sight of Nick and excused himself to go talk to his brother. Sara, meanwhile, had mingled with different people in the room, beginning with Aunt Vi, who kept insisting Sara taste her chocolate chip cookies, because they were the best. She explained how she used to bake them for Rafe when he was a little boy and wanted Sara to sample them, too. After biting into one, Sara discovered they were indeed warm, gooey and the best she'd ever had.

The only family in the room consisted of Pirro and Vi, and Rafe and Sara. The rest of the guests appeared to be friends of Angel's. Apparently, she was sticking to her rule of not celebrating occasions with Nick's parents.

Sara immediately caught herself, realizing

she'd grouped herself as family. Because she felt as if she really belonged here in Hidden Falls. It was going to be hard to leave them when it was time to go back to the city to testify. Hard but necessary, since this wasn't her hometown, nor was this her family.

Keeping the harsh reality in mind, she made her way through the room toward the small bar area where Pirro played bartender for his daughter. At least he had a job that would keep him busy talking, his mind occupied, so he wouldn't have time to worry.

Coop waved to her from across the room, and she walked over to meet up with him.

"How's it going?" she asked.

"Nice people in this town," he said, a grin teasing the edge of his mouth.

She shook her head and laughed. "You know that's not what I meant."

"Amanda was surprised to see me here, but I think she bought the story that I came to see you."

"Good. Are you at least relaxing while you're here?" she asked.

He shrugged. "With all the action here, my mind is going nonstop."

"Now *that* I understand. So, when are you going to introduce me to your friend, the editor?" Sara asked, tilting her head toward where a blonde with long, wavy hair was

305

talking to Angel.

"I will. As soon as I can introduce both you and Rafe together. Speaking of Rafe, where did he disappear to? Because you two promised to give me some PDA, remember?" Coop tilted his cup back and finished the last of his drink.

Sara glanced around, but she didn't see Rafe. "I think he's outside talking to his brother. He'll be back soon. In the meantime, you and I can catch up. So, how's Lexie?"

A warm smile took hold, transforming Coop's entire face at the thought of the woman he loved. "Busy with Web site updating and making sure her grandmother takes her blood-pressure medication."

Sara smiled. "You like her grandmother, don't you?"

Coop nodded. "She's a piece of work and a very special woman."

"And house-hunting? How's that going?"

"Still looking. Lexie's not used to having a place of her own, since she's always stayed at her grandmother's when she's in town. She's having trouble narrowing down what she wants, but we'll get there."

"Spoken like a patient man, head over heels in love. I'm really happy for you, Coop."

"Thanks. So . . . what about you? Have you and Rafe —"

"Have she and Rafe what?" Rafe asked, coming up beside them and wrapping his arm around her shoulder.

He pulled her tightly against him, cocooning her in his warmth.

Well, Coop wanted a public display of affection, Sara thought. Rafe was providing one, and to Sara it felt so right.

"Coop was just asking if you and I were having a nice summer," she quickly improvised.

"We're having a great summer." Rafe leaned close and pressed a kiss against her cheek.

Her knees trembled, and she reached for and squeezed his hand. "That's right. We are. So, when do we meet Amanda Stevens?"

"Right now." Coop turned and gestured toward the reporter across the room.

Amanda walked toward them, and Sara took in the attractive woman with wavy blond hair and porcelain skin.

"Coop! I still can't believe we're both here at the same time."

"Well, since we are, I'd like you to meet my friends, Rafe Mancuso and Sara Rios," Coop said.

"From the Bachelor Blog!" Amanda exclaimed. "It's so nice to see you both together."

"You recognize us?" Rafe asked.

Amanda smiled. "Of course."

Sara wondered if the words that fell so easily from the woman's lips could be true and the only reason she knew of them. Not because she was secretly chronicling their lives.

"How do you feel being the subjects of the blog?" Amanda asked.

Sara felt Coop's eyes boring into the woman as if he could find answers that way.

"Can I be honest?" Sara asked.

Amanda nodded. "I wouldn't want it any other way. It's off the record anyway. I'm just curious. I know Coop complained about his experience as the bachelor, but he certainly ended up with the right woman for him. So the blogger scored in that relationship."

Now Sara flip-flopped in her musings. Amanda gushed about the idea of the blog in a way that made Sara wonder if Coop was right, and the other woman had an agenda and she really was the blogger.

"I met Lexie because she had an interest in a ring I was given as a reward, not because the blog paired us together," Coop pointed out, just as he had when Sara made similar comments back in the city.

"Details," Amanda said with a laugh. "Now, back to you two. You never answered my question," she said, wagging her finger in a chiding motion toward Sara and Rafe.

"I think we'd prefer privacy," Sara said honestly. "But when I look into his eyes, I'm so happy sometimes I don't care if the whole world knows!" she exclaimed, pulling Rafe into a spontaneous hug.

Over her shoulder, Coop's eyes filled with laughter and gave her an invisible thank-you for playing along with his game.

"And I couldn't agree more," Rafe said with more restraint than Sara had shown.

"That's sweet. I don't think there's any-thing better than true love," Amanda said.

Sara settled in back at Rafe's side, and he slipped his hand into her back pocket, pull-ing her close. The gesture had the effect of cupping her behind in his hand, resulting in a rush of arousal that nearly had her sighing in pleasure.

Somehow she managed to refrain and cleared her throat.

"I agree. Love is wonderful." Sara looked up at Rafe with adoration before turning back to Amanda. "So, how is your article on Angel's going?"

"This place is so charming," Amanda said, her gaze taking in the small family room area where Angel was entertaining. "The home cooking is divine. I really think Angel's is a hidden gem in Hidden Falls. That's a great tag line, don't you think?"

Sara nodded. "I'm glad you can give Angel the recognition she deserves. It's so lucky that you found this place in the blog."

"Isn't it?" Amanda agreed. "Oh! There's Stu, my photographer. I want him to take some shots of everyone gathering around at the end of the day. Nice and homey. It was great to meet you." Amanda waved and took off after her photographer.

"Great performance. I'd applaud, but that would call her attention back to you," Coop said, obviously pleased.

"Do you think it was enough that she'll give herself away?" Sara asked.

Coop shrugged. "It's a start."

Rafe had been uncharacteristically silent, and Sara realized he wasn't paying attention to them but to Pirro. "Why don't you go talk to him?" she suggested. "I know you'll feel better, and maybe he will, too."

Rafe glanced at his watch. "It's almost time to go anyway, so I'll give him a last-minute pep talk. Excuse me." He started toward the older man, then turned back to

Sara and placed a long, lingering kiss on her lips.

A long, long kiss, she thought, winding her arms around his neck and reciprocating until he broke off contact and walked away.

"He's really into the role," Sara said, laughing even as she was aware of the tingling that aroused her straight down to her toes.

Coop shook his head. "He's not playing, Sara. The man's crazy about you."

"And I'm not discussing this here and now. Answer a question for me instead."

Coop frowned at her cavalier dismissal of the subject. "Fine. Shoot."

"Why would a beautiful woman with a fabulous editorial career turn to sensational journalism for a story?" she asked of Amanda, the probable writer of the infamous Bachelor Blog.

"Because she believes in love, fairy-tale endings and happily ever after. Even if she still hasn't found it for herself just yet, she believes it's out there."

"Next thing I know you'll be saying she also believes in unicorns and the tooth fairy," Sara said with a grimace.

"You never know. She is playing Cupid."

Sara studied the woman, who spoke animatedly, waving her hands as she made her point to both her photographer and Angel. "So she really believes she's doing a service with this blog."

Coop nodded. "I believe she does."

"Then maybe the solution is as simple as informing her she isn't."

"Huh." Coop glanced at the other woman.

"If she's rational, reasonable and has ethics, she might listen to you."

"Your captain already appealed to the editor in chief and came back with a no," Coop reminded her.

"Then appeal to her as a friend. Use your persuasive skills. It's certainly worth a try."

From across the room, Rafe gestured toward Sara. "Time to go," she told Coop.

She shivered, wondering if she'd ever be ready for this sting. She'd never worked a job with so many personal elements involved. She wanted to wish Pirro luck before he began his role.

And she prayed everything went off without a hitch.

Earlier today, Pirro had driven to the Hilton to inform the two drug dealers that he'd made contact and his dealer was eager to get together with them tonight.

Agent Lopez had wired Pirro, then instructed him to follow his normal routine to the meet, so he drove alone in his car to the farthest stretch of land on the edge of town and parked beneath a thicket of trees. Behind him were a series of old abandoned tunnels, which used to run between the United States and Canada. Years ago, the state police had detonated explosives, causing the tunnels to cave in on themselves, making them impassable in either direction and ending an illegal drug trade. Pirro had originally picked this location because it was far from town and remote enough that no one would stop by and no local cops would canvas the area.

Ironically, Pirro had chosen to meet his dealer near the tunnels, never once considering that he was engaging in the same illegal act. All he'd wanted to do was make his friends as happy in bed as he was. And look where that had gotten him, he thought as he nervously paced the dirt-packed ground and waited for the drug dealers to show.

"Calm down and stop pacing. You're making me nervous," the DEA agent waiting alongside him said.

"Where are Rafe and Sara?" he asked, his gaze darting around the dark night.

"We're here!" they both called out in hushed tones from their position behind the bushes. Earpieces enabled them to hear everything.

Backup, they'd explained to him.

"Are you satisfied?" Agent Lopez asked. "Now, like I said, you need to relax."

Pirro stopped in his tracks. "I'm sorry, Agent Lopez. I'm just nervous."

The other man placed his hand on Pirro's shoulder. "Remember what I told you. Stop calling me *Agent* Lopez, and act normally or this will never work," he said in a low whisper.

The sound of a car driving over the unpaved road announced Biff and Todd's arrival.

"Oh, my God. They're here. Oh, my God." Pirro's stomach churned. Nausea overcame him. "I'm going to be sick," he muttered aloud.

"Pull yourself together!" Agent Lopez ordered. "Here they come. Now, act normally, introduce us and I'll handle the rest."

"You make it sound so easy," Pirro hissed.

Agent Lopez had no time to reply.

Biff and Todd strode up to them, briefcase in hand. If Pirro didn't know better, he'd think they were two college kids on their way to school. Unfortunately, he did know better. They were drug dealers, arsonists, and he was about to screw them over.

Pirro knew he was supposed to perform the introductions. Instead, he leaned over and threw up all over Biff's expensive leather shoes.

Or maybe they were Todd's.

CHAPTER EIGHTEEN

Sara and Rafe knelt in the bushes, guns drawn and ready. Just in case. Earpieces enabled them to hear the discussion a few feet in front of them, and from what Sara could tell, Pirro had just puked.

"On my shoes! Man, what's wrong with you?" Todd yelled.

"Gross." This from Biff. Sara recognized their different voices.

"I'm sorry. I'm just nervous," Pirro said.

Rafe met Sara's gaze and winced.

She placed her finger over his lips in a silent *shh.*

"Let's just get this over with," Todd muttered.

"This is A— Lopez," Pirro said, quickly catching his mistake.

Sara let out a long breath.

"I'm Biff, and the one with puke on his shoes is Todd."

"A. Lopez."

"What happened, your parents couldn't think of a first name?" Biff laughed.

"He's making fun of my name? Where'd yours get Biff? Wasps 'R' Us?" Agent Lopez shot back.

The man brilliantly deflected. Sara stifled a laugh. From the look in Rafe's eyes, he was doing the same.

They trained their gazes — and guns — back on their targets.

"Pirro here says you can get us the goods?" Biff asked.

Lopez needed them to talk specifics, and he couldn't mention drugs or do anything that would smack of entrapment.

"Depends on what you want."

"Oxy to start. If the quality is good, we'll go from there. Do you have any on you?" Biff asked.

Lopez had the pills in a brown paper bag, and Sara heard the crinkling of paper.

"Looks good to me," Todd said.

"How much?" Biff asked.

"Forty-five grand for one hundred pills." Some more crinkling of paper.

"That's small potatoes. If our boss likes the quality, we plan to use his trucks to transport a hell of a lot more for distribution in the city," Todd said. "Can you handle the demand?" he asked Lopez.

"Of course."

Sara heard the crinkling of paper again.

"Where are you going with that?" Biff asked.

"I thought you said it wasn't enough," Lopez said.

"It's a start. We'll take it, our boss will test it and we'll be in touch for more. Here."

Sara envisioned Todd giving Agent Lopez the money.

The crackling of paper told her Biff had snatched the drugs.

"Freeze!"

At the sound of Lopez's voice snapping out the command, Sara and Rafe pounced, surrounding the two men.

Sara's knee popped under the strain of kneeling for too long, but she held her position, gun trained on Biff and Todd.

Pirro had long since dropped to the ground, crying in relief.

As Lopez read Biff and Todd their rights, Rafe and Sara cuffed the two men.

It was over as quickly as it had begun, a successful operation from beginning to end except for the painful certainty that Sara wouldn't pass the rigorous exam necessary for her to return to active duty at the NYPD.

Following the bust, Coop was given his

318

promised interview and was free to run the story after Agent Lopez vetted the information Pirro had given to make sure their case didn't suffer from the older man's embellishing.

Rafe and Sara finally arrived back at his place. "I don't know about you, but I'm exhausted," Rafe muttered.

"Wiped out." She collapsed, propping her leg on the arm of the nearest couch.

Eyeing her in concern, he headed for the kitchen, returning with an army of supplies, which he deposited on the table. "Scoot over."

With an adorable smile, she wiggled herself closer to the couch, making room so he could sit beside her.

"Here." He first handed her ibuprofen for the pain and obvious swelling, which she gratefully accepted.

"Thank you," she said, swallowing the pills with the glass of water he also gave her.

"You're welcome. Now, ice." He held out an ice pack. "Want me to do it for you?"

She nodded.

He placed the ice pack on her knee, wrapping it around to cover as much of the swelling as possible. He tried to be careful and not put too much pressure on the already sore joint.

She winced at the initial contact.

"Cold or pain?" he asked.

"Both."

He felt her pain directly in his heart. Rafe knew Sara was tough. She could handle physical discomfort and wouldn't fight the medical necessities. It was the emotional turmoil that was so much harder, eating away at her day by day. More so now that she'd obviously seen how difficult fieldwork would be, especially in a place like Manhattan where the physical requirements to return might be more than her knee could handle.

He was smart enough not to mention it now. Instead, he sat with her in silence and waited twenty minutes for the ice to do its thing. Then he rose, held out a hand and helped her to the bedroom, where they could both stretch out. Once in bed, she curled into him, relaxed and immediately fell fast asleep.

She obviously felt safe with him. Trusted him when she was weak. If pressed, he'd say she loved him in her own way — which would be enough for him if he wasn't always waiting for the end *she* believed was inevitable.

Rafe awoke feeling refreshed, considering

he'd fallen into a deep sleep with his arms around Sara for the better part of the night. He didn't think he'd rolled or shifted positions once. Since she was still out cold, he headed for the kitchen. After making coffee, he sat and drank his liquid caffeine. Though he tried to scan the newspaper, the phone began ringing nonstop. Family members wanted to talk about Pirro's role in last night's bust, and the slant they had on the story shocked even Rafe.

Pirro became an overnight hero and legend in his own mind. Apparently, he told the family he'd been an undercover police informant all along in order to catch big-time drug dealers in New York. And since Agent Lopez had left town along with his prisoners, Biff and Todd, there was nobody to dispute Pirro's version, at least until Coop's story broke in the *Daily Post.*

Except for Sara and Rafe.

And they weren't talking.

If Pirro wanted to bask in the limelight, who was Rafe to steal his glory? Especially since Pirro had promised to get his Viagra legally from now on, and to never supply his friends again. Agent Lopez called to tell Rafe that Biff and Todd had panicked in lockup and had immediately named names in order to cut a deal.

With the stress of the drug dealer off his plate and his aunt's marriage back on track, that left Rafe with the outstanding threat to Sara's safety as his sole concern. But even the captain seemed convinced John Morley wanted to scare her and keep her from testifying, not harm her and add another murder to his long list of charges.

Even so, Rafe wasn't taking any chances. He planned to stay by Sara's side, a strategy that had already played into Coop's agenda. With their public display of affection at Angel's last night, this morning's Bachelor Blog had proven Coop's hunch. Because only someone in the room could have reported today's blog contents — up-close-and-personal coverage of Rafe and Sara's evening prior to the bust.

THE DAILY POST
THE BACHELOR BLOG
Love blooms in a small upstate town. Bachelor hunk Officer Rafe Mancuso is recuperating from his injuries thanks to the tender loving care of fellow officer Sara Rios. At a small intimate gathering, the couple could be seen entwined in each other's arms. It even appears Officer Mancuso likes to cop a squeeze when he thinks no one is looking! Good thing the

blogger has spies everywhere. An intrepid reader sent in the following picture. Ladies, this bachelor's heart is taken. It shouldn't be long now before our sexy bachelor pops the question and takes himself off the market. Stay tuned . . .

Below the text, the blog featured a photograph of Rafe's hand slipped into the back pocket of Sara's jeans, *copping a feel.*

He groaned and tossed down the paper. "Whatever happened to the concept of privacy?" he muttered.

"Coop did ask us to play things up," Sara reminded him, joining him at the kitchen table. "Want me to freshen it up?" She gestured to his coffee cup with the carafe in her hand.

He nodded. "Thanks."

She refilled his cup and sat down with her own. "So Coop was right? Amanda is the Bachelor Blogger?"

"Unless someone else at the party reported in. I only saw her photographer snapping pictures."

Sara took a long sip of coffee before answering. "Seems pretty careless for someone who wants to keep her anonymity, if you ask me."

He couldn't help but stare. She was here,

and he was grateful. And though he wondered how much longer *this* could last, and
knew he had little or no control over the
answer, he refused to dwell on the negative.
He might as well enjoy what he had now.
While he still had it.

"I agree with you. It's careless. But maybe
Amanda figures we'll never question who
sent it in. It could have been anyone on their
cell phone last night," he said, trying to put
himself in the blogger's shoes.

"And maybe she doesn't care if Coop
figures out it's her because he also works
for the same paper?" Sara pursed her lips in
thought.

"Could be."

"How's your knee?" he asked, glancing at
the brace she'd put on again this morning.

"I'm hanging in."

He nodded and changed the subject. "So,
what's on our agenda for today?" He
glanced at the sun streaming through the
kitchen window. "How about we go out on
the boat?"

A slow smile touched her lips. "Can we
do the same thing we did last time we were
on the boat?" she asked, her smile turning
naughty.

"We sure can." He still had vivid dreams
about making love to her on deck. His jeans

grew tight at the thought.

He rose from his seat. Grabbing both mugs, he carried them to the sink, rinsed and set them on the rack to dry.

Then he walked over to where Sara stood and pulled her into his arms. "Have I mentioned that I'm glad you came here for protection?" He buried his face in her neck and inhaled her sweet scent.

"I don't think you've mentioned it," she murmured.

"Well, I'm telling you now." And on the boat, under the sun, he'd show her just how glad he really was.

Over and over again.

Sara was beginning to hate the telephone. For as long as she'd been in Hidden Falls, the phone had been the bearer of bad news. Today was no different. No sooner had they packed up food supplies for the boat, when Rafe's cell phone rang.

They stared at each other for a long time before he finally gave in and glanced at the incoming number.

With a groan, he hit the send button. "Hey, Captain. What's up?"

Sara came up beside Rafe and waited as he listened to her superior.

"Uh-huh. Yep. I understand. I'll let her

know." Rafe hung up the phone and turned to face her. "Morley's making noises from his jail cell about how his lawyer is working on another bail hearing."

Sara made a face. "So? No judge in his right mind will let that man out on bail."

"The D.A. wants to make sure of that, so she's filing a motion for an expedited hearing on the charges. If Morley's willing to waive a jury trial, you may be heading home sooner than we thought."

Sara's heart sank. She wasn't ready to leave this place just yet.

Or leave Rafe behind.

With a sigh, she shoved her hands into the pockets of her denim shorts. "When?"

"They'll let you know as soon as they do. But the captain said to tell you they'll arrange for police transport to and from the courthouse."

Sara rolled her eyes. "Come on. You just called me a *surprise* witness. Morley won't know when to expect me."

"Precautions wouldn't hurt," Rafe reminded her.

"Okay, an escort is fine." But she refused to dwell on something that hadn't happened yet. "Now, can we leave before someone else calls and further kills the mood?" She

picked up the shopping bag full of sand-
wiches.

He grabbed the cooler they'd loaded with
soda, water and ice.

Sunshine and the soothing bobbing of the
boat beckoned to her. Not to mention time
alone with Rafe to do whatever they wanted
to beneath the midday sun.

"Race you to the car," Sara teased. She
darted around him, grabbed the door
handle.

And bumped right into Coop, who was
about to ring the doorbell.

"Nooo!" Sara said, seeing her boat trip
evaporate before her eyes.

"Nice greeting." Coop eyed their package-
laden hands. "I'm interrupting something,
aren't I?"

"Yes!" Sara said.

"Is it important?" Rafe asked.

"Unfortunately, it is." Coop looked sheep-
ish, but firm.

Sara groaned.

Rafe shot her a look lit by disappointment
of his own. "It's okay. We can go on the boat
later. Come on in," Rafe said to Coop with
a lot more graciousness than Sara was feeling.

But she knew Coop was only here for a
short time, and if he was here, it must be

important.

"Come in," she said, pushing aside her disappointment, but shooting Rafe a look that warned him she'd hold him to their speedboat ride.

"What's going on?" Rafe asked Coop.

"I've been thinking about something Sara said the other day. About how if Amanda really believes she's doing a service with the blog, maybe she'd stop if she discovered she wasn't."

"What's wrong? You couldn't pinpoint her as the source of today's blog?" Sara asked.

Coop frowned. "Pretty much. I'm sure you realized the same thing when you read it this morning."

Sara nodded. "We had this discussion earlier. Any of Angel's friends could have seen Rafe tuck his hand into my pants pocket."

"And the photo? Could have been anyone discreetly using a cell phone, her photographer included," Rafe added.

"Exactly. But I still believe she's the blogger. So I want the three of us to appeal to Amanda's human side to stop plugging your every move, because she's putting you in danger," Coop explained. "I know Amanda, and I have to believe we can get through to her."

Rafe shook his head. "Isn't that —"

Coop held up a hand, halting Rafe midthought. "Before you call me idealistic or naive, Sara knows I'm anything but. I just don't want to waste time playing a game with her when the truth could protect you faster."

Rafe inclined his head. "That's the smartest thing I've heard all day."

"I also wanted you to read my article before I turn it in. Give you a chance to make sure you're okay with how I laid out Pirro's role."

Rafe raised an eyebrow. "And I just might have misjudged you, as well."

Coop shrugged. "I never let anyone vet my stuff before. Consider it a favor for a friend." He winked at Sara.

She immediately felt guilty for being annoyed he'd shown up unannounced earlier. "Thanks, Coop."

"No problem. Just leave me with Rafe's e-mail. Now, can I steal you two to go talk to Amanda before she leaves town?" he asked.

Rafe nodded. "No time like the present."

Coop started for the door.

Rafe grasped her wrist, and she turned toward him. "Rain check?" he asked.

She couldn't contain her smile. "Wouldn't

miss it for the world."

Sara believed in glomming the good, because she never knew how long it would last.

Sara, Rafe and Coop caught up with Amanda outside Angel's as she was packing her car for the ride home. Rafe and Sara held back while Coop asked her to stay, at least long enough for a talk.

From her nod, Sara assumed she was willing.

Coop waved them over, and they joined Amanda and Coop by the car.

"Coop says you all want to talk?" Amanda asked, sounding confused.

Sara inclined her head. "If you don't mind delaying your trip for a little while."

Amanda shrugged. "I'm in no rush."

"Then why don't we go back inside. I'm sure Angel won't mind if we use her living room." Rafe gestured toward the house.

Amanda walked down the path, her ponytail bobbing against her back as if she were a young kid, not a newspaper reporter who wielded power with the written word.

Once they were settled inside, Amanda spoke first. "So, where's the fire? What's the emergency and why do you all need to talk to me?"

Angel's living room was a warm, inviting space and Sara hoped Amanda took her cues from the feeling. Considering the woman had already refused to stop her blog when Captain Hodges asked directly, she couldn't imagine why she'd do so now.

"We want to talk to you about the Bachelor Blog," Coop said to Amanda.

Sara studied the other woman intently.

Amanda met Coop's gaze. "I don't understand. Did you want me to talk to Stan about the blog?" she asked.

"That's our editor in chief," Coop explained to Sara and Rafe. "And no, it's not Stan we want to talk to about the blog. It's you."

"Okay . . . ?" What seemed like genuine confusion crossed Amanda's face.

"We want you to stop writing about us," Sara jumped in impatiently.

"But you're making no sense. If you don't want me to mention Rafe and Sara in the article that includes Angel's B and B, you have nothing to worry about. But Coop, you know I have nothing to do with the Bachelor Blog." She nervously tucked her hair behind her ear.

Nervous because she was lying? Or nervous because she was genuinely confused? Sara wondered.

"Actually, I know no such thing," Coop said. "What I know for a fact is that the blogger is anonymous to everyone but Stan. My gut tells me it's you."

Amanda's eyes opened wide. "That's ridiculous. I'm the *features* editor!" She curled a long strand of hair around and around one finger.

Coop shook his head. "You could be the blogger, too. The blogger who heard from Angel directly about where Sara was staying and the features editor who is also doing an article about great summer escapes and happened to choose Angel's."

"That's a reach," Amanda said, her leg swinging back and forth in front of her.

Sara sighed. They needed to appeal to her more directly. Maybe if Sara personalized the situation, Amanda would confess her role and end Sara's and Rafe's stint in the blog.

Sara leaned forward in her seat. "Look, my boss already asked you to stop discussing our whereabouts in the blog because you're jeopardizing my safety, and you said no. But Coop thought now that you've met me, you'd reconsider."

A look of disbelief crossed her face. "Nobody asked me to stop. Nobody mentioned anything about anyone's safety. I don't understand," she said, her voice shaking.

Sara met Coop's gaze. That was as much of a confession as they were likely to get.

He rose and walked over to where Amanda was seated. "Stan didn't tell you Captain Hodges called?"

She shook her head.

Rafe let out a low growl.

"Son of a bitch." Coop was more expressive. "That bastard was willing to risk Sara's life as long as his paper is making money."

Amanda, gaze narrowed, looked from Sara to Rafe then back to Coop. "What do you mean? What exactly is going on?"

"Have you been following the news about the Morley case?" Sara asked.

"Other than the fact that he allegedly killed his wife? Not really." Amanda blushed at her ignorance. "I don't really follow hard news."

"She's more of a fashion girl," Coop said fondly.

Obviously, now that he knew Amanda hadn't deliberately refused to help, Coop had forgiven her. Sara understood why. All Sara cared about was making Amanda understand the situation.

She explained the Morley case and how Amanda's blog had been inadvertently alerting Morley's people to Sara's whereabouts. "My apartment's been tossed, and I've had direct warnings not to come back and testify since I've been in town."

Amanda spread her hands wide. "I'm so sorry. I had no idea." She drew a deep breath. "I'll stop posting about you immediately."

Rafe rose from his seat. "That's a start, but I was hoping you'd be willing to do more." He took charge, and Sara couldn't tear her gaze away.

"Such as?" Amanda asked.

"Yes. Such as?" She had no idea what Rafe had in mind, but she couldn't wait to hear.

"Sara's due to return to New York soon to testify. When she does, I want you to print your final blog about us. Tell the world we're not only engaged, but we went to Bermuda to get married. Throw them off her trail so she can return to New York safely."

"Brilliant," Sara said in awe of Rafe's idea.

Coop nodded. "I'm impressed."

All three looked to Amanda for an answer.

The woman stood and paced the floor of the small living room. "I'm horrified Stan didn't tell me the police called and asked me to back off."

"Join the club," Coop muttered.

Sara knew her friend and also knew he'd

cemented his decision to leave the paper sooner rather than later.

Amanda turned to face them. "Of course I'll do it. I owe you that much, if not more. You tell me when, and I'll be ready to run with it," she promised.

"And in the meantime?" Sara asked.

"I'll finish up the bachelor who's also featured now, run with your story when you're ready . . . and call it a day. I can't work for someone with no morals."

Sara was satisfied. They had a deal. They had a plan. When the time came, she could go home.

CHAPTER NINETEEN

On the way back from Angel's, Rafe stopped at Pirro and Aunt Vivian's house so he could check on the older man. Sara admired his dedication to his family. She'd even venture a guess that he felt less confined and constricted by them than he had in the past. He liked to complain about their intrusiveness, but in his heart he adored each and every one of them. Today, realizing the events of last night had been overwhelming, Rafe had wanted to see for himself that Pirro was doing okay and that he'd mended things with his wife.

Their cars were in the driveway. When nobody answered the doorbell, Rafe grabbed Sara's hand, sending a jolt of awareness spiraling through her. Enjoying the feeling of being a couple, she let him lead her around back where they found Vi and Pirro holding court on the patio. Rafe's parents were there, along with friends and neighbors.

"Is it a holiday from work that nobody told me about?" Rafe asked, glancing around at the crowd.

"I gave everyone the day off in honor of Pirro's heroism," Rafe's father said, holding up a bottle of beer.

Rafe shook his head and laughed. "Then hand one over so we can toast to Pirro, the hero."

Sara grinned. She and Rafe had agreed not to spoil Pirro's version of events. Apparently, they'd been celebrating, too. Sara was happy to join them. Especially with going home to New York looming large in her thoughts now, it was especially sweet to spend time with Rafe's large family. Too soon, she'd be home alone.

The way she liked it.

Didn't she?

"Rafe, a word?" Pirro walked over and pulled Rafe aside.

"I'll be back," he promised.

Sara nodded. "I'll be fine."

"No, no. You come, too. You're part of this," Pirro said. He adjusted his baseball cap by the brim and led them to the far corner of the yard.

"I'm glad you came by. I have something for you."

"We came to check on you," Rafe said. "I'm glad to see you're surrounded by family and doing well. Last night was rough."

"About last night." Pirro pulled his cap off and looked Rafe in the eye. "I know I'm embellishing the story a little."

Sara grinned. "Not by much."

Rafe shot her a grateful look.

"What else can I do? Tell my wife I was so scared I brought up her dinner all over that animal's shoes?" Pirro asked, his face flushed red with embarrassment.

Rafe shook his head. "It's our secret, I promise. Want to know another secret?"

Pirro raised an eyebrow.

"The first time I shot someone, I wet my pants."

"Really?" Pirro asked.

Rafe inclined his head. "Let's go back and celebrate, okay?"

Pirro nodded. "Okay. But first, here." He reached into his pocket and pulled out a handful of blue pills. "Here. My final illegal stash. I made an appointment with my doctor for Monday. I'll get them from him."

Rafe put his hand on Pirro's shoulder. "That's a wise decision."

"Wiser than the ones I've made so far. And I wanted you to know I realize that now. I'm grateful to both of you for getting me out of the mess I made, and I wanted to give you the last of them." Pirro closed Rafe's hand around the pills.

"You're a brave man, Pirro DeVittorio," Sara said. "I'm honored to know you."

And she meant it.

"I feel the same way about you, Sara Rios."

Rafe placed one hand on each of their shoulders and led them back to the party, where Pirro rejoined his wife.

Rafe turned to Sara. "Do you have a place to hold these until I can safely get rid of them?"

She held out her hand, and he poured them into her palm. She slid them into the pocket of her shorts.

For the rest of the afternoon and into the evening, they mingled with Pirro and Vivian's guests and ended up staying for a barbecue. Sara spent a good amount of time with Mariana, listening to Rafe's mother tell her stories about when he was young.

To everyone's surprise, Nick arrived with Angel, and they both appeared to be in a good mood. Despite her usual pessimism about relationships, Sara still held out hope for the couple.

The beer and wine flowed, and by the time the night drew to a close, Sara was lightly buzzed and definitely enjoying herself.

"Ready to go?" Rafe pulled her against him and whispered in her ear.

All thoughts of the party and guests fled in favor of enjoying Rafe and whatever time they had left.

She leaned into him and nuzzled her lips against his neck. "Lead the way."

They said their goodbyes, which as usual when among his family took longer than either of them would have liked.

Until finally, he threaded his fingers through hers and tugged on her arm. "Let's go home."

Ripples of yearning rushed through her, not just for Rafe, but for the word he'd uttered and the elusive feeling of belonging that was always just out of reach.

Rafe spent the next few days as if they were his last. He spent the hours eating, sleeping, sailing, making love with Sara — and waiting for the call that would send her home. But as the days passed without a word from New York, he stopped thinking about it and began to live in the fantasy that this could last.

Early afternoon, he returned from doing a few errands to find Sara sitting on the couch, his favorite blanket pulled over her legs, and a tub of ice cream in her lap as she ate from the carton. *Jeopardy* was on the television and Sara called out questions between spoonfuls of Ben & Jerry's Chocolate Fudge Brownie–flavored ice cream.

Locking the door behind him, he tossed his keys on the counter and strode into the room. "Is there enough to share, or should I grab my own?" he asked.

Her gaze darted between him and her favorite snack. "You can share," she said begrudgingly.

He ignored her obvious reluctance to share. Instead, he grinned and, in a split second, crossed the room and jumped into the spot next to her on the couch.

"Well?" he held out a hand for the utensil.

An adorable pout settled on her lips as she spooned out a small bit of ice cream, but she didn't hand it to him. She held out the spoon for him to eat from it.

He opened his mouth and let her feed him.

She then went back to her own mouthfuls.

"That's it? That's all I get?"

She tipped her head to one side. "Do you really want to come between me and my Chocolate Fudge Brownie?"

341

"Do you really want to make me beg?"

"Begging's good." Her eyes twinkled with mischief.

"Taking what I want is much better."

She raised an eyebrow.

He plucked the carton from her hands and placed it on the table, then came over to her, swiping his tongue over her lips and finally sealing his mouth on hers. He teased the seam of her closed lips until she opened and he thrust his tongue inside, taking all the Chocolate Fudge Brownie he desired.

His yearning grew, desire building as the passionate lip-lock went on and on, all the seductive powers he possessed going into this one kiss. She writhed beneath him and let out a low moan of appreciation. Then, wrapping her arms around his neck, she fully participated in sharing her beloved ice cream with sexy nibbles of her teeth and hot laps of her tongue.

She didn't seem in any rush to take things further, and he was enjoying the playful moment too much to rush them. He deepened the kiss, and his body pressed against hers, his hips settling between her thighs, increasing the sensation of his hard erection throbbing in his jeans and pulsing against her soft, feminine body.

He wound his tongue around hers, thrust-

342

ing in and out, mimicking the most intimate sexual act until their bodies began to rock in unison to the same tempo. His hips wound in circles, thrusting against her, harder and harder, until she began to pant and moan beneath him. Rafe didn't know how he'd hold back, but he'd damn well try, and he pumped his hips into hers, attempting to give her the pleasure she sought, the orgasm that was so obviously within reach.

Harder, faster, harder, faster. He grit his teeth and somehow held on as she trembled and finally screamed her climax, her entire body quaking with the force of it.

She reached up and began yanking on his jeans. He took the hint. He undid his button and stripped naked while she did the same. And then he was over her again, his hands thrusting through her hair at the same time he plunged hard and deep, his engorged member sliding into her hot, moist sheath.

She arched her back, bent her knees and not only accepted all of him but pulled him impossibly deeper. He thought he'd explode right then.

Her fingers gripped the back of his hair, and he pulled out, only to thrust in harder.

"Rafe!"

She called out his name, a mix of pleasure and pain, and he understood. He couldn't take it, either, but he definitely couldn't stop. In. Out. In. Out. All the while, her ragged breathing sounded harsh and wonderful in his ear.

In. Out. In. Out. She gasped, her breaths more rapid now.

He couldn't hold on another second, but he had to take her with him.

In. Out. In. Out.

"Come with me," he said, his words gruff, barely out of his mouth before the most intense orgasm shook him, body and soul. Quaking tremors rippled through him, over and over, along with *"I love you,"* words he'd never meant to utter but couldn't control.

Sara lay awake in Rafe's arms, cuddled together on the couch. He'd passed out on the couch, falling into a deep sleep. He didn't move a muscle when the phone rang, nor did he roll over as Sara wiggled free. She missed the call and let it go to voice mail, but the message left by the captain couldn't have been clearer.

Drive home tomorrow. Court the day after.

Not a minute too soon, Sara thought.

In fact, the order had come way too late.

Too late to protect them from the inevitable heartbreak she'd known would come. There was a way to make it easier, though.

Sara saved the message for Rafe to hear. Then she took a quick shower, tossed her things into her suitcase and was ready to leave within the hour.

She knew from Coop that Amanda's fake story about Rafe and Sara's honeymoon departure was ready to run on the Bachelor Blog with the hit of the send button. As soon as she was in the car, Sara would call Coop and have him tell Amanda that it was time. The Internet would spread the story in seconds. The *Daily Post* would follow up with it on the evening edition. Morley and his men would think Sara had fled the country rather than testify, and nobody would be expecting her back in New York.

Ready to leave, she paused only to stop by the couch where Rafe slept. She took the knitted blanket on the arm of the sofa and covered him. Then she knelt by his side. A lock of hair had fallen over his forehead, giving him a boyish look she rarely associated with him, making him seem more vulnerable than she knew him to be. Hurting him was the last thing she'd ever want to do, and she believed that her leaving without forcing them to rehash their opposing views was kinder to them both.

But kinder did nothing to diminish the pain slicing through her heart, because *she loved him, too.*

She didn't miss the irony, either. She, the big bad cop who wasn't afraid of anything — except for believing in love and happily ever after.

She pressed a kiss to his cheek and rose to her feet. Nausea filling her, she grabbed her bag and headed for the door.

She didn't leave him a note. She wouldn't know what to say, and the answering machine message would provide enough of an explanation.

Nick had just left their second try at marriage counseling. Another session of him doing the talking and Angel maintaining her silence.

Nick had had it.

He'd done what was expected of him by his brother and the rest of the family. He'd put himself out there and opened himself up to his wife. He'd reached out and tried to understand — and even accept Angel's need to run her own business. All before she'd ever given an inch in meeting him halfway.

He was finished trying. If she wanted to

fix their marriage, she'd have to come to him.

Rafe jumped up and realized he'd fallen asleep on the couch. Loud banging on his door told him what had woken him, and when he stood, he discovered he was still naked.

Where was Sara?

He pulled on his jeans while the knocking on the door continued. "I'm coming!"

He headed for the door and let his visitor inside. "Nick! What are you doing here?"

"I have to talk to you." He glanced beyond Rafe and looked around the room. "Where's Sara?"

Rafe rubbed his eyes, still groggy and half-asleep. "She's probably in the shower."

Nick shook his head. "Her car's gone."

That woke him up. "What?" He started for the door, but Nick's voice stopped him.

"Her car's gone."

Rafe's gut churned. "Maybe she went to the store."

His churning gut denied that possibility.

They'd made love, and she'd taken off?

What the hell . . . He looked around the family room for a note and didn't find one.

He headed for the bedroom next. Sure enough, all signs of Sara were gone. From the open suitcase on the floor, to the tooth-brush in the bathroom and piles of clothes on the floor in between.

Gone.

Rafe walked back into the other room.

"There's a message on your answering machine," Nick said, pointing to the kitchen counter.

Feeling like a ball of lead had settled in his stomach, Rafe strode to the machine and hit Play. The captain's voice flooded the room. "Court date scheduled for nine o'clock in the morning day after tomorrow. Hit the road in the morning. See you soon."

"Well, that explains the why," Nick said too cheerfully.

Rafe shot him a dirty look. "We'd agreed that when it was time to go back, we'd go together. She had all day tomorrow to get on the road."

They'd made love, and she'd taken off.

That explained the why. He'd told her he loved her and then, stupidly, contentedly, fallen asleep.

"What the hell was I thinking?" he muttered.

"I'm sure I don't know what you're talking about."

Rafe ran a hand through his hair. "Tell me why you're here."

Nick groaned. "Because I'm participating in one-sided marriage counseling, and it's pissing me off."

"And you want my advice?" Rafe let out a harsh laugh. "What do I know about love? Sara's gone." And it damn near killed him that she could walk out the door after all they'd shared.

"Then get in your car and follow her home." Nick pointed to the front door. "She can't have that much of a head start. Go after her."

"You say it like it's simple," Rafe muttered.

"Same way you've said it to me." Nick slung an arm around his brother's shoulder.

"I'll go after Sara if you go over to Angel's and put your foot down," he said to his brother.

Rafe shook Nick's hand. "Good luck."

"Back at you."

They'd both need it, Rafe thought. Neither one of them was guaranteed the outcome they desired.

Sara wasn't a crier. She normally didn't shed tears, yet from the minute she pulled out of Rafe's driveway, after she'd called Coop and given the okay on the fake blog story, the waterworks flowed. Sara understood the tears meant something deep and meaningful. Something she would have to deal with. She even considered turning around and going back, but she was so overwhelmed with emotion, she couldn't figure out what she was feeling, or even what she'd say to Rafe if she returned.

The one thing she knew for sure, the only thing, was that she had to be in the city to testify. So she kept driving before she could put her focus back on herself and her feelings for Rafe.

She'd barely driven ten minutes out of town on the highway when she caught sight of a car pulled over on the side of the road. A white distress flag had been tied to the antenna.

Sara slowed down to see if the person in trouble was still with her car, and, sure enough, she saw a woman with long hair sitting on the side of the road. The day was typically balmy and warm, the road basically empty, and who knew how long she'd been sitting there waiting for someone to stop and help.

Sara's cop instincts kicked in, and she pulled over, just in front of the woman and her vehicle. Leaving her car running, Sara walked around toward the woman in distress.

"Can I help you?" Sara called out.

"You certainly can."

The woman had jumped to her feet, and, as she came closer, Sara realized she looked familiar. "Joy, right? I met you at Angel's Bed-and-Breakfast, remember?"

"Of course I remember. You're the reason I came to this godforsaken town." Joy reached for her back pocket and withdrew a gun.

Sara made the same move, coming up empty.

Off-duty and upset about Rafe, she hadn't even thought about taking out her weapon to help a solitary woman on the side of the road.

Bad move, Rios, she thought to herself.

"Hands in the air," Joy said.

Sara slowly complied, raising her hands as Joy's words finally registered. "What do you mean, *I'm* the reason you're here?"

CHAPTER TWENTY

From the time on the answering machine and knowing she'd taken the time to shower and pack, Rafe figured Sara had at least a twenty-minute head start. He hadn't needed his brother's nudge to get him to go after her, but at least he'd gotten Nick to go to Angel.

He didn't know what it was with the Mancuso brothers, but their love lives were in the toilet.

Or were they?

Ever the optimist, Rafe refused to believe he wouldn't get through to Sara. He deliberately hadn't pushed her about her feelings, wanting to give them time to cement whatever *it* was. So, just maybe, he could get past her panic after all.

He merged onto the main highway out of town and settled in for the long ride to New York. Ten minutes later, he saw a car that had pulled over on the side of the road. A car that looked just like Sara's.

Concerned, he slowed down and pulled over, backing up until he was in front of the car. A quick look at the license plate confirmed it was Sara's car.

Panic sliced through him, but he instructed himself to stay calm. Think. If she'd pulled over because of car trouble, wouldn't she still be here now?

Unless she'd called someone to pick her up. But anyone in his family would have alerted him. In case he was wrong, he dialed Angel, Nick, even his parents, and Pirro and Aunt Vi. Nobody had heard from Sara, but they promised to call him if they did.

His mind immediately went to worst-case scenarios. Could Morley's men have gotten to her?

Before panic enveloped him, he forced his training to kick in. *Rethink the situation,* he thought. Sara hadn't heard from any of Morley's men since the festival. The threat was out there, but there was no one with whom to attach a face, no one they'd seen out of the ordinary in town. So, though they'd had a plan, they'd become complacent. Sara even more so, since she'd taken off without a word.

Their plan — a plan which Sara had already deviated from — dictated that when she was summoned back to New York, they'd call Coop and have him tell Amanda to run the fake blog. Then they'd drive back to the city together.

Heart pounding, Rafe tried the reporter, hoping he'd heard from Sara. Sure enough, she'd been in touch and had told him to have Amanda go with the story, which she had. The blog post had been up for about half an hour. And Coop hadn't heard from Sara since.

Promising to call when he found her, Rafe hung up.

He strode over to Sara's car and tried to get inside. The door was locked, but a quick look through the windows told him nothing appeared amiss.

Next Rafe walked the perimeter of Sara's car, taking note of the obvious skidmarks where another car had peeled out of there. Skidmarks that looked fresh.

Bingo.

She hadn't been alone.

Shit. He immediately called the state police and reported that an NYPD police officer was missing, along with a brief roundup of the circumstances that had brought her here from the city. He detailed the location of the abandoned car on the side of the road, with the license plate.

He directed any further questions to Captain Hodges, then turned back to his own search and investigation.

Where the hell could they have taken her?

Rafe took one last slow walk around the area, keeping an eye on the ground for clues. He knew Sara well enough to know she wouldn't go without a fight or at the very least without attempting to give him something to go on.

He saw an old bottle cap, gravel, dirt and rubber from a worn tire tread. He was about to give up when he caught sight of something blue. He knelt down and picked up a couple of blue pills. Pills that looked exactly like the Viagra Pirro had given him last week.

Any one could drop Viagra, but could it be coincidence that he'd given her the same brand of pills for her to hold? She'd put them in her shorts pocket, and Rafe had forgotten all about them once they'd gotten home. Had she thrown them out? Or left them in her pocket?

Sara wasn't big on doing laundry. She'd hand washed her bras and other things, but for regular clothes, she stalled as long as possible. Like him. And those shorts had been the ones she was wearing earlier in the day.

If she had left them in her pocket, would she have dropped them for him now?

And why?

If Morley's men had come after her, she'd have no reason to leave the pills as a clue. He'd know or at least assume who'd taken her just by finding the abandoned car. She could have dropped her ring or her watch, or something more personal if she was just looking to confirm to him she'd been kidnapped.

But the pills?

He couldn't see her dropping the tablets by accident, either. It just didn't make sense.

In the distance, he heard sirens and knew the cops would be showing up to canvas the area. Rafe had no desire to get caught up in their manhunt and questioning. He could do Sara more good by being out looking for her than if he let himself get tied up here.

Shoving the pills into his pocket, he climbed into his car and headed back to town, all the while racking his brain, trying to come up with an explanation.

Why? Why would Sara deliberately drop the pills? There had to be a specific reason. What was she trying to tell him?

Think! he ordered himself in frustration.

Pills. Morley. The two things didn't mesh. But the pills had led to Biff and Todd being arrested . . . so maybe her kidnapping wasn't related to Morley after all. Biff and Todd were barely adults; prepsters looking to make an extra buck by being frontmen for drug dealers. And those big guys wouldn't be happy that Pirro had ratted them out to his nephew, a cop, with a cop girlfriend.

Rafe gripped the steering wheel harder. Maybe Sara's disappearance had everything to do with the drug sting instead of the more obvious Morley connection. Rafe's reliable gut instinct told him that the drug connection made perfect sense. It also sickened him, since drug dealers would be a lot more violent than Morley's men.

He glanced at the clock on the dashboard. It still hadn't been that long since Sara had been taken. Rafe could still find her in time if he could figure out where they'd taken her. Once again, Rafe's mind turned to the pills as his clue. And the only place that came to mind were the deserted caves where the sting had gone down.

But a drive there would waste valuable time if she was somewhere else. Suddenly his cell phone rang. He glanced at the number and hit Send. "Talk to me, Nick."

"Aunt Vi just called Angel in hysterics because you'd called her to say that Sara was missing and on her way out of town, but she could swear she saw her in the passenger seat of a woman's car headed toward the old abandoned caves."

His pulse kicked up rhythm, and he stepped on the gas. "Why didn't she call me?" he asked.

"Because she's Aunt Vi, and she's always going to take the long way around a problem. Can I help?" Nick asked.

"No, I've got it. Thanks." He disconnected his brother and redialed the state police, asking for immediate backup.

The abandoned caves would be the perfect place to get rid of a body, he thought, and nausea overwhelmed him. Ignoring the feeling, Rafe tore off the highway and through town, headed for the outskirts.

All the while, his head throbbed from the fear and panic racing through his brain, but one thought was prevalent above the others.

Rafe prayed he wasn't too late.

Sara knew how to handle a perp, but Joy had taken her off guard. Worse, Sara still had no clue why Joy had been waiting for her, why the other woman had abducted her or what she wanted with her now. The one thing Sara did know — sitting in the passenger seat of Joy's car, gun pointed at her stomach — was that she only had until they reached the tunnels to figure a way out of this mess.

"Can you tell me *why* I'm here?" Sara asked again.

"I said shut up!" Joy waved the gun as a reminder of why Sara should listen. "I need to concentrate until we're out of town."

Sara turned around to look out the side window.

"Eyes straight ahead. Hands in your lap, and don't make eye contact with anyone as we drive through town," Joy warned, slowing to heed the twenty-mile-per-hour speed limit.

Sara did as she was ordered. Just as she had from the minute Joy had pulled out the gun. The old standby rule, never leaving a place of kidnapping, went by the wayside when Joy had waved the weapon in Sara's face and forced her into her car.

The only information Sara had gleaned so far was that Joy had been watching her from the day she'd arrived in town, and right now they were headed to the tunnels where the drug bust had gone down — apparently Joy had seen that unfold, as well. At least Joy's revelation about viewing the bust caused Sara to remember she had Pirro's Viagra in her pocket. She'd had a split second to come up with the idea to leave Rafe a clue, dig out the pills and drop them on the ground before Joy had shoved her into her car and set off.

Whoever Joy was, she was more than a handful and way more than Sara had planned for. And that was the problem. She'd let her guard down around Rafe and kept it down in the one area of her life where she should have been more careful.

She never should have left Rafe sleeping and taken off on her own. When he woke up and realized she was gone, Sara would be lucky if he even wanted to come after her.

Sara had to assume she was on her own.

Joy finally pulled the car to a stop beneath the same trees where Rafe and Sara had hidden during the bust.

Joy climbed out of the car, came around and pulled Sara out, too. "Step away from the vehicle."

Eye on the woman with the gun, Sara walked into a clearing, all the while looking around for something to use as a weapon. But there were no rocks or large tree branches nearby. There wasn't an escape route, either, since Joy had full control of her gun, if not her faculties. Even if Sara made a run for it, Joy could take her down with one clean shot.

The one thing Sara knew she had to do was buy time. "Can I *talk* now?" she asked Joy, who'd ordered silence until they reached their destination.

"Oh. You're one of those. You just need to know everything before you die." Joy sighed, sounding put out and annoyed.

But as Sara knew, criminals usually loved to tell about their exploits and reveal how brilliant they were, and she assumed Joy was no different.

"Fine. Did you really think you'd get away with that stupid blog post telling the world you're off on your honeymoon?" Joy asked.

Sara raised an eyebrow. "Why wouldn't I?"

"Because like I told you, I know better. I've been here watching you."

"But you haven't told me *why*." *And the why might be the clue to getting out of here,* Sara thought.

"Because John and I have a life to live, and I'm not going to let you get in the way." Joy flipped her hair back defiantly.

"So, you're John Morley's mistress," Sara said, comprehension dawning.

"Fiancée."

"He didn't wait long after offing his wife, did he?"

Joy narrowed her gaze. "All you need to worry about is that I outsmarted you. Cop versus cop, I come out ahead."

Aha. Now they were getting to the bragging. "You're a cop, too?"

Joy shifted her gaze, looking around to make sure they were still alone. "I was a corrections officer."

Was. "What happened?"

"I was wrongly discharged for mental incapacity." Joy sniffed as if the charge were offensive. "They just didn't appreciate an independent woman."

Sara figured the higher-ups in Joy's department had read the woman correctly, considering she was armed, dangerous and holding Sara hostage.

"But Morley did, right? He appreciated everything about you," Sara said, pushing Joy for more information.

"Of course. We planned everything. With Alicia gone and her money unfrozen, John could fix his business problems, and we'd live happily ever after."

Sara thought she heard a car, then decided she was imagining things. "Sounds . . . perfect," she said, refocusing on Joy.

The other woman nodded. "If only Alicia had died immediately, you wouldn't be in this mess. Blame her." Joy obviously missed

Sara's sarcasm completely.

"So, John sent you after me?" Sara asked, because Joy being here didn't track with the man who'd approached her at the dance.

Joy rolled her eyes. "You are slow. Of course not. We women have to take things into our own hands, don't we? He sent a man to scare you, but I've researched you. I know you don't scare."

"If you've been watching me, why did you wait so long?"

"I just knew to wait for the right moment. Just like I knew that blog story was a fake."

Sara bit the inside of her cheek. "Can't put anything over on you."

Joy flushed with victory. "I knew John would buy the story and call his men off, but I'm smarter than that."

"So you keep telling me." The woman sounded more obsessed and insane than smart, but Sara respected dangerous even more. "Tell me something. How did you know when to pull over on the side of the road and wait for me?"

"When I heard John's court date had been moved up, I knew to keep a closer eye on you. As soon as you loaded the suitcases into your car, I took up my position and waited. I knew it would only be a matter of time until you drove by, and I was right."

Joy's eyes gleamed with pride.

Sara applauded. "Good for you."

"I was worried I'd have to deal with your boyfriend, too, but you played right into my hands."

Swell, Sara thought. She didn't need the reminder that she'd made Joy's life easier by stupidly bailing on Rafe and their well-thought-out plan. "And if Rafe and I had left town together?"

Joy shrugged. "I'd have gotten to you in the city," she said matter-of-factly. "Okay, enough talking. Consider it your last request fulfilled." She repositioned her hand, looking ready to shoot.

"So, now what? You'll shoot me and leave my body by the tunnels and . . . what? Hope nobody connects you to me?"

"How will they?"

Sirens suddenly sounded in the distance. A combination of panic and relief washed over Sara.

Shock registered on Joy's face. "How would they ever find us?"

Sara swallowed hard and decided to gamble. "You're not as smart as you thought. I left Rafe a clue," she said, goading the other woman, hoping to keep her talking and off balance so she wouldn't shoot.

"And there's no way out, so drop your weapon." Rafe came up from behind, taking Joy off guard.

Sara, too. Apparently she *had* heard a car in the distance earlier, and Rafe had snuck up on foot.

Surprised, Joy swung toward Rafe, then back to Sara, who had safely stepped out of reach.

Joy was caught in between them both and chose to focus on Rafe.

Each had a gun drawn on the other.

"Stalemate," Rafe said.

"She's Morley's girlfriend," Sara informed him.

"Fiancée." Joy's correction sounded inane in light of the situation, but the distinction clearly mattered to her.

From behind Joy, Sara met Rafe's steady gaze.

She'd left him, and he'd come after her anyway. There would be time later to reflect on what that meant. For now, she knew what she had to do.

She just hoped she didn't get Rafe shot in the process.

Sara gave Rafe an imperceptible nod.

"Drop!" she yelled at the same time she dove for the back of Joy's legs, barreling into her and taking her down at the same time a gunshot sounded, deafening in its roar.

And heart-stopping in that Sara had no idea whose gun it came from, or who, if anyone, the bullet had hit.

Rafe read Sara's mind, anticipated her action and was ready to duck when the order came. He hit the ground and rolled away from the woman's aim. The shot missed, and he quickly rose to his feet.

Sara had the upper hand, but the other woman still had the weapon, which they were grappling for. Rafe stepped on the woman's arm, and the gun fell from her hand. Sara scrambled on hands and knees for the weapon, grabbed hold of the gun and rose to her feet.

It was over by the time police cars surrounded them and screeched to a halt. It took another forty minutes to get the cops up to speed, the story straight and Joy taken into custody.

Over an hour passed before Rafe and Sara had a minute alone.

From the moment he'd found her car on the side of the road until she'd taken possession of Joy's gun, his only thought had been Sara's survival. Once he'd accomplished that, the deal he'd made with his brother, to go after their women, took center stage. But Rafe had realized there was nothing left for him to say. He'd put everything out there for Sara, and by walking out on him earlier, she'd thrown it back in his face.

So, when he finally could speak, it wasn't gratitude for her safety or praise in how she'd handled Joy that came out.

"I don't know what the hell more you want from me!" Rafe exploded in anger instead.

Sara blinked in surprise before she quickly regained her composure. "I'm sorry."

Her words didn't deflate his feelings of hurt and betrayal. "For what? For not trusting me enough to get you home? For not believing in me enough to stick around? Or wait — maybe it's for not loving me enough for all of the above?"

Sara opened her mouth, then closed it again. She drew a deep breath. "I do."

"What?"

"I do love you." Her voice trembled. Her eyes shimmered with unshed tears. "It's the trusting in the future I have a hard time with."

He shook his head in disbelief. Only Sara could turn an *I love you* into something he couldn't celebrate.

"Well, guess what? It's just not good

enough. I've put myself out there for you, shown you exactly what we could have together if you'd let down your guard — and you still question it?" He raised his hands in the air. "I'm finished. Come back to my place and get some sleep. I'll follow you back to New York in the morning." He turned to head back to his car.

"Rafe, wait." Sara's voice stopped him.

He turned around, but he wasn't interested in whatever she had to say. "Look, I think we're finished talking. And don't worry. I'll be sleeping in the extra room, so there will be no mixed signals from me from here on in."

Because he couldn't be in the same bed without touching her, and he wasn't about to give more knowing he'd receive absolutely nothing in return.

After leaving Rafe's, Nick stopped in town for flowers and headed over to Angel's like a man on a mission — only to be stopped by a call from his brother telling him he'd found Sara's car on the side of the road with no sign of her. Since then, the flowers sat on the counter — their meaning undiscussed — while Nick and Angel held vigil and waited for news on Sara.

"Good news?" Angel asked once Nick had

hung up the phone with Rafe.

Nick shrugged. "Depends on your defini-tion. Is Sara safe? Yes, she is. Are they back together? No, they aren't." The news was a kick in the gut on many levels. Because Nick had believed in Rafe's ability to go after Sara and win.

Angel walked over to where Nick sat on the couch in the family room. "As long as Sara's okay, the rest will come," she said, her tone full of certainty.

"Will it? Really? Why are you so sure they can make it if we can't? We have history. Not just in years together, but in shared experience and memories, good and bad. Yet we sit in that therapist's office, and, if not for me, we'd be sitting in complete silence." And he couldn't take it another second.

"Why did you come here? Before we got the call about Sara, you showed up with flowers. Why?"

"Because I love you. Because you're my wife, for better or for worse, and I want you back. And because I finally realize I'm not the one who placed this damn business between us — you did!" He rose and grasped her by the arms, so their faces were inches apart.

"You hate this place."

"Only because you use it as a wall between us!" He counted to five, gathering his courage. "We lost another baby, and we never talked about it. You never cried. And I never pushed you. Instead, you turned to this business, and I complained that it took you away from me. But that's not it at all."

Angel shook her head. "Please don't make me do this," she said, her voice breaking along with his heart.

But he shook his head, bound and determined to force the issue once and for all. It was the only way.

"We lost two babies, and I'd never ask you to get pregnant again, to go through that kind of agony and loss again, but we lost something together. We lost the dream of a family. We didn't grieve together. Hell, Angel, I don't know if you even grieved alone!"

"I grieved in my own way."

"But you didn't cry."

"Because I was afraid if I did, I'd never, ever stop!" she yelled at him, her voice breaking along with the damn wall she'd built up and kept between them.

Her shoulders shook, and she slid to the ground, aching sobs escaping. All Nick could do was settle in beside her, hold her tight, and be there while she mourned.

He prayed that when this was over, they could make a fresh start — and that this time, it would be together.

CHAPTER TWENTY-ONE

Sara headed home to tie up the loose ends in her life. There was nothing like seeing your life flash before your eyes to make a person want to reevaluate what was important.

She had no choice but to tackle her issues in priority order, starting with business and John Morley. From the moment she arrived back in New York, she had police protection. Sara testified against Morley, and with her testimony on record, she was finally safe from Morley and his men. He wouldn't add cop killer to his list of crimes after it was too late to do any good.

Next up, a long-overdue visit with her father. She'd missed him while she was upstate. She'd called ahead, and he was expecting her, so she knocked and let herself in with her key.

Martin Rios greeted his daughter with his customary booming hello and huge hug.

"I've missed you!"

"I missed you too, Dad." She stepped back and looked him over. Robust and handsome, with dark hair and a mustache, her father . . . Well, he was her father.

And she wanted to crawl into his arms and tell him everything that had gone wrong.

"Uncle Jack tells me you've been a busy girl. Come sit down and fill me in."

Sara bit the inside of her cheek and did as he asked. She sat down with her dad, filling him in on the antics of Pirro that had led to the drug bust, the kidnapping and rescue by Rafe, along with a description of Rafe's big, fun family, including Angel and the blogger story, ending with her fake elopement.

By the time she was finished, her father stared at her in awe. "Well, well."

"Well what?"

He slapped his thigh with one hand. "Well, you've gone and done it."

"Done what?" she asked, exasperated and lost.

Her father cocked his head to one side, studying her as if seeing her for the first time. "You've fallen in love with your ex-partner, that's what!" Martin smiled, his grin as wide as his face.

Sara wasn't nearly as amused. "What

makes you say that?" She'd hoped to bypass her unresolved love issues during this visit.

"I'm not sure if it's the dreamy look in your eyes when you talk about him, the fact that you used his name in almost every sentence, that my loner daughter is head over heels for his big family or all of the above."

"Is it that obvious?" She ducked her head in embarrassment.

"I'm afraid so." But he was still grinning like a hyena. "Why do you look like this is a bad thing?" he asked.

"Why do you look like it's not?" His attitude left her truly perplexed. "I feel like I've lost my way. Aren't you worried for me?"

Her father shook his head. "Unless this man's an axe murderer disguised as a cop, I don't see the problem."

"This from the man who lived happily ever after alone?" Sara shook her head and laughed. "Come on, Dad, you can tell me what a huge mistake it is to even consider tying my life to one person, and another cop at that."

His big brown eyes grew wide. "Is *this* what you think I want for you? A lonely life shared with someone only on occasion?" He swept his arm around, the gesture meant to encompass the small apartment she'd grown up in.

"Lonely?" she asked, stunned at his choice of that one word.

Her father leaned forward in his seat. "Did you think I celebrated when your mother left?"

They'd never discussed it before. Sara had only known what she'd seen growing up — a contented man with available, short-term women when the opportunity arose.

Sara swallowed hard. "I thought you were relieved the fighting had ended."

He let out a low groan. "I suppose that's true. And I really had no choice but to adapt. I was also pretty determined to never get hurt that way again." He shook his head in obvious dismay. "But I never thought about how it looked to you. That's where I fell down on the job as a parent, I guess."

Sara smiled. "You weren't much of a talker."

"I'd hoped I made up for it as a listener. But I guess that left you reading between the lines."

She nodded. "It did. Are you telling me I didn't read correctly?"

"If you think falling in love or making a commitment to someone is a bad thing, then something definitely got lost in translation, and I blew it."

Sara shook her head at his logic. "Dad, it wasn't just you. We don't have one family member who isn't divorced." She held up a hand before he could interrupt. "Except for Reni. Still, one out of however many others is hardly a reason to believe in marriage and relationships."

He reached out and lifted her chin in his hand. "Didn't I raise you to believe in hard work above all else?"

"Of course."

"Well, marriage and commitment take work. I was willing to do the work. Your mother wasn't. End of subject." He dropped his hand and looked away. "Except that the same goes for any couple in the world today."

Sara narrowed her gaze, surprised she'd misunderstood her father for so many years. "But wouldn't you say being a cop makes it twice as hard to make a relationship work?"

"Yes. So what?"

"So, two cops would make it twice as impossible." She stated what she'd always believed was obvious.

He placed his hand on her shoulder, and she met his caring gaze. "Nothing is impossible. Not if what you and this man share is worth the effort."

Rising, her father walked over to a large cabinet and opened a drawer. He sifted through the contents and pulled something out.

"What's that?" Sara asked.

He walked over and sat back down beside her. "It's a picture. Look."

She glanced down at the framed photograph she didn't recall seeing before. The picture captured her family — her father, her mother and Sara as a toddler. All three of them smiling and happy.

A memory and recollection Sara didn't have. "I've never seen this before!"

"Another mistake of mine. It hurt too much for me to look at it, so I buried it, just like I buried my feelings," he admitted.

She swallowed over the painful lump that kept getting bigger in her throat. "Why are you showing me this now?"

His wise gaze leveled on hers. "Because I'm trying to tell you I wouldn't have missed these years with you and your mother for anything in the world. And I'm just sorry you never knew that before now," he said, his voice gruff.

Sara found her voice just enough to say, "I love you, Dad." She pulled her only parent that mattered into a big hug.

"I hope you've learned a valuable lesson

today." He pulled back and cleared his throat.

She caught the telltale tear in his eyes before she stood and turned away to wipe one of her own from her cheek.

A few days later, fresh from an orthopedist appointment for her knee, Sara walked into her apartment just as the telephone started ringing. She grabbed the receiver before it went to voice mail. "Hello?" she asked, out of breath.

"Sara? It's Angel. Did I catch you at a bad time?"

"Not at all," Sara lied. She cradled the portable between her head and her shoulder while she put her bag and keys down and locked her door.

Then she curled up on a club chair to take the call. "What's going on?" Sara asked, happy to hear from the other woman.

"I had news I wanted to tell you myself," Angel said. "I just felt like you understood so much, and we really connected . . ." Angel's voice trailed off, as if she suddenly felt funny about the admission.

"I understand. I've been thinking about you, too." *About everyone from Hidden Falls,* Sara thought.

Including Rafe.

Especially Rafe.

Sara drew a deep breath. "So, what's your news?"

"Nick and I are giving our marriage a second chance," Angel exclaimed.

Sara's heart literally skipped a beat. "That's wonderful! How? What changed?"

Had Nick finally given in and accepted his wife's need for a career and a focus outside her marriage?

"We both did. Ever since Nick stayed here and saw how alive this place makes me feel, he's tried to be more understanding. But most of all, he came over and forced me to face things I'd buried deep," Angel admitted in a soft voice.

"Things about losing the babies?"

"Mmm-hmm. He resented the B and B mostly because I put it between us because I didn't want to face the pain over our loss. When Nick put it out there and made me face it, everything changed. I'm able to talk about it now without shutting him down, and he's able to accept this place. Or at least he's trying to, which is all I ever wanted. He's even helping me out here. Like it's *ours!*"

Sara felt herself smiling. "You sound so happy, and I'm thrilled for you! What about counseling? Are you still going?"

"Believe it or not, now that we're communicating, it helps us compromise on different things. It's work, but it's so worth it."

Sara had heard those words a few days before, when she'd visited with her father. *Marriage and commitment take work. I was willing to do the work. Your mother wasn't.*

Now Angel was repeating them, too. She and Nick were compromising — working — to make their marriage succeed. Because she obviously felt what she and Nick shared was worth the effort. Rafe had done the work. He'd shown her he was willing to meet her halfway and fight her demons, but she'd been the one to bail. Like her mother. And that wasn't the person she wanted to emulate, let alone be.

Nothing is impossible . . . Not if what you and this man share is worth the effort.

"Sara, are you still there?" Angel asked.

"Sorry, I got lost in thought," Sara admitted. "I'm here."

"Okay. Well, I have to get going, but keep in touch, okay?"

"I will."

"Umm . . . and Sara? You didn't ask, and I swore I wasn't going to say anything, but Nick tells me Rafe's miserable without you. Gotta go. Bye."

"Bye." Sara stared at the phone in her hand.

She was miserable, too, and she wanted nothing more than to show up on Rafe's doorstep, but she couldn't make that move. Not until she'd tied up the remaining loose ends hanging over her. She needed to know what she was dealing with physically.

Another MRI, sets of X-rays and a doctor's appointment merely confirmed what Sara already knew. Although she had already regained some mobility and would get some more over time, thanks to the scar tissue and beginnings of arthritis in the joint, she'd never pass the NYPD physical that would have enabled her to return. She hadn't needed the confirmation to tell her what she wanted to do next. She'd already made up her mind.

Somewhere between her stay at a small B and B in upstate New York and falling in love with Rafe and his big, welcoming family, Sara's dream of being a New York City cop had morphed into something different. Something she couldn't have imagined wanting, let alone yearning for, a few weeks ago.

Sara wanted out of Manhattan and the big-town anonymity she thought she'd enjoyed. She wanted to trade big-city law enforcement for the small-town equivalent, spending her time helping people she knew and cared about as opposed to protecting the anonymous many she didn't. Even if she had been miraculously cleared for duty in Manhattan, she'd already decided her days there were over.

What she didn't know, couldn't yet know, was which small town would become her new home. The answer depended on Rafe and his ability to first forgive and then to compromise. Because she couldn't imagine living in Hidden Falls, surrounded by his family, without him.

Cleared for active duty.

The words should have been a welcome relief, but lately Rafe didn't give a damn about much of anything. He was going through the motions of his life, and there wasn't a thing he could do about it. He finally understood why he'd found his brother drinking at Billy's Bar all those weeks ago. Rafe would be there himself now if he wasn't in Manhattan. The bars here were too crowded for him to find the peace and solitude he was looking for.

He sat down with an open carton of Chinese food and began to sort through his mail when a knock sounded at his door. He wasn't expecting anyone, and he barely knew his neighbors. He sure as hell wasn't in the mood for company.

When the knocking grew louder, he shoved the carton aside and walked to the door. Looking through the peephole, he was shocked to see Sara on the other side.

He opened the door warily. "Hi."

"Hi." She smiled.

He braced his hands on the door and the frame. "To what do I owe the pleasure?"

She drew a deep breath, obviously not sure of her welcome. "I was hoping we could talk."

He inclined his head, unwilling to give until he knew why she had come. "So talk."

"Right here?" As she looked around, taking in the dark, dank hall, her ponytail swished from side to side.

Already his fingers itched to wrap around the soft strands and pull her close. He clenched his hands into tight fists instead.

"Right here," he confirmed. She'd already left an indelible imprint on his vacation home.

He had memories of their time together, and he wasn't just imagining what her skin felt like — he *knew*. He had dreams of her in his sleep and visions while he was awake. His apartment was the only place he could look around and not see Sara. He'd like to keep it that way.

"Fine. How have you been?" she asked.

"Just swell. You?"

She shrugged. A delicate lift of her shoulders that sent ruffles around her collar shimmying. He couldn't stop staring, wondering what she was doing here and ordering himself unsuccessfully not to care.

"I've been keeping busy. I testified against Morley," she said.

"I heard." The captain assumed he still wanted to be kept in the loop, and since Rafe had no desire to broadcast his personal life to his superior, he'd shut up and listened.

"And I heard you've been cleared to return to active duty. I'm glad."

"Thanks." He swallowed hard. "I understand you weren't as lucky." He knew what her career as an NYPD officer meant to her. "I'm sorry."

"It's funny, but I'm not. I once thought losing my career meant losing myself." She slid her hands into her front jean pockets. "And now I don't."

He knew he shouldn't ask, just as he knew he would. "Why not? What changed?"

What had shifted in her mind? In her life? Sure, she'd said she felt selfish after realizing what Angel had lost was nothing compared to her career, but that was before Sara knew for sure she wouldn't pass the physical to return.

She met his gaze, her eyes wide, clear and honest. "I changed. Or maybe what I mean is, you changed me."

He'd had enough talking like strangers in the hall. Reaching out, he grasped her hand and pulled her inside, shutting the door behind them. "Go on."

Sara nodded, knowing this was her one and only chance to reach him. They may have proclaimed their intention to go into this with their eyes open, but he wasn't as jaded as she was. Despite his father's affair, he'd had a rosier view of marriage and relationships.

He'd had hope.

She hadn't.

But she wanted to put those days behind her. She wanted to be more like him. "Here it is. I told myself I was happy alone, that I didn't need or want a big family. But then I drove up to your small town and met your relatives and found a place where I really felt like I belonged."

He listened, watching her carefully, his expression neutral and unreadable, like the trained negotiator she knew him to be. If she was going to win, she had to put all her cards on the table and hope it wasn't too late.

"I guess I didn't know a good thing when I had it." Sara rubbed her hands up and down her bare arms. "What I felt for you scared me so much I pushed you into an agreement for sex. Like it meant nothing. Like you meant nothing. When, in reality, you meant everything." She shook her head, ashamed of how she'd treated him, and when she blinked, a tear fell.

He reached out and caught it with his finger, but still he said nothing.

She gathered yet more courage and continued. "I had this negative view of marriage and relationships, and I didn't think we had a shot at a future."

"What changed?" he asked again.

"A wise man told me that nothing worth having comes easily. He made me realize that what we shared is worth the effort to make it work."

He shook his head and laughed.

She knew it was despite himself.

"Who do you know that's so smart?" he asked.

She smiled, too. "My father. You'd like him."

"I'm sure I would. He raised you, didn't

he?" His tone had softened, and she sensed she was finally reaching him.

"Do you understand what I'm trying to tell you?" She stepped forward, moving closer, hoping he didn't turn her away. "I was wrong to think we weren't worth the effort. You're worth it."

His strong hand cupped her face as he looked into her eyes. "I thought you were worth it, too, or I wouldn't have put myself out there for you."

"I'm still worth it," she said, hoping he still believed that, too. Her heart pounded harder in her chest. "I'm just different than I was a few short weeks ago."

He eyed her warily, obviously still unsure of whether he could trust her.

She held his gaze, stared at his handsome face and silently promised to rebuild that trust — and never give him a reason to regret it. "I finally realize I've been lying to myself about not wanting a relationship or a family. I want all those things. With you."

And she desperately wanted him to agree.

"I want to believe you," he said in a gruff voice.

"Then do."

Rafe wished it were that easy. He'd put his entire being on the line for her once before. What could convince him to let down his guard again?

"I quit my job," Sara said, taking him off guard. "Well, technically that's not right. I wasn't cleared to come back, but I would have quit even if I had been."

Rafe shook his head. "Now you've lost me."

She drew a deep breath. "You are looking at the first chief of police of Hidden Falls — assuming the town council amends the charter and the funding goes through. But I can't do it alone. I want you to come with me. The town needs their own police department, and we could create and run it together."

Rafe was floored, her words barely sinking in. "Leave the city? Move to Hidden Falls?" He stared at her as if she'd lost her mind.

Yet this crazy notion did what nothing else she'd said had accomplished so far. He finally believed she meant what she was saying. That she was coming to him, to this relationship, in it for the long haul. He leaned against the wall for support.

"Look, I know it's sudden, but it's well thought-out," she said, unaware of his sudden-shifting belief. "Trust me, Rafe. I've already started inquiries and talks with the mayor, and the sheriff's office. Everything's in motion. I know you moved to the city to get away from your family, but I'm asking you to go back. With me."

"Sara," he began, nearly speechless over the depth of what she was offering.

But she wasn't listening. She rambled on, obviously afraid if she let him get a word in, he'd shut her down and she'd lose everything. Little did she know, she was about to gain it all instead.

She shook her head. "Let me finish, please. I know your family can be overwhelming, but you know you love them and they need you close by. I know I'm asking a lot, but that same wise man also reminded me that marriage and relationships are about work and compromise. And heaven knows I'm working as hard as I can to show you I've changed. I'm trying to be an optimist. I'm looking toward a future with you."

Rafe shook his head, needing to be sure. "Am I hearing you right?" Even when she came to him in his dreams, he'd never heard her offering him the entire world.

She nodded. "Each and every word that's coming from my heart. The same heart I'm giving you now. But if you say no, I'll find a new hometown to settle in so you won't have to worry about dealing with me every time you go home." She spread her hands, then dropped them to her side.

He couldn't contain his smile. "Are you finished?"

She glanced at him through damp lashes. "That depends. Do you believe me?"

"I believe you, and most importantly, I believe in us. I always have."

"I'm not too late?"

"I never stopped loving you, so how could you possibly be too late?" He held out his arms, and she stepped into his embrace.

She laid her head against his chest, and he closed his eyes, savoring the moment.

"I've asked a lot of you today. Are you willing to make those compromises? Or do we have to renegotiate terms?" she teased. "Because I'd go to the ends of the earth to make us work."

"That's all I needed to hear," he said, letting out a groan of pure contentment. "But are you sure you want to live in Hidden Falls?"

"Someone has to keep Pirro and the rest of the family in line." Sara tilted her head back and grinned.

"I have to admit I didn't see that one coming, but you're right. I have come to terms with my family, and I miss them. Besides, I think I've done enough hostage negotiating to last me a lifetime."

"As long as you spend that lifetime with me." Her eyes sparkled with love.

Rafe nodded. "That's all I ever wanted." *She* was all he'd ever wanted.

"You're all *I* ever wanted, and it feels so good to say it out loud."

He sealed his lips over hers — a kiss and a lifelong commitment he intended to keep.

EPILOGUE

THE DAILY POST
THE BACHELOR BLOG
Ladies and gentlemen, due to unforeseen circumstances this is the last installment of the Bachelor Blog, but let it be said we ended with a bang. Reports of our last bachelor eloping with his lady were greatly exaggerated. But all is not lost, and romance still blooms.

The new Mr. and Mrs. Mancuso were officially married in the groom's hometown of Hidden Falls, New York, where the couple has relocated permanently. The setting for the ceremony? The oft-mentioned Angel's Bed-and-Breakfast, a quaint family inn run by Angel and Nick Mancuso — our hero's brother and his wife.

The Hidden Falls town council reported that funding to create a new police department in Hidden Falls is underway. Which

Mancuso will be named chief of police? I wish I could say stay tuned. . . . Instead, I'll say farewell. It's been a pleasure reporting on New York City's most eligible bachelors and helping some very special couples to find each other. Just remember, fairy tales do happen. And your happily ever after could be right around the next corner.

ABOUT THE AUTHOR

Carly Phillips started her writing career with the Harlequin Temptation line in 1999 with *Brazen,* and she's never strayed far from home! In 2002 Carly's book *The Bachelor* was chosen by Kelly Ripa for her Reading with Ripa book club, making it the first romance to be chosen by a nationally televised book club. Carly has published thirty books, and, among others, she has appeared on the *New York Times, USA TODAY* and *Publishers Weekly* bestseller lists. An ABC soap opera addict, Carly lives in Purchase, New York, with her husband, two teenage daughters and two frisky soft-coated wheaten terriers who act like their third and fourth children. You can find Carly online at www.carlyphillips.com; www.plotmonkeys.com and www.myspace.com/carlyphillips.

We hope you have enjoyed this Large Print book. Other Thorndike, Wheeler, Kennebec, and Chivers Press Large Print books are available at your library or directly from the publishers.

For information about current and upcoming titles, please call or write, without obligation, to:

Publisher
Thorndike Press
295 Kennedy Memorial Drive
Waterville, ME 04901
Tel. (800) 223-1244

or visit our Web site at:

http://gale.cengage.com/thorndike

OR

Chivers Large Print
published by AudioGO Ltd
St James House, The Square
Lower Bristol Road
Bath BA2 3SB
England
Tel. +44(0) 800 136919
www.audiogo.co.uk

All our Large Print titles are designed for easy reading, and all our books are made to last.